# Lady of Bones

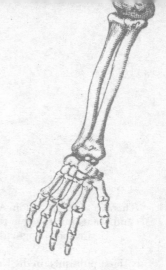

# Lady of Bones

## CAROLYN HAINES

**MINOTAUR BOOKS**
**NEW YORK**

First published in the United States by Minotaur Books, an imprint of St. Martin's Publishing Group

LADY OF BONES. Copyright © 2022 by Carolyn Haines. All rights reserved. Printed in the United States of America. For information, address St. Martin's Publishing Group, 120 Broadway, New York, NY 10271.

www.minotaurbooks.com

Library of Congress Cataloging-in-Publication Data

Names: Haines, Carolyn, author.
Title: Lady of bones / Carolyn Haines.
Description: First edition. | New York : Minotaur Books, 2022. |
   Series: A Sarah Booth Delaney mystery ; 24 |
Identifiers: LCCN 2022003423 | ISBN 9781250833723 (hardcover) |
   ISBN 9781250833730 (ebook)
Subjects: LCGFT: Novels.
Classification: LCC PS3558.A329 L33 2022 | DDC 813/.54—dc23/
   eng/20220127
LC record available at https://lccn.loc.gov/2022003423

Our books may be purchased in bulk for promotional, educational, or business use. Please contact your local bookseller or the Macmillan Corporate and Premium Sales Department at 1-800-221-7945, extension 5442, or by email at MacmillanSpecialMarkets@macmillan.com.

First Edition: 2022

10  9  8  7  6  5  4  3  2  1

For Dorothy Morrison, partner in magic and mischief

# Lady of Bones

# 1

Standing in the kitchen at Hilltop, I listen to the laughter and conversational murmur of my closest friends. Softened by the durable walls of the old plantation house, their voices drift from the parlor through the dining room and find me as I prepare a snack platter for our Halloween celebration.

My friends are all gathered at Hilltop, the ancestral home of my partner in the Delaney Detective Agency, Tinkie Bellcase Richmond. We're here to decorate for Halloween, but as the soft cooing of the baby reminds me, also to celebrate the arrival of Maylin Richmond, the miracle baby. After years of trying to conceive, Tinkie and Oscar succeeded, and little Maylin is their awesome reward. She is a gift to all of us.

Maylin's auspicious arrival—in the backyard of a local resident while Tinkie and I were working a case—still makes my heart stutter when I think of all the things that could have gone wrong. This child is a part of me in a way I never anticipated. Though not of my blood, I would lay down my life for her. It's a peculiar awareness to feel such powerful love for a little bundle who may or may not even see me clearly.

The tidal surge of emotions Maylin evokes makes me pensive, and perhaps a little melancholy. Loving someone or something is dangerous. Love is an open door to pain. Folks say that only death and taxes are inevitable. Some call it the cycle of life—birth in the spring, full glory in the summer, the slow decline in the fall, death in winter. Seasonal and unrelenting. It's a stupid system, in my opinion. We should be allowed to linger in summer, to live hale and hearty until we decide to step on a rainbow and ascend to our just rewards. This business of loving deeply and suffering greatly seems too punitive. We become the walking wounded, and in time, the pain lessens and joy seeps in around the edges. But I am always aware of the potential for disaster.

I've finished arranging the tray with the spicy black-bean dip and an orange cheese dip, my contribution to color-coordinated food. Yes, I used food coloring to get that perfect orange hue, so sue me. There is normal food and there is holiday food. Sometimes, sprinkles and food coloring are just essential.

I put the bowl of chips in the center of the tray and start toward the parlor with it. By the sounds of the merry laughter, my friends are truly celebrating. Tonight I will rejoice in Maylin and push away the blues, doubts, and apprehensions.

Balancing the tray on one hand, I reach for the doorknob to the parlor and freeze. Someone behind me calls my name, but there's no one else in the room.

"Sarah Booth Delaney." The haunted voice comes at me again.

I whirl around only to encounter the very thing I dread most. A hooded figure dressed in a black robe and holding a scythe looms over me. The hood prevents me from identifying the intruder, but I catch a glimpse of white skeletal bone, and I know Jitty has left Dahlia House to pay a call on Hilltop. Seeing her here as the grim reaper terrifies me. There is so much potential for loss if Jitty is here as an omen or a warning. Everyone I love is in the parlor behind the closed door. I won't let Death touch any of them.

"I don't know what's up with you, but go home." I sound fierce and mean, and I am. As much as I love the family ghost who haunts me, I do not like her attire.

"There can be no rebirth without death." Her voice is hollow and ominous. "Death is never a final ending."

Jitty, who constantly taunts me with riddles and symbols, is at it again. "We've had *a* birth," I remind her. "A true miracle of a baby girl. A *re*birth is totally unnecessary. Go home. What are you doing here, scaring the life out of me? I swear, Jitty, I think you just killed my right ovary. Think of all the eggs you just broke."

"There is a season for all things, and a time to every purpose under heaven."

"I like the Byrds as much as anyone else, but now isn't the time for quoting pop music, Jitty." Perhaps I'm grasping at straws, but I'm hoping this grim reaper outfit is Jitty's costume for the swiftly approaching Halloween holiday. Jitty is, after all, a ghost. She is also a part of my family, and I take her messages to heart. "Why are you dressed like that?"

"Darkness hovers near," she says. "You know as well as I do that on All Hallows' Eve, the veil between the living and the dead is at its thinnest." Her voice is sounding closer to normal.

"Will I be able to talk with my mother and father?" Jitty is my link to the Great Beyond, where my parents await me. But a little message now and again would not be amiss.

Jitty pushes back the hood of her black cloak and the bone-white skeleton begins to flesh out. It's a marvel of the spirit world to see the beautiful enigma that is Jitty form before my eyes. Before I can compliment her, she speaks. "You ask the same questions over and over, Sarah Booth."

"And I will continue to do so until I get the answer I want," I tell her.

"Aunt Loulane says you are the stubbornest girl she ever wrangled."

"You tell Aunt Loulane for me that stubborn is a survival skill. If I weren't so stubborn I'd be a grease spot on the highway." I can't help grinning. After my parents were killed, Aunt Loulane gave up her entire life to come to Dahlia House and raise me. I owe her a lot. "Pass it along to Aunt Loulane that she's the reason I'm so stubborn. She gave me the will to keep living." I wasn't exaggerating.

"She says to tell you that mules are stubborn but young ladies should be more tractable and bend with the wind. Otherwise you'll be a spinster for life."

"I don't for a minute believe Aunt Loulane said that!" I'm indignant until I catch the glint of mischief in Jitty's eyes. Jitty is always making up stuff and pulling my leg.

"She didn't say that," Jitty says, cackling, "but for a minute you went for it." She makes a motion of a fish snapping at a fly. "I coulda caught you if I'd really tried. You're like a big fat old trout, Sarah Booth."

She's dropping back into her country dialect—though Jitty can speak the King's proper English with British accent and all when she chooses. In fact, she speaks a number of foreign languages when it suits her. Being dead has given her a wealth of talents that are mostly wasted on me.

"What are you doing here dressed as the grim reaper?" I repeat.

"It's Halloween, duh."

Jitty is almost two hundred years old, but she can still adopt the speech patterns of the young. Her "duh" drips with disdain. "I know it's nearly Halloween, but this isn't a costume party. We're celebrating Maylin's birth."

"Seems to me that baby's been celebrated every minute of every hour of every day since she was born."

Did I detect a little jealousy on the part of my haint? Delicious! "Well, she's heir apparent to the Delaney Detective Agency. Tinkie has done the impossible. She's reproduced. Something I'm not sure I'm cut out for. Maylin may be the culmination of the Richmond *and* Delaney lines." I know that will get her going.

"And what about the baby you're supposed to have to carry on the Delaney name? That baby won't have any heritage if you give it all away!"

"Gotcha!" It is rare that I can play Jitty. "Now tell me what you're doing here dressed like something out of a bad movie."

"Death don't play. That's what I came to tell you."

Jitty's words almost made me gasp. I'd expected some flip answer, not the deadly serious tone she'd used.

"Is someone going to die? Someone I love?"

"You know it's against the rules of the Great Beyond for me to tell you. All I can say is that Death is going to figure prominently in your life for the next few weeks. Hades isn't the place you want to visit, but you may need to do that, Sarah Booth. It's all part of the plan." She pulls her hood back up, casting her face in shadow. "Time to boogie."

"But—"

Three bats come out of nowhere and fly around my head as Jitty begins to fade and dissipate, like cigarette smoke in the wind.

"Don't you dare leave now!" I want to grab her and force her to tell me what she means by her getup and her behavior. Even knowing it won't do any good to reach for her, I try, only for my hand to whisk through empty air.

"Death is never a final ending." Her words come back to me like a cold blast. And I can't tell if she's serious or having some fun with me.

"Jitty?"

There was no answer, so I pushed open the door to the parlor and stepped into a room filled with laughter and light. Maylin's little hands and feet waved in the air. She was tucked into her plush leopard-print carrier, but she actually turned her head toward me. I totally believed that she knew I was her Auntie Sarah!

"You're pale," said Cece, my brilliant journalist friend. "Something wrong?"

"No, I just heard something outside." As if to validate my lie, the doorbell chimed.

"I wonder who that could be." Tinkie rose to answer the door, but I stopped her.

"I'll get it." I handed the tray to Cece and headed for

the front, pinching color into my cheeks. Cece was too observant.

The doorbell chimed again, a long, impatient summons. I swallowed back my annoyance and pulled the door open. The tawny-haired woman standing on the porch slowly lifted a hand to her heart. She stared at me as if I'd grown a second head.

"Can I help you?" I asked.

"You're the spitting image of her. It's like seeing a ghost."

I've never been a fan of riddles, and I was already agitato from Jitty's torment. "Who are you and what do you want?"

"You're Libby Delaney's girl, Sarah Booth, aren't you?"

My mother had been dead for more than twenty years, and it was rare to hear her name on the lips of a stranger. Many people had forgotten her. "Yes, I am." I swallowed against the lump in my throat. "Did you know my mother?"

The woman's tired features lifted into a smile. "Oh, I knew Libby quite well. I played Ethel to her Lucy when we decided to get into trouble." She held out her hand. "I'm Frances Moore, but everyone calls me Frankie. I knew you a little bit, too."

"Frankie." I murmured the name because I knew it so well. I could hear her laugh ring out from the kitchen where she and Mama sipped coffee or planned some adventure. Frankie's name was written on lots of photos around our house—of two young women at the beach, or at lunch in a fancy restaurant or dive, or gadding about in the Roadster. Blond Frankie with her huge sunglasses and hats, and my mother with her scarves and red lips. They were a pair. I remembered looking at the photos with my mother, who would laugh and tell me all about Frankie and how much they'd loved to stick their thumbs in the eye of propriety and authority. "Mama loved you so much." Emotion hit me in a solid wave.

"And I her," Frankie said. "I moved to Paris when you were in grammar school. I wanted to come back for your parents' funeral, but my husband was dying. I couldn't leave him. I should have stayed in touch with you but, to be honest, my heart was broken. I lost my heart-sister and my husband in the same year. Not to mention James Franklin. I adored your daddy, too."

I didn't have much to say—I was too caught up in the feeling of loss.

Frankie stepped inside and put a hand on my arm. "I need your help, Sarah Booth."

From the parlor I heard Tinkie call out, "Sarah Booth, what's going on? Is someone at the door?"

I cleared my throat. "Yes, someone is here."

"Well, bring them in," Tinkie sang out. "We have champagne and some strange orange dip you made. I know cheese doesn't come in that shade of orange."

"Frankie, come on—"

She held me with a gentle grip. "I need your help and I need it now, Sarah Booth. I don't have time to mess around. My daughter is missing and I fear she's going to be killed." Frankie's knees wobbled and she slumped against the doorframe. "I'm sorry. I'm just exhausted and worried sick."

I grasped her elbow and assisted her through the foyer and to the parlor. All conversation stopped when they saw me and the pale, stumbling woman I brought in.

"Pour that woman a drink," Harold Erkwell said, and

then splashed two fingers of bourbon into a glass and handed it to her.

Frankie took the drink and knocked it back. She pushed out her breath on a sigh. "I'm okay. Just tired and worried."

I made the introductions of Frankie to Tinkie, Oscar, Coleman, Cece, Jaytee, Millie, Harold, and baby Maylin.

"I apologize for crashing your celebration of the baby," Frankie said, "but I need the help of Delaney Detective Agency. My daughter has gone missing in New Orleans and I fear she's fallen into the hands of some evil people."

Oscar sat up and put his hand on Tinkie's back. "My wife just gave birth. I'm afraid she's—"

"I can't leave Maylin," Tinkie cut in. "We're breast-feeding. But I can give Sarah Booth all the support she needs for internet research or making calls or investigating financial areas. We'll help you find your daughter."

Frankie turned to me. "Will you help me?"

Beneath the tired, worried woman I saw the younger version of my mother's best friend. "Of course I'll help you. Tell me everything you know about where your daughter went and who you think has her."

# 2

Harold poured another drink for Frankie, and this time she sipped it slowly. The color had returned to her cheeks, and she was sitting up straighter. To give her a chance to pull herself together, I told my friends about how Frankie and my mother were such good buddies and adventurers. When Frankie threw me a grateful smile, I nodded at my partner to pick up the questioning. Tinkie was sometimes softer, easier than I was in dealing with distressed people.

"Tell us about your daughter," Tinkie prompted. The rest of the crew circled around Frankie, waiting for the details. She'd certainly captured our interest. Only Coleman remained in the background, leaning against the mantel by a fire that needed stoking.

"My daughter, Christa, is a journalist working out of

New Orleans for several online magazines. A few months ago she was contacted by the University of Missouri. They invited her to submit an investigative piece for a chance at a free master's degree. The degree is nice, but the introduction to a level of professional journalism was the real reward for the program. Christa went all in."

So far the young woman sounded smart and dedicated. "What story was she working on?"

"Human trafficking." Frankie blinked back tears. "It sounded dangerous to me. The people who do that kind of thing are ruthless, and Christa was trying to put together cases of missing women. She was digging into some really bad people, and she said she was gathering proof that women were being taken from the streets of New Orleans. She just didn't know why or who was doing it."

"She had evidence?" Coleman spoke softly but it was clear to me he was paying close attention.

Frankie nodded. "She said she did. She found some information." Her voice broke. "It gets even worse." A single tear glided down her cheek. "A friend of Christa's disappeared from the French Quarter four days ago. Christa thought she might have been taken by a group of people who believe crazy things. She was devastated by Britta's disappearance but she was pragmatic, too. She was determined to find her roommate and bring her home safely, but she recognized the potential. If what Christa believed was true, the story could be her ticket to any newspaper she wanted to work for."

"So Christa suspected more than sex trafficking. Something even worse?"

Frankie nodded. "That's what Christa was investigating. A cult."

"What kind of cult?" I felt a chill pass over me.

"Everyone, give her a chance to tell her story in her own way." Tinkie gave all of us the stink eye. "Can't you see she's worried sick?"

"Do you have a photo of your daughter?" Cece asked. Her voice was kind, but as a journalist, she was already planning how to publicize Christa's disappearance and get as many feet on the ground looking for her as possible.

"I do." Frankie quickly found one on her phone. We passed it around, all looking at the beautiful young blonde with bright blue eyes and a wide smile. No one said it, but we were all thinking that she was a perfect candidate for human trafficking herself.

"She's a pretty girl," Tinkie finally said. "How old?"

"Twenty-four. Sarah Booth, you were ten when Christa was born. My daughter was kind of a surprise to all of us, but she's the best thing that ever happened to me." Frankie's voice broke. "We have to find her."

"How long has she been missing?" I couldn't shake the memory of Jitty as the grim reaper. Was this the tragic death her visit foretold?

"Two days," Frankie said.

I looked at Tinkie and we nodded. Two days wasn't so bad for a twenty-four-year-old woman who might be out kicking up her heels and having an adventure. We'd done worse when we were in our twenties. Still, I couldn't ignore the fact that the day Tinkie got her daughter, Frankie's girl had gone missing.

"Are you sure she's missing instead of just . . . laying low?" Coleman asked the question we'd wanted to ask but had hesitated to do so.

"Christa is a free spirit," Frankie conceded. "But she would never scare me. Not like this. No matter what she might be doing, she would answer my calls or texts.

She knows I'm worried." She looked around at my friends. "I'm very appreciative that you're so concerned for me and my daughter. It means a lot."

Group sharing was over. Frankie needed to talk to me and Tinkie alone. We had personal questions that only she could answer about her daughter, and about their relationship. "Why don't we step into the kitchen," I said. "I was going to make some black and orange deviled eggs." I waved a hand. "We're decorating Tinkie's house for Maylin's first Halloween."

"It's just as well you let those deviled eggs alone," Tinkie said. "Black eggs are not appealing, Sarah Booth. It would scare Maylin."

"How old is the baby?" Frankie frowned.

"Two days," Tinkie said, and it was apparent from her expression that she had the same thought I did. Maylin had arrived in her life just as Christa had disappeared from Frankie's. "Doc Sawyer says she can't really see yet and certainly won't remember this holiday, but we'll have photos to show her. We're going to celebrate every single moment we can with her."

The tears fell from Frankie's eyes. "I understand that completely."

I took her arm and steered her into the kitchen. After I eased her into a chair at the counter, I closed the kitchen door behind Tinkie. After seeing the photo of Christa, I was more than a little worried about her. Beautiful young women often attracted trouble they didn't deserve. "Tell me about the human trafficking story she was pursuing," I said, settling across from her. Tinkie sat beside her.

"I didn't like this story from the start," Frankie said. "It smacked of danger, but Christa was determined. The basis of the story was that young women were being taken from the French Quarter. Girls who had drifted there or didn't have family. Some were artists, performers, or just looking for opportunity in a city with a reputation for music, food, and fun."

"Christa wouldn't be the only journalist to dig into that dirt," I said.

"That was bad enough. The whole sex trafficking thing. Until her roommate, Britta, disappeared."

"Her roommate?" Tinkie exchanged a look with me. "Christa thought she was sold into the sex trade?"

"This is when I got really worried. Christa believed Britta had been taken by some people for a nefarious reason. For a ritual."

"Tell us about it," I said. "Take your time. But just tell us everything Christa said to you."

Frankie swallowed and blinked back more tears. "The night before she disappeared, Christa called me. She said she'd found disturbing details about young women vanishing from the streets. She said the sex trafficking story had been done to death, but she'd found something even better."

"What did she tell you about her story idea?"

Frankie frowned. "Not all that much. We were supposed to get together, but she disappeared before we could make it happen."

"You said the angle she was working involved her roommate?" Tinkie said, nudging her back on track.

"Yes, sorry. I get . . . Anyway, Christa met Britta Wagner in the French Quarter. She's German, a very talented artist, and a wanderer." Frankie shrugged. "Young people get the wanderlust, and Britta was charming and so bold. She was traveling all over the United States but had decided to spend the fall in the French Quarter. She and

Christa hit it off and leased an apartment together. They grew close quickly."

"And what happened?" I didn't want to seem pushy, but Frankie was so distraught it was hard for her to keep on point.

"Britta went missing. She set up her art stand at Jackson Square just like she did every day. You know how the artists gather along the fence and hang their work and paint. She was showing her watercolors—so very talented—and she was supposed to be there to meet Christa. Only when Christa went there at the appointed time, she was gone. Her stuff was right there but no sign of Britta. Christa checked at home, but Britta wasn't in the apartment and none of her friends knew what had happened to her."

This was sounding worse and worse. "She's been gone how long?"

"Four days," Frankie said. "Christa reported her missing, and she called Britta's parents. They're planning to come to New Orleans as soon as they can make some financial arrangements. They're obviously hoping the kidnappers will ask for a ransom. They're worried sick, just like me. Christa told the Wagners she'd find out what happened to Britta. And she'd found a couple of good leads. Or at least that's what she told me." Her voice broke. "I'm afraid the people who snatched Britta have also taken Christa. I think Christa was onto the truth—that there is someone in New Orleans taking young women off the street and not for sex." She looked me straight in the eye, her pain laid bare. "I think they may be selling them for something worse."

# 3

While Tinkie calmed Frankie down, I slipped from the room to talk to Coleman. He had no jurisdiction in New Orleans, but he had law enforcement friends all over the country, even the world. He stepped outside and made a phone call to some friends in New Orleans while I returned to get more details from Frankie.

"Did Christa have any idea who might be involved in abducting Britta? Coleman is checking with New Orleans to see if the NOPD has found anything about either of them."

"She only said that Britta was talking about a very handsome man who'd stopped by her stand when she was painting. He complimented her work and asked if she would accept a commission to paint a particular landscape. Britta was cautious and asked him to bring a photo of the scene he wanted her to paint because he wanted her to go with him to see 'the gardens,' as he called them. Britta was pretty savvy about the dangers of going anywhere with someone she didn't know."

"Even if she'd decided to go with a strange man, she wouldn't have left her easel and all of her work and art supplies on the square." I had to point that out. The French Quarter locals were good about watching out for each other, but thousands of tourists roamed the area. Not everyone was honest, and art supplies were expensive and in high demand. "If the paints and canvases were left alone for any length of time, they would likely be stolen."

"That's exactly what Christa said." Hope sparked in Frankie's eyes. "Britta wouldn't have left her stuff like that. She sold her artwork consistently, and she was hanging ten or more paintings in her booth. She would never have just abandoned them." Frankie leaned forward, her intensity increasing. "Christa's theory was that Britta was taken—and Christa was worried. She believed the man Britta described as interested in a commissioned painting was involved with a group of youth-obsessed cultists." She looked up and her expression was grimly determined. "Christa believed the cult was working out of the Garden District."

That was a long jump in logic, from a young girl disappearing to being kidnapped by what Frankie was calling a cult. "A religious cult? Like the Branch Davidians or Jim Jones?"

Frankie wiped away the tears but they kept coming. "This is going to sound even crazier than Jonestown, but Christa said there was a group of people in the Garden District who practice a strange religion. She said they believed they could attain immortality."

"Seriously?" I couldn't help it. Anyone with half a brain knew that aging couldn't be stopped. People had been trying to stop the process for centuries, and some of the so-called cures were pretty gruesome. Hungarian Countess Elizabeth Báthory—a name I would *not* mention to Frankie—was said to bathe in and drink the blood of young virgins to preserve her youth. Didn't work, but no one really knew the number of children she murdered, though some accounts speculated as many as six hundred and fifty young servants. "In this day and age there are people who think time can be stopped?"

"Wait a minute," Tinkie said. She looked down and seemed to be considering her next words. "I may have heard of these people. Remember Emma Jane? We called her 'Pouty.'"

I rolled my eyes. "How could I forget? The biggest narcissist in high school. She married while in college and that's the last I heard of her."

"She married a doctor in New Orleans, a plastic surgeon. About four months ago, she called to invite me to lunch. She was in Zinnia on her way to some fashion show in Memphis. When we met, she said she'd found an exciting new group of people who'd unlocked the secrets to endless youth. She thought I might be interested since I was 'getting on up there.'"

Emma Jane had always been consumed with her appearance. I distinctly remembered her at a spend-the-night party, locking herself in the bathroom, checking for wrinkles, wattles, and unwanted hair growth. She was thirteen and already consumed with the horror of decay.

"Why did she call you?" I asked. Emma Jane and Tinkie hadn't been friends. Not really.

"She never came out and said why, but it would appear

that those in the 'congregation' of this youth movement are urged to bring other people in. To sustain and grow the flock, as it were. Finding new converts is necessary to stay in the good graces of the group."

"Like some kind of weird bait-and-lure pyramid scheme?" I asked.

"Yep," Tinkie said. "I never called Emma Jane back. I'd honestly forgotten about it until we started talking about these missing girls."

"Will you help me find my daughter?" Frankie asked. "I can pay you. I can front you some money to go to New Orleans and I'll come and help you."

Frankie was my mother's closest friend for many years. I didn't want to take her money. "Let's see what Coleman can find out from the police department," I said. "Now we need to ask some questions, Frankie. Give us as many details as you can remember."

She nodded. "I'm ready."

"Since you think Britta's disappearance is linked with Christa's disappearance, let's work on that." Tinkie was all business now. "As far as we know, Britta just disappeared from Jackson Square right around lunch, four days ago, right?"

"Yes. That's how I understand it," Frankie said.

"No signs of violence? No one saw anything that indicated an abduction?" Tinkie pressed.

Frankie bit her bottom lip in an attempt to control the trembling. "That's my understanding, but Christa was finding it difficult to believe."

"Lay out the sequence of events as far as you know." Tinkie put a hand on Frankie's knee to show her straightforward questions weren't out of callousness. Right now, though, we needed facts.

Frankie inhaled deeply. "This is what Christa pieced together. Britta set up her artwork on the Square at seven that morning. She left her booth to walk across to the Café Du Monde to get some coffee and beignets about ten o'clock. She came back, sold a painting of St. Peter's Cathedral in the fog, and then that mysterious handsome man showed up offering her a commission. She told him to bring a photo of the landscape he wanted her to paint and she'd give him a price. He left and she continued to work. Then she was just gone. Gail Senseny, the artist next to Britta's space, didn't see anything or remember Britta saying she was going anywhere specific."

Telling the details seemed to have a calming effect on Frankie. She was making more sense and being meticulous in recounting what Christa had told her. The information was secondhand, but it was all we had to go with, and it would give us the all-important timeline of when Britta disappeared.

"Christa knew all of this how?" I asked Frankie.

"When Britta didn't show up at the appointed time, Christa figured Britta had a customer, so she got two lunches to go and took them to the Square. Britta's stuff was there but she was nowhere to be found. That's when Christa talked to Gail." Her eyebrows rose. "I remember something else. Gail told Christa that Britta had gotten a phone call from a man she called Renaldo. Shortly after the call, she said she'd be right back and left. But she never came back. That was four days ago."

"And then Christa did what?" I asked.

"She waited for a couple of hours, and when Britta didn't come back, she packed up the equipment and art and took it all to the apartment she shares with Britta."

"And then?"

"Christa waited all that night. She went to all their normal hangouts. No one had seen Britta. It really was like she'd vanished into thin air. At noon the next day, when it had been twenty-four hours, she filed a missing persons report. She had Britta's passport, so that was helpful. But there was no sign. She was at the booth one minute, then she was gone."

"And that was four days ago?" I clarified.

"Yes. I talked to Christa that afternoon. She was sick with worry and talking to all the street artists. She was canvassing the restaurants and bars and the art galleries. The local people see things that tourists don't. But only Gail recalled seeing Britta leave her booth area. She talked on the phone, and the next time Gail looked over, she was gone."

"And when did Christa disappear?"

"Two days ago. We'd planned to go over her story and I drove over to meet her for an early dinner. I'd talked with her that morning and she was so distraught about Britta I felt I should be with her. We agreed to meet at the Blue Moon. I waited an hour. She didn't show. When I went to her apartment, no one was there and the door was wide open. I've been frantic, and the police didn't want to take me seriously. Then I remembered hearing about you and the detective agency. I knew Libby's daughter was the one person I could count on."

I felt the weight of her trust heavy on my shoulders. "Let me get you some food, Frankie. Why don't you plan on staying with me tonight? We can go to New Orleans tomorrow." I leveled my gaze at Tinkie. "It'll only be me. Tinkie truly can't leave her baby."

As if on cue, Maylin's cry came from the parlor. Not ten seconds later, Oscar appeared with the red-faced baby. He held her out to Tinkie. "She's really upset."

Tinkie took her with complete calm. "She's hungry." She stood up. "If you'll excuse me, I'll be back in a few minutes."

"Join us in the parlor, please." I couldn't let Frankie stay alone, missing her daughter.

"I don't want to interfere—"

"Nonsense," Oscar said, offering his arm to escort her. Oscar and Harold both had excellent, courtly manners. But the man I wanted to talk to was Coleman. I fell behind Oscar and Frankie and then took a left into the foyer, where I could signal Coleman out. He eased out of the parlor without attracting any attention.

My face must have told him of my distress because when we had some privacy, he drew me into his arms and held me. "I remember Frankie. She was your mother's conspirator in mischief. I'm so sorry about her daughter."

"Did the NOPD have any information?"

"They did." He led me to the staircase and we took a seat. "Christa did file a missing persons report on her friend. And Britta's parents have contacted the German ambassador's office. He's making inquiries about Britta. Now that Christa has also gone missing, the police are taking it far more seriously."

That was good to know.

"Do they have any leads?"

"They were kind of tight-lipped about leads, but tomorrow one of my good friends is working. I'll speak with him and get as much info as I can. Are you going to take her case?"

"I have to." There was a bond between Frankie and me and my mother.

"And Tinkie?"

"She can't go to New Orleans toting a baby. She can do

the things she does best here." But I had an inspired idea. "Why don't you come with me, Coleman? You're due for a change of scenery. Other than our trip to Columbus, which was only a few days, you haven't had a break in forever. While I'm working, you can take in the city. And maybe help me out in a pinch."

Though I'd caught him by surprise with my suggestion, I was happy to see he was considering it. "I actually think that's a good plan, Sarah Booth. We'll be close by, yet New Orleans is like a foreign country in some regards. And I'll be there to keep you out of trouble."

He wasn't going to be wild about the forever-young cult angle, but Coleman would go wherever the leads took him. If Coleman went, it would also relieve Tinkie of any guilt she might feel at staying behind with her baby.

"It's a deal, then." I stuck out my hand and we shook. "Partner. I'll leave early with Frankie and you can follow as soon as you clear things at the sheriff's office. This is going to be good for both of us."

# 4

Frankie and I were packed and loaded to leave Zinnia by seven the next morning. Exhausted by emotions and worries, Frankie had gone to bed as soon as we got to my ancestral home, Dahlia House. Coleman and I had stayed up to talk, planning his escape to New Orleans and the first steps of my investigation into what happened to Christa and Britta.

I kissed Coleman goodbye on the front porch with a promise to meet him for dinner. Frankie had surprised us with a reservation at the Belle Fleur Apartments, part of the complex where Christa and Britta lived. It was a lovely place tucked into the boundary of the French Quarter, with private gardens and easy access to everything. Coleman and I would be staying in the lap of luxury.

But it wasn't luxury I was thinking about as I got behind the wheel of my car and watched Frankie shift into the passenger seat. Coleman had offered to drive her car to New Orleans so Frankie and I could have the time to talk. He was a real champ.

We'd barely cleared the driveway when Frankie turned to me. "Your mother always had a thing for convertibles. Did she ever tell you about the time she stole the local mortician's classic T-Bird convertible?"

Oh, I had not heard this story, but I was eager to. "Tell me."

Frankie's words took me back to a time when I was young and safe. "Did she really steal a car?" My mother was a practical joker, but this was actually a crime.

"It depends on how you view it. Mr. Jenkins, at the time, was a good thirty years older than your mother. She was just seventeen. He offered her the car to use, and he left the keys in it. I do believe his intention was that she would drive the car when he was with her. Libby had other ideas and saw the car, the keys, and opportunity. She gave rides to all the high school kids, then she took the car back."

"I gather Mr. Jenkins wasn't happy."

"An understatement, but Libby was smart. She knew Jenkins wouldn't push the matter. It was a scandal that he'd tried to bribe her to spend time with him by offering the car."

"That's all true, but my mother's conduct wasn't exactly . . . ethical." I was smiling despite my statement.

"Fiddledeedee," Frankie said, waving a hand to dismiss my worries. "Jenkins was an old lech and he got what he deserved. I could tell you Libby stories all day long."

"But we really should talk about Christa and where to start looking."

"Once Christa is found, I'd like to spend some time with you, that good-looking sheriff, and my daughter. I want to share some of my memories with all of you. Libby and Franklin Delaney were a force of nature, Sarah Booth. You have no idea how many people they helped. How brave and fearless they were when they stood up for right." She sighed. "I miss them both, and you were so young when they died. I want you to know, fully, who they were."

"I'd like that very much."

The first thing we did when we hit New Orleans was to go to Christa and Britta's apartment to look for Christa's laptop. If she was working on a story, she'd have notes, and those would likely be on her computer. While Britta's art supplies and paintings were in the apartment, we couldn't find any evidence of Christa's work. No computer. No notebooks. Nothing except her clothes and personal items.

Frankie maintained her composure, but I could see the tears in her eyes, and it made me feel helpless because I couldn't offer any solid clues. While we knew Britta had disappeared from Jackson Square, we weren't even certain of the location where Christa was last seen.

"Did Christa ever mention any friends here in the Quarter?"

"She was seeing a man, but I don't know how serious it was. Christa wasn't one to share her personal life. She was private like that. We talked, but she didn't give details. Not even to me. But she had lots of friends living near her."

For the first time, I felt that Frankie was holding something back from me. Now wasn't the time to push, but I didn't really have a choice. "Do you know the name of Christa's love interest?"

"Carlos Rodriguez." Frankie shrugged one shoulder. "Don't tell Christa, but I had Carlos checked out. He had some trouble with the law when he was younger. He grew up in New Orleans in a really tough part of town. Now he's a photographer, very respected. Christa never said, but I thought perhaps he was working with her to illustrate her story. Christa knew I'd be upset about his past, so she kept all of this on the QT."

"What kind of trouble with the law?" I didn't actually get a whiff of suspicion, but Carlos was at least a lead.

"His family had some connection to a drug cartel, but Carlos was never implicated. He got in trouble in high school for selling weed. No heavy drugs."

"Okay." Coleman would be invaluable in the research of Carlos. "I'll look into that, just to make sure we're turning over every rock." I didn't want to make Frankie hopeful or concerned, and I didn't know which way she'd break over Carlos. She might feel compelled to protect her daughter's choices. Or she might be thinking what I was thinking—drug cartels had been known to kidnap Americans and ransom them back.

"Did she have a mentor at the university?" This might be another good angle.

"Dr. Sonya Welch. She's been a true supporter. I don't see how she could be involved. She's in Missouri at the school."

"But she was directing Christa's research for her application?"

"Yes." Frankie picked up a red jacket. She held it and buried her face in it. "It still smells like Christa's soap and shampoo." Her voice broke. "She would never worry me like this if she could contact me."

That much I believed to be true. "We don't know that anything tragic has happened," I reminded her. "All we know for certain is that Christa isn't where she should be. The same for Britta. When will her parents arrive?"

"Probably sometime tonight or tomorrow. They were getting the first available flight here, but international travel takes some planning."

"Why don't you make some coffee for us," I suggested. The pot was right on the counter and it would keep Frankie busy while I quickly canvassed the neighbors, who I could hear outside on the shared front porch. As much help and good company as Frankie was, her daughter's neighbors and friends were more likely to be open and honest with me if I was by myself.

Christa's apartment was located in a fourplex of up-and-down units painted bright teal. The rooms were large, light-filled, and lovely, and the apartment complex sat on a large lot full of beautiful live oaks. A lot of wonderful New Orleans neighborhoods had been built on the grounds of old plantations. I didn't know the history of this particular area, but it would be easy enough to discover. Listening to laughter and chatter coming from the front porch, I realized Christa and Britta's apartment seemed to be a gathering place for young people.

I made my way to the front door and peeked out to discover a cluster of twentysomethings sitting in wicker rockers, talking and laughing. They greeted me with smiles and hellos as I approached.

"Can we help you?" a woman asked.

"I'm a friend of Christa's. She was supposed to meet me, but it seems she's out of pocket. Have y'all seen her?"

A tall brunette stepped forward. "We haven't. In fact, we were saying earlier that we haven't seen Christa or Britta in . . . at least two days. What's going on?"

"I'm not certain. Her mother is here, too. We're both a little worried."

"I'm Addie Graham," the brunette said, and then made introductions around the group. "We're all friends. I know Christa was working on a story for a scholarship opportunity, and Britta was painting landscapes. She was pulling in the cash, too. Both of them were busy with various projects, but they were always home at night."

"We're supposed to have a potluck tonight. Christa was going to bring her famous crème puffs for dessert," the man Addie had introduced as Burt Steele said. "They never missed the weekly dinners."

"Any idea what Christa was working on?" I played it casual.

"She never talked about it," Addie said. "She was excited, though. I'm also a freelance journalist so it makes sense she wasn't blabbing about her great idea, but often we did share concepts and research methods." Her face brightened. "She did ask to borrow some books I had on the Garden District."

"And she had a couple of appointments to talk to that priest near City Park," Burt volunteered. "I remember that because Christa wasn't exactly the religious kind, but she was suddenly really interested in Catholicism and saints."

"I think that was part of the investigative story she was working on," Addie said. "But I didn't pry. Christa was ambitious. Very ambitious. And she didn't . . ." She faltered to a halt.

"Didn't what?" I asked.

"She didn't trust easily," Addie finished. "Carlos was always saying that he could almost feel her wanting to trust, but then she'd pull back. He thought it had to do with her father's death when she was little."

"By the way, where is Carlos?" Burt asked. "He probably knew Christa's plans."

"I haven't seen him, either. His place is on Barracks Street," Addie supplied. "I think it's 428 Barracks Street, but he was usually over here at Christa's. That is until she got so caught up in her investigation that she didn't have time for anyone."

"She was pretty intense about the scholarship," Burt said. "Before she started working on this big story, she was easygoing and fun. She changed." His face showed concern and some annoyance. "And not for the better. It happened quickly, too."

"When was the last time you saw Christa?" I asked.

"I saw her in the Copper Kettle," Burt said. "She was waiting for Britta." He stood up. "What's going on? Has something happened to Christa or Britta?"

"Well, they're missing," I said, playing down my worries, "but maybe they took a trip. That's what I'm trying to find out."

"And who are you, really?" Addie asked. "What's your relationship with Christa?"

"I'm her mother's friend." That was all I was willing to tell.

"Christa was close with her mom, Frankie. She wouldn't take off and leave her mom hanging in the wind. What's going on?" Addie was getting angry now.

"I'm not certain." As much as I wanted to engage their help in hunting for the missing women, I hesitated. They seemed like good friends, but I didn't trust easily either.

While I was trying to think of something to say, Burt walked to the edge of the porch, his focus on a black Lexus SUV. He pointed across the neutral space to the opposite lane of traffic. "I think that's the guy who was trying to hire Britta to paint a landscape."

The minute he pointed, the SUV took off, tires squealing. I barely got a glimpse of a chiseled jaw, dark hair, and piercing eyes before the vehicle was gone. "Do you know that man?" I asked.

"No," Burt said. "But Britta pointed him out to me when I was at her booth. I thought at the time that he was hanging around, watching her. He made me uncomfortable."

"Tell me more," I urged.

"Britta was really excited about the commission he offered. She wanted to do it very badly, and she was talking about how much he'd offered."

"How much?" Talking about money was crass, but this could be important.

"He promised her twenty thousand for the watercolor landscape. He brought her a photo and dropped it off at her booth where she was working, but he wanted her to see the scene in person."

"And you saw him talking to Britta?" This could be helpful.

"I guess I came up to her booth about an hour after he'd left the photo. He was still lurking around, which seemed weird. I didn't like it."

"Did Britta seem unnerved?"

"She was too focused on the painting, already sketching it out, getting ideas. That was her process. She didn't notice him still watching until I asked about him. She just said he was intense about getting her to do the painting."

He frowned. "The landscape in the picture was really beautiful."

"What was it of?"

"A garden. It was blazing with colors and exotic plants with a white shell path that curved and seemed to go slightly downhill, like maybe to a stream or small bayou. And there were terrific statues of what I assume are gods and goddesses. The kind you'd find in Greece. And incredible fountains." He frowned. "It did look magical."

"Do you know where it was?" This might be helpful information.

He shook his head. "Britta said the man was very secretive. He said the garden was an oasis in a desert of man-made disasters." He hesitated. "And he said something strange. That the gods had smiled on this garden location and given it special powers. I remember that because when Christa was asking about Britta and I told her about the man, she thought that was significant. How he used the plural of gods."

"Can you remember anything else?" I asked. Burt had been more helpful than he knew.

"Only that it's creepy that man was just here, staring at the apartment where Britta lives. How did he know where she lives? I'm sure she wouldn't have told him." The color drained from his face. "Unless she was forced to do so."

"Do you have any idea where this garden might be?" I wasn't hopeful but I had to ask.

"No idea. It's so beautiful, it seems like some of the magazines would have featured it, and I keep pretty close tabs on the local art venues. I'm always looking for interesting places that might want an outdoor sculpture. I'd love to create something for this space."

"Would Britta have gone to this garden if she knew the address?"

Burt shook his head. "Not alone. Britta is careful. She's been all over the world, living on her own, traveling by herself. She's smart and savvy in the ways of the world. She was wary of the man who offered the commission even though she wanted it. She didn't go with him to look in person, but the project enthralled her."

"Shush!" Addie whispered. The group stared at the front door and froze.

# 5

Frankie walked into the strained silence on the porch. "What's wrong?" she asked.

"We're all just trying to piece together a timeline of when we saw Christa and Britta last," I answered. "These folks have been very helpful." I smiled and they responded in kind, though everyone looked a little uncomfortable.

"Did Christa tell you the history of these apartments? They're on the edge of what was once a vast working farm. This area was not within the city limits." Addie changed the conversation like a pro.

"No, she never mentioned it," Frankie said. "Is there a story?"

"New Orleans was perhaps the largest slave market in the United States, and Canewood Plantation built holding pens. The enslaved people couldn't be kept in the city proper; there wasn't room. So they were brought here and gotten into better condition for the sales. Many were malnourished and mistreated from the journey to New Orleans and their life working on various plantations. It's a horrific bit of history. I'm surprised she never told you. Christa liked the darker stories, and you were so close." Addie shook her head. "You always supported her in everything she did. It was wonderful to see."

"I tried to give Christa all my support and my best advice," Frankie said. "She never mentioned this tragic history. Was she interested in it?"

Leitha, a quiet brunette, spoke up for the first time. "I don't think that was Christa's focus. She was onto something else. Something that involved religious beliefs. Or at least that's what I think."

"What makes you think that?" I asked. I was hesitant to pursue this in front of Frankie, but the conversation had taken the turn without my help.

"I studied mythology in college and she was asking me about different resurrection beliefs. I had to assume that was her interest."

"Like Easter?" I asked.

"Exactly. Almost every religion has some type of resurrection element. The Greeks had Persephone, who rises from Hades every spring to bring the Earth back to life. Osiris for the Egyptians. Resurrection is a common theme in most religions."

"Was there any particular resurrection belief she showed interest in?" Frankie asked.

Leitha shook her head. "It was more of a broad canvas of belief systems, but she was after something. She just didn't say what it was."

"Thanks, that's really helpful," I said.

"The coffee is ready," Frankie said. "Would any of you like a cup?"

Addie took the initiative to break up the conversation. "No, thank you, Mrs. Moore. I have to run by the library and pick up some books. I should hustle." She stood up and was joined by Burt and Leitha.

"If we can do anything to help hunt for Christa and Britta, please let us know," Burt said. "We'll keep our eyes open, too."

"Thank you, Burt. Addie, I'll be staying here in the apartment for a day or two. Until Christa shows up, at least. If you hear anything, just drop by."

"Will do, Mrs. Moore." Addie slung her purse strap across her chest. "See you all later."

Frankie and I watched the young people break up and go in different directions. She turned to me. "They're worried about Christa and Britta and they aren't very good at hiding it."

There was no point denying what was clear to see. "They are. But it's good to have them on the lookout. They'll haunt the places our missing women are most likely to go." I put a hand on her shoulder. "Places we might never think of."

We walked back into the apartment and sat down in the breakfast nook, filled with beautiful and thriving plants, to drink our coffee. I asked Frankie questions about Christa and tried not to be too intrusive or negative. I needed to know her likes and dislikes, her beliefs, desires, treasures—the little things that spoke of her individualism. That would give me an idea of possible patterns of behavior.

When I finished the coffee, I was ready to lay out some

plans for the rest of the afternoon. It wasn't going to be easy to convince Frankie to stay in the apartment, but I felt I could be more successful alone. "Would you stay here?" I asked her. "It would be a terrific help if you went through Britta's things to see if you can locate a photograph of a garden. Burt was telling me about that big commission and the strange man who offered it."

"Are you trying to give me the slip?" Frankie was nobody's fool.

"I can work more effectively alone. It's true. Everyone will hold back, not wanting to worry you."

She nodded. "I know. Just call me if you learn anything."

"I promise." I grinned. "I'm working for you."

"I know," she said, "but it's hard to be the one sitting at home waiting."

I knew that for a fact. "I promise I'll call if I hear or find out a single thing."

I hated to leave her alone, but I wanted to talk to the boyfriend, Carlos. I figured he'd be reluctant to talk in front of his girlfriend's mother. Especially considering the things I wanted to ask him about.


Instead of driving, I left Frankie the car and called an Uber to take me to Barracks Street and the address I'd been given for Carlos Rodriguez. Parking in the Quarter could be a nightmare, and I wasn't eager to test my parallel skills.

The shotgun house on a tiny patch of lawn was nicely kept, and when I knocked at the door, it was answered by a handsome man in his late twenties or early thirties. "Carlos Rodriguez?" I asked.

"Yes, who are you?"

"I'm a friend of Christa Moore."

I didn't get a chance to say more because he cut in over me. "Where is she? Have you seen her? Is she okay?"

Either he was really worried about her or a very good actor. "I was hoping you might be able to tell me." My statement caused his face to fall into lines of worry.

"I haven't seen her. We were supposed to meet two days ago and she didn't show. I was . . ." He looked down. "I've been worried."

Now I really did feel sorry for him, which wasn't my job. I had to remind myself of that. Carlos looked forlorn, but I'd met too many con artists and tricksters to buy into his sadness one hundred percent.

"When was the last time you talked to her?"

"October twenty-fourth. I remember the date because she said Britta had been missing for two days and she thought she had some leads that had opened an important door for the scholarship story she was working on. She was consumed about that story and she was bird-dogging it hard. She wasn't eating or sleeping. I called her that morning, early, and she agreed to meet me. I told her I'd help do anything she wanted, and I thought maybe she'd let me in, allow me to help. But she never showed and when I went to her apartment, everything about her work was gone. Her day planner, her notebooks, her computer. She had a desktop and a laptop and both were gone. I knew something was very wrong."

"Tell me about this story she was working on," I said. I wondered if she'd told Carlos something she hadn't told her other friends or her mother.

"Wait a minute." He stepped back. "I don't know

who you are or why you're asking all of these questions. Maybe I shouldn't talk to you at all."

Thank goodness Tinkie had insisted on Delaney Detective Agency business cards. I handed him one. "I'm working for Christa's mother. She's at Christa's apartment right now and you can call her and ask if you'd like."

"I don't know her," he said. "Christa was going to introduce us at Thanksgiving." He flicked the business card and stared at it again, completely unimpressed.

"Carlos, you can be a help or a hindrance. If you really want Christa back, talk to me."

He pushed the door open and I stepped into an apartment that lacked the neatness of Christa's digs, but was clean and contained amazing framed photographs. Carlos had a great eye and a sense of light. "Wow. Those are terrific."

"Christa had them framed and she hung them." He turned away, but I still caught a hint of sadness on his face. "She believed in me when no one else did."

And I hoped to goodness he had not repaid that belief with betrayal. It seemed that Carlos may have been the last person to talk to Christa, and his lack of knowledge about the story she was pursuing left me troubled. I shared everything with Coleman. Well, almost everything, and the things I didn't spit out always got me in big trouble.

"Can you give me a list of Christa's hangouts? I need to hit the street. The more time that passes—"

"The worse it looks," Carlos said. "I know. The first forty-eight hours are crucial. I'll write some places down for you, but I've already been everywhere I thought she might be. And I've left word with people to call me." He didn't flinch when he asked, "This is not looking good, is it? First Britta, and now Christa. Did someone target them?"

"I don't know. I just got here today. I'm following every lead we have, but there isn't a lot. Someone knew to take her computers. That's the thing that really alarms me." I wasn't pretending about that. Had Christa stumbled on something big?

"She's like a terrier," he said. "Once she gets hold of something, she doesn't let go. Not even if she's afraid."

"Was she afraid?" I hated to even ask the question.

"She was very afraid for Britta. That creepy guy hanging around. Renaldo, or something like that, I think is his name. The whole commissioned painting, the twenty thousand dollars. That's a lot of money for a relatively unknown painter. Britta is talented, no doubt about that. But twenty grand?"

"What did Christa say?"

"She was worried her friend had been abducted. She called Britta's parents and the police. She called the German embassy. She did everything she knew to do, but no one really took her seriously. Britta was a vagabond. She's been everywhere. After a while she pulls up stakes and moves on. That's what the officials said."

"But she left all of her work and supplies?"

"Yes, Britta's stuff is there, but Christa's is gone. That makes no sense."

I liked Carlos, and I hated to ask, but I had no choice. "I have to ask you about your background and family, Carlos. I hope you'll be honest. I'll check it so there's really no point lying."

He nodded and held my gaze. "Christa didn't want to tell her mother about me or my past. She was afraid

Frankie would judge me before she got a chance to really know me."

"So tell me what there is to know. I'll speak with Frankie this evening."

"My uncle is a very dangerous and mean man. He runs a cartel in Colombia and he's killed a lot of people. He almost killed my father when my dad refused to help with the drug business. That was years ago, when I was an infant. That's why we left the country and came here. My father, though, was a good man. He refused to be involved in that business. He was an accountant and got a job as a bookkeeper for a family-owned chain of grocery stores in the Ninth Ward. That's where I grew up with my older brother, Eduardo."

I could tell by his face that the story was about to take a dark turn. I wasn't wrong.

Carlos shook his head slowly. "Eduardo broke my father's heart."

Despite my best intentions not to be sucked into a sob story, I couldn't help my emotions. "What happened?"

"Eduardo grew up, and he took my uncle up on his offer to become part of the business. He moved to Houston and rose high in the ranks of a dangerous gang." He cleared his throat twice. "Eduardo was shot in the head, execution style. It broke my father's heart and he died of a heart attack a month later."

"I'm sorry, Carlos. That's tough."

"My brother made his choices. The money and power . . . he couldn't walk away. I found photography. That's what saved me."

His story was inspiring—if it was true. With Coleman's help, it would be easy enough to check out, so I hoped Carlos wasn't stupid enough to lie to me.

"Frankie is staying in Christa's place right now. Why don't you stop by this evening and talk to her?"

"I'd love to do that, but I don't want to do anything to increase her worry."

"I think she'd feel better if she met you." I had another thought. "Do you have any photographs of Christa?"

"Of course! I'd like to bring her one."

"She'd like that. May I see some of your photos of her?" I realized that I didn't have an image of my missing client with me. I'd simply failed to ask Frankie for a photo, though I knew she had snapshots on her phone. A professional photo would be much better anyway.

"Come this way." He led me down a hallway filled with incredible black-and-white photos of dramatic New Orleans scenes. The photos truly captured a sense of movement; of time stopped for a split second before it resumed.

He turned into a bedroom and I stopped in my tracks. The wall I faced was a heart-stopping montage of Christa. Some were candid shots of her clowning around, some perfectly lit studies of her beautiful bone structure and startling blue eyes. I thought of the human trafficking angle Frankie had said Christa was working on and my heart sank to my toes. Also concerning was Carlos's apparent obsession with her. He was a photographer, and image was everything. But I had to wonder if he'd taken his interest in Christa over the top.

"I know. She's so beautiful," Carlos said. "There is not a minute of the day when I don't think how lucky I am that she cares about me."

I studied the photos and stopped in front of one taken on the abandoned steps of what had once been a large home. There was nothing left now but the steps and some charred timbers. New Orleans had many beautiful areas where the older homes were maintained perfectly. "Where was this taken?"

Carlos thought for a moment. "It was in the Garden District."

"How long ago did you take it?"

"Maybe three days. It was such a great shot I had it printed immediately. I was going to give it to Christa. She loved that property." Carlos's enthusiasm seemed genuine, and I could see why Christa would love the photo, but it wasn't the human element that drew me.

I moved to another group of stunning photos. The wrought iron fence and gate were unusual. The spears of the gate were topped by Cerberus, the three-headed dog of Greek mythology, the dog that guarded the entrance to Hades and stopped any souls from departing. It couldn't be just coincidence that I'd just been told Christa was interested in resurrection religions.

"That's the same place. Christa was fascinated by it," Carlos said. "She was really digging that fence. It's how I got that terrific pensive look on her face. I swear, she would have climbed that fence if I hadn't stopped her."

"Where is this?"

"Third Street. There's not much left of the house, that I could tell. The vegetation is in the way, but I've heard it was once magnificent. I think they did a TV series set in the house."

"Address?"

He shook his head. "I'm sorry, we were walking down the street and I was so busy photographing Christa that I didn't pay attention. But it was Third Street."

"With that fence, I can find it."

"Why would you want to?" he asked.

That was a question better left unanswered until I had

more information. I was literally saved by the bell when my phone buzzed, Coleman on the line. Now wasn't the most auspicious time to get a report on Carlos, since he was standing right in front of me, so I said my goodbyes and took off on foot before I called Coleman back.

Pedestrians bustled by and I saw a leather shop on the corner—a sure sign that I was headed straight toward the tourist section. This was a part of town that still allowed traffic, and I was busy dialing Coleman when I felt the hairs on the back of my neck prickle. Turning around, I saw a black SUV about three blocks back, cruising slowly. The only occupant appeared to be the driver. The car took a sharp right and sped away the minute I started staring at it.

Could the same guy who'd been watching Christa's apartment now be following me? It wasn't a comforting thought.

I found a small café and went inside to call Coleman.

"I was getting worried," he said.

"I'm fine. I didn't want to talk in front of Carlos. Are you on the way to NOLA?"

"Headed down the highway now. About two hours away. I found out some interesting details about Carlos Rodriguez. Do you want to wait until I get there?"

"Spill it now, please."

"Carlos comes from a crime family, but Carlos seems to have steered clear of serious trouble except for a juvenile arrest. After that, he has a clean record."

Carlos had been truthful in all that he'd told me. I could tell there was something else to the story, though. "But?" I prompted.

"Just be careful, Sarah Booth. Carlos may be a great

guy, but these people have the power to make bodies disappear. If Frankie's daughter got crosswise . . ."

He didn't have to finish. These were people with a lot of money at stake, and they cared about money far, far more than human life. I was just glad I hadn't taken the call in front of Carlos. I couldn't have kept my thoughts from showing on my face.

"Where are you now?" Coleman asked.

"Duet's Café. I'm headed back to Christa's apartment on Esplanade. The place Frankie rented for us is very close. Why don't you meet us there? Frankie has been looking through Britta's things. All of Christa's work tools and computers are gone."

"I see." Coleman didn't elaborate. "Be there in less than two hours."

"I can't wait to see you." And I wasn't exaggerating. I needed a dose of Coleman to get me over the dark forebodings I'd begun to develop about my case.

# 6

Waiting for Coleman to arrive, I had time to give Frankie a detailed report of what I'd discovered and my first impression of Carlos. To her credit, she was eager to meet the young man. When Coleman arrived in her car, Frankie withdrew into a bedroom so I could give him the greeting he deserved—a kiss that sent sizzling signals from my lips to my toes. I was really glad to see my fella, and he was happy to see me.

"Has Cece called?" Coleman asked when we stepped back from each other.

"No." I hadn't expected to hear from my journalist friend. I'd only been gone from Zinnia for ten hours. "Is everything okay with Tinkie and the baby?" Thinking of little Maylin made my weary heart dance for a moment.

"They're fine. Cece just had some insight into the people seeking eternal youth that Tinkie mentioned to you. Emma Jane, or 'Pouty,' as you called her."

I had my research cut out for me on that angle. People who sought to remain youthful forever seemed like morons to me, but a lot of people with a lot of money had nothing to do but worry about wrinkles. So be it. There were all kinds of cults out there. Sex, youth, car, religious, political—the list was endless. And charlatans of all stripes had learned to capitalize on foolish people who wanted their dreams and fantasies validated. Yes, you can live to be two hundred and remain flexible, just take this potion or vitamin or soak in this elixir.

"Earth to Sarah Booth." Coleman had a knowing grin on his face.

"Sorry. I took a little trip to an alternate universe."

"I could tell."

"So what's our next step?"

He nodded toward the bedroom. "I have some information on Britta."

I couldn't conceal my eagerness to hear what he'd found. "Tell me."

"I'm not sure Frankie needs to hear this, but then again, she's your client and she isn't paying you to filter the information to protect her."

This didn't sound good at all. "Would you please ask Frankie what she'd like to do for dinner? While you're talking to her I'll call Cece. I think we have to tell her everything we find."

"I agree." He gave a little mock salute and went to

knock on the bedroom door while I stepped out on the porch and called my friend.

Cece was on deadline for the next day's paper, but she took a moment to fill me in on what she'd learned with a few phone calls. There had been youth cults in New Orleans since Ponce de León braved the wilds of the Gulf Coast and went searching for the fountain of youth.

"Tinkie is going to talk with her friend who mentioned it." Cece sighed. "Who has time for this foolishness?"

"I don't know, but thank you. And I'll remind Tinkie that Maylin is her first and only priority. If she can give me a way to contact Emma Jane, I can take it from there."

"The real reason I wanted to talk to you is to tell you that Tinkie is chafing about not helping on the case."

"She is helping, and I'll tell her so."

"Good, and if you find out there really is a youth cult in New Orleans, you have to call me instantly. Can you imagine what fodder that will be for *The Truth Is Out There*? Millie is practically frothing at the mouth to head to New Orleans to dig into this. You know she's already conjuring up a 'what-if' story, as in what if Elvis's body was saved and he's been returned to the years of his lean and hip-swiveling youth."

"'What-if' could be dangerous in Millie's hands." I knew Millie had a blast writing the weekly column in the local newspaper that featured celebrity gossip, crazy reported happenings, and local people. The column was so popular it had turned some Sunflower County residents into social influencers.

"What if Elvis met a youth cult? What if aliens provided DNA that led to eternal youth? Surely you see the potential." Cece was droll, but we both saw the big potential for great copy and fun.

"Does she even need to talk to anyone? She can just make it up."

"If she can tie the story to a local Sunflower County name, all the better."

"I'll keep that in mind." And I would. Millie's columns, written with Cece, were just fanciful enough to make me laugh. I couldn't stick around, though, as Coleman and Frankie were coming down the hall toward me. "Gotta go, Cece. Talk soon. If I get any leads on fountains of youth, injections, diets, or plastic wraps to sweat off the pounds, I'll let you know."

"Ha ha, always the clown. Be careful," Cece said and signed off. It was time to deal with the information on Britta, and, judging from Coleman's face, it wasn't going to be what Frankie wanted to hear.

New Orleans was a city where it was hard to find a bad meal, and we ended up in the courtyard at the Napoleon House, a palm-filled wonder. The drink in my hand was a Bloody Mary with just enough Creole spice to make it zing. We ordered jambalaya with crusty French bread and settled back to talk. I let Coleman proceed at his own pace. He was good at reading people.

"Frankie, what did Christa tell you about Britta?"

"She's from Düsseldorf." She checked her watch. "I guess her parents are coming in tomorrow or they would have called by now."

"Do you really know much about her?"

It was a red alert question, and Frankie saw it clearly. "What's wrong? What did you find out?"

"Checking with my law enforcement friends, I did find some things that are concerning."

I reached across the table and held Frankie's hand. She looked terrified, and I didn't blame her.

"What kind of things?" she asked.

"Britta has been in trouble with the law. Several times. In different countries."

"For what?" Frankie asked, her voice cracking.

"Blackmail."

This wasn't what I'd anticipated, and Frankie looked as if she'd had the wind knocked out of her lungs. "What? Blackmail? What are you talking about?"

Coleman gave me a helpless look. He believed in telling the truth, even when it was distressing. "It seems that Britta has done paintings for several wealthy clients. Along the way she's picked up some personal information that she then used to blackmail her clients."

"How many?" I asked.

"Only one charge filed here in the States. In Florida. Boca Raton, to be exact. There are indications she pulled the same stunt in Germany, but it's more difficult to get the details of that. The Florida authorities have been looking for Britta."

"Do you think that's why she disappeared from here?" Frankie asked.

"I don't know," Coleman said. "But we have to have all the facts out on the table to make our decisions. Could Christa somehow be involved in this?"

Frankie shook her head. "No. Not in blackmailing anyone." She hesitated. "Unless that was justice. Christa has a real issue about what is just and what isn't. If someone hurt Britta and she blackmailed them to get even . . ."

Frankie's honesty showed me exactly how much she loved her daughter. And how well she knew her.

Coleman nodded. "I'll get more details. If Britta picked

the wrong person to apply pressure to, it's possible they're behind her disappearance."

"And if Christa was with Britta, she wouldn't abandon her friend even if given the chance."

This new information put another whole level of danger around the missing women. While it gave me new directions to seek information, it was not the kind of lead I liked. If Britta had picked the wrong person, she might be dead. And Christa might have been pulled into trouble along with her. I didn't intend to say any of this to Frankie, but I could see the deep worry on her face.

"Did you have any luck with the police?" I asked Coleman.

"They have missing persons reports on both women. Christa filed one on Britta, and it looks like Carlos Rodriguez and Frankie filed one on Christa. There wasn't much information for the officers to go on. Britta did disappear from her booth at Jackson Square, and no one seems to know much about Christa. Rodriguez said he was supposed to meet her and she never showed."

That was exactly what he'd told me. Coleman also had information on Carlos's family connections. That information matched as well. The consistency led me to believe Carlos was a truth teller, which gave me a slight bit of relief from worry.

Our dessert arrived, but Frankie had little appetite, though she tried hard to hide it. Darkness had fallen while we were in Napoleon House, and the lights of the French Quarter sizzled red, blue, and green neon at some of the corner daiquiri bars. Many of the shops and bars were decorated for Halloween, with dancing skeletons, ghouls, witches, and ghosts. One grim reaper reminded me of Jitty's visit at Hilltop. She'd warned of trouble, and now I was sitting in a pile of it.

Frankie insisted on staying at Christa's apartment alone. She was still hunting for the garden scene photograph, and Coleman and I were just across the beautiful lawn. We went to the apartment and Coleman pulled me into an embrace.

"I'm worried about those young women," I said.

I could admit it to Coleman, even as I tried hard to be strong for Frankie.

We walked out onto the porch, which also faced Esplanade, and Coleman brought us each a nightcap to sip while we talked. Before we got settled, though, Tinkie called.

"I've made an appointment for you. Breakfast tomorrow at the Ruby Slipper," she said without even giving me a chance to say hello. "Take that photographer, Carlos, with you. Pouty will meet you at nine o'clock sharp for an interview for a fashion piece. She'll expect to be photographed, so make it look real."

"Okay."

"Pouty's the wife of Dr. Leo LeMuse, plastic surgeon to the celebrities. She kept her maiden name. Anyway, a lot of Hollywood people come to him in New Orleans when they need work and don't want to be beset by the paparazzi."

"That's a made-up name."

"Of course it is. LeMuse is totally made up. I think Leo's real name is something like Muskrat or Musty or something equally glum. Pouty's mother was a Cotterille, of the Cotterille family. The ones who own about twenty thousand acres of rich Delta soil."

"I know the family." The Cotterilles had less than a sterling reputation for business practices. "Is Pouty as awful as her name and her family?"

"Oh, she's much, much worse," Tinkie said, laughing. "But vanity is her Achilles' heel. She's the one who invited me to meet members of the forever young group. She wants to be in a big fashion publication. Flatter her."

"Thanks, Tinkie!" For that kind of information, I would make Pouty think she was the Queen of Sheba if I had to. "How is Maylin?" Even the thought of that little girl made me smile.

"I think she's grown an inch," Tinkie said. "Oscar says so, too. Hurry home or she'll be a teenager before you know it."

We said our goodbyes and I returned to the porch and Coleman. Snuggling against his side on an old glider, I dumped my worries and for a moment basked in the joy of his company. The soft autumn night of New Orleans, with jazz music in the distance, was the perfect opportunity for a bit of canoodling, and Coleman was an expert at it.

# 7

Carlos was eager to help find Christa, and he showed up at the Ruby Slipper in the grand old Pelham Hotel with three huge camera bags, lenses, flash equipment, and the perfect attitude for a fashion photographer.

"Growing up in the Ninth Ward taught me how vital attitude is," he explained. "When you wear the same pair of jeans and worn-out sneakers to school every day, kids notice. They can be mean. We all learn defense mechanisms. I perfected the sneer." He demonstrated and I had to laugh. He was clever and fun. On the ride to the café—I'd chosen to Uber rather than try to park—I'd had another talk with Tinkie and we'd refined my cover story. I was ready for Emma Jane "Pouty" Cotterille LeMuse.

When Pouty arrived, pushing into the restaurant like

royalty expecting everyone to genuflect, Carlos rolled his eyes at me. We were in for a tough morning, but we were loaded for bear.

Pouty's perfectly blank expression made me wonder if her facial muscles had been paralyzed. I wasn't one to judge, because I didn't give a hoot. I was, however, impressed with the burnt-orange frock coat over black leggings. She was a kind of Halloween Prince, with a frill of a ruffle at her throat that showed vivid colors of forest green, yellow, and red. The gold buttons of the fitted frock coat were a master touch. She was a walking advertisement for fall. In her mid-thirties or beyond, her body was lean, sharp, and honed. She looked really good. Even her multitone hair, which must have taken hours to achieve, shimmered in the light with a natural effect. I couldn't detect a single wrinkle or misplaced eyebrow.

The waitress brought menus, and Carlos and I ordered. "I don't eat," Pouty said. "Once past the lips, forever on the hips."

"How do you stay alive?" Carlos sounded sincere, but I couldn't tell.

"I drink protein shakes. Yummy."

It occurred to me she might be a good ventriloquist. Her lips barely moved. "I love your outfit," I said, trying to find some common ground to break the ice.

"Tinkie told me to wear something with fall flair. If this won't suit, we can run over to the house. I have closets full of great clothes. Since I never gain weight, everything always fits me to a T."

"Yes, it does." I signaled Carlos to start shooting some photos. That would loosen her up.

Indeed, the moment the camera came out, she was able to smile. Even her teeth were pearly white, straight, and evenly spaced. I wanted to tap them to see if they were real, but I was afraid she'd snap my finger off. I didn't trust that the unblemished creature seated at the table with me was truly alive. She'd been a cute enough kid in school, but this woman was a finely wrought sculpture.

"So Tinkie said you were helping the marvelous Cece Dee Falcon with a story about high fashion in New Orleans." She stared at me really hard, letting me know that she found my black jeans and teal sweater far from fashionable.

"Exactly. I'm doing the groundwork and Cece will follow up and write the piece. She wanted me to get the initial questions out of the way, and for Carlos to have a chance to shoot you to find the best angles."

"Essentially, you are a peon," she said with a mean little quiver at the corners of her mouth.

"That's a rather unkind way to phrase it, but yes."

"Normally I don't have time for peons, but I didn't fully understand what would occur this morning, and I do owe Tinkie a favor. Lucky you."

"Oh, I was just thinking how lucky I am. Now, tell me the structure of your day, please. I need to know how you manage to look so fabulous on a daily basis."

"You think it's plastic surgery and chemical injections." She smiled really big, and I thought of the wolf in *Little Red Riding Hood*. It was clear she *could* smile, when she chose to. She simply didn't choose to very often.

"Mrs. Cotterille, or do you prefer Mrs. LeMuse?" I let the question hang.

"My husband is LeMuse. I am an individual with my own name. You can call me Pouty."

"Excellent," I said. "I'm helping Cece and Tinkie out,

simply doing as they asked. Could you give me an idea of what you do every day?"

She inhaled deeply. "I get up and exercise. Then I read for an hour, something that improves my mind or deepens my connection with spirit. Then I have a protein drink, exercise again, then select what my husband will have for dinner and tell the cook, then I might go shopping. I have art instruction in the afternoon. Then dinner for Leo and then some time to help Leo relax. He's always exhausted and needs attention."

"Lovely," I said. "Do you have any hobbies, other than art?"

She hesitated. "I can play the ukulele, but Leo doesn't like it. He says it's a child's instrument and a waste of my time. Please don't mention it in the article."

For the first time she sounded like a real person, and I nodded. "I won't. I can't sing, but I always wanted to play the guitar."

"My fingers aren't long enough for the frets on a guitar. Leo says my fingers are . . . . unnaturally short. Leo said he could elongate them, but—it just sounded like a bad idea. He didn't like it when I refused."

I had to give her credit for that. She might have ended up unable to use her hands at all if something went wrong. "The ukulele is a far better choice than hand surgery."

Carlos was busy snapping photos as we talked. When the food was served, he sat down and we ate while Pouty talked about growing up on the Cotterille land in the Delta, and how everyone hated her family.

I had an inkling of why the Cotterilles weren't all that popular but I didn't mention the poor wages, the snooty attitude, or the dozen other things that had made Pouty, fair or not, the subject of spleen. Annoyingly, I was beginning to feel a little sorry for her. She'd gone from being the daughter and heir of a tradition that was not her choosing into the marriage bed of a man who seemed to demand perfection in his wife. Both roles were soul killing. Who would Pouty have been had she been born Pouty Smith or Jones or Welford and had half a chance to grow into the person she wanted to be? Or maybe I was projecting my values onto her. Maybe she was exactly who she wanted to be. I had to put that aside and get on with my "interview."

"What's your beauty routine, if you don't mind sharing?"

"Be sure and mention that I get my hair done at The Hair Cottage and give my stylist Trish Patterson all the credit. She is brilliant at styles and color. She could even help you."

The glint in Pouty's eye told me she knew exactly how mean she was being. Poof! My sympathy vanished. "So, you study art and play the ukulele. What about nail sculpting or maybe studying your image in the mirror? That could take a lot of time."

Carlos pushed back from the table and bent to pick up some cameras from his bag. He coughed to cover up the laughter that had almost escaped. He was a good ally to have in this job.

"Why don't we move to some outdoor locations?" he suggested. "I'd like to see your hair in natural light. I'll bet it really shimmers."

"Of course!" Pouty was on her feet in an instant.

Carlos took a few shots in the lobby of the beautiful old Pelham Hotel, and then we went out into the golden October sunlight. He found an old hitch where carriage horses had once been tied and Pouty was frolicking around it. Carlos worked the angles, from high to low. He was dedicated to getting good photos, and I hoped he'd be able to use some. So far, I'd gotten nothing useful from Pouty and I knew it was my fault, not hers. She was willing to talk, I just hadn't been able to find my way to the subject of a group of people worshiping eternal youth. I had to do better.

I caught up with the two of them a block down the street. Pouty did love the camera, and I had to admit she was a very good model. She was beautiful and had that special quality that made people look at her. Folks on the street were stopping to watch Carlos and Pouty work.

We crossed Canal and went to the Audubon Butterfly Garden and Insectarium. When Carlos stopped to change a lens, I approached. "Pouty, Tinkie said you were talking about a group of new friends you'd made. She said she was interested in checking it out because you were dedicated to healthy living and staying young."

"Tinkie's interested?" She snapped on the bait like a starving trout. She really wanted Tinkie to participate.

"Yeah. She just wasn't clear about what this group was. Like, is it a yoga group, or a wellness group, or a financial group, or medical, or spiritual, or what? She asked me to get the details."

From her expression, it was clear Pouty suddenly didn't want to talk. I decided to play hardball. "I'm coming into an inheritance from my uncle Crabtree's side of the family, and Tinkie said we might want to join together over the winter. She said she would do it if I did. You know, get healthy inside and out. Tinkie is determined that I get pregnant before I'm too old to have a baby. Little Maylin has turned her into quite the doula."

Pouty rolled her eyes. "Your body would never recover from carrying a child and giving birth. I suggest you avoid that completely. By the way, how is Tinkie doing? I mean, is she still fat? The last time I saw a photo she was as big around as she was tall."

Nobody criticized my partner and got away with it, but revenge would have to wait. I smiled. "Tinkie is almost back to her fighting weight. It was all baby. Doc said Tinkie would snap back to normal in a matter of weeks, especially since she's breastfeeding."

The horror on Pouty's face was priceless. "Her breasts will sag for the rest of her life."

"Tinkie has enough money to fix anything that bothers her. But nothing can replace Maylin."

"If you say so." Pouty looked down at her manicured nails. "The answer to your question is all of the above. Our group has nutritional, medical, emotional, mental, and spiritual healing sessions."

"Growing up, you went to church. Is that the kind of spiritual you're talking about?" I played dumb.

"I know living in Zinnia you aren't exposed to a lot, but there are a million different ways to worship. If you broadened your education, you'd know that different cultures find different things important."

"I always loved Greek mythology. Especially the story of Persephone."

"Yes, the pantheon of gods and goddesses, a religion where women get equal time. That should appeal to you, Sarah Booth, independent woman that you are. Women are ignored or forced into the role of servants in many religions."

"Exactly," I said. "So what is it you worship, and how much does it cost? Not to be crass, but Dahlia House needs some work and I have to plan out my inheritance budget. Oscar says I can't touch the principal, only the interest."

Pouty was intrigued. "How much are you getting?" she asked.

"My attorney told me not to talk about it. He said unethical people would be after my windfall." Again, Carlos had to turn away to hide his smile.

"Then it's a good sum?" Pouty was nothing if not persistent.

"Oh, yes. Life changing. But money is so boring to talk about. Tell me all about this spiritual path you've found. Do you have a teacher or a guru or a bishop? Give me the scoop. I told Tinkie I'd ask. Everything is more fun with a good friend, don't you think?"

"For some people." Pouty leaned in closer. "We believe that our physical bodies, though they seem temporary, could be made more durable. Living a healthy life, in mind, body, and spirit, will slow the aging process." She paused dramatically. "Perhaps even stop it."

"Stop it? Wouldn't you be dead then?" I could act, but not even I could pull off a wide-eyed belief in eternal life, which was exactly what she was talking about.

"You're a skeptic. Well, I was, too, until I talked with Rhianna. She's brilliant, Sarah Booth." Pouty had finally dropped her superior attitude. She was a Rhianna, spiritual leader, fangirl.

"I don't want to be skeptical. Tell me more."

"You have to commit one hundred percent. I don't know that you're ready for that."

"I don't know, either." I held up a finger. "Wait a minute. If this Rhianna can truly stop the aging process, what does your husband say about this? He makes his living keeping age at bay for a lot of men and women."

"Leo hates Rhianna and everything about the People of Eternity."

"The what?"

She looked a little taken aback, and I realized she'd given me more than she'd intended. "That's the name of the group. The People of Eternity. POE for short. As an artist, Poe understood the allure of death, how the promise of that sweet release could tempt. He often wrote of cheating death and of immortality. Rhianna teaches us that we don't have to die to achieve that eternal life."

"What do you mean you don't have to die?"

"We transcend. We simply step into paradise young and firm and never aging." Her face suddenly clouded and she looked away.

"How exactly do you manage that?"

She shook her head. "You need to talk to Rhianna. I have your phone number. I'll ask her to call you. She has unusual abilities, and if she senses you're a good fit for the group, she'll be in touch."

"Thank you. That sounds perfect." I'd pushed as hard as I could. I changed tactics. "What does Leo say about the prospect of eternal life? I mean, other than he hates Rhianna."

"Leo doesn't believe in an afterlife or anything else. We're in the process of divorcing." She shrugged one shoulder. "For so many years, I thought Leo was the smartest person I ever met. He truly is a genius with a scalpel. But that's not enough any longer. I think he's bogged down in the old way of thinking. Rhianna says it happens to a lot of people. They excel for years, but success makes them cautious and afraid to try new things, to think in new ways, to see life through a different lens."

"I'm sorry to hear about the divorce." I hadn't planned

on this turn. I'd actually assumed that the antiaging cult group was likely her husband's idea.

"Leo is fine with it. He has a new project. She's twenty and her whole body will be his canvas. Just like mine used to be."

I thought her voice had a catch in it, but I couldn't be certain. She had resumed the blank expression, giving nothing away. Was it possible this willingness to believe in eternal youth came from being hurt? "No man is worth losing a minute of sleep."

"Thank you, Sarah Booth. That's unexpectedly . . . kind."

She'd also perfected the ability to make me feel like a heel. Aunt Loulane had always cautioned me about being judgy. "Thanks for helping me, Pouty. Even if I don't qualify to belong to your group, it sounds fascinating. I mean, the way we grew up, we didn't really have a big choice in what we believed. We were expected to do what everyone else did. I think it's refreshing that you're broadening your horizons."

"I didn't expect that from you."

I'd given her little reason not to think I was provincial. "It's okay. We all grew up with the same . . . expectations."

She laughed out loud. "Hardly. Your mother, Sarah Booth, you'll never know how I envied you your mother. She saw *you*. Not a Mini-Me version of herself. Your mama didn't try to shape you and force you into the mold she'd failed to fit."

Color me dumbfounded. "Thanks, Pouty. I had no idea you knew anything about my mother."

"You were always so weird, we never talked."

The truth was that I wasn't particularly social in high school. I was dreaming big dreams of Broadway even then. Maybe I'd come off as stuck up. That notion made me uncomfortable. "I just wanted to be an actress. That's all I thought about."

Carlos had joined us, his camera now at rest. "I caught some of your conversation. I want to know more. Tell me about the group you belong to."

"You're not really interested in my spiritual group, are you?" Pouty was suddenly suspicious.

"Maybe. Maybe not." Carlos shrugged. "My grandfather was a healer. He believed in many strange things that my family left behind when we moved to America. There are big mysteries in the world. My grandfather believed that humans have the power to heal themselves of all illness. In a sense, that is a form of immortality, wouldn't you say?"

Pouty nodded. "To have the power to heal yourself is a big belief." She studied Carlos a moment. "Very big, if you actually comprehend it."

"I think I do," Carlos said. They were in a staring match, and I was beginning to feel a little concern. I didn't know Carlos, but I had a terrible thought. What if he was part of this cult?

"Are you talking about things like the fountain of youth?" I asked.

My question broke the intensity and Pouty cast a sidelong glance at me. "In a way. But it's not that simple. And I can't really tell you much. We've taken a vow of . . . not silence, but of letting Rhianna take the lead in explaining this to others. If she's interested in talking to you, she'll call."

"And perhaps I could be included?" Carlos asked.

"It's very expensive to join." Pouty had shown a more

human and compassionate side, but when it came to money she was still a bitch.

"I have family resources if I choose to ask for them." He was unruffled. "Can you tell us more about how this transition from life here on Earth to paradise happens?" Carlos asked.

"I don't know all the details. Only Rhianna understands how it works. But it's going to happen very soon, and there will be a ceremony to welcome the change. All of us will be helped, and the best thing is we'll have a choice. We can transition without suffering physical death." She smiled. "I guess we all do want a story that ends with eternal life. Even better, eternal youth. That's what we want. Leo is going to be puke green when he finds out people no longer need his bag of tricks to look good forever. Now I have to get home to my exercise routine. I have to keep this body in tip-top shape since it's going to last me through eternity."

# 8

Carlos had left his car at the Pelham, so I walked back with him. He was silent for several blocks, but then he stopped me. "What do you think happened to Christa and Britta? Do you think they're hurt?"

"I don't know. Did Christa ever talk about her investigation or the People of Eternity?"

He frowned. "The last time we were together, she mentioned a youth cult. I should have paid more attention."

"Can you remember anything?" I tried not to sound skeptical, but Carlos was, I presumed, her lover. Surely she would share details of her big story with him. His reticence at coming forward with information made me suspicious. And then he'd offered the information that he could get money if he wanted from his family. Of course,

I'd lied about my inheritance, too. That was likely all Carlos was doing. I just didn't know for certain, and that made me uneasy. The only lead I had left in my quest for Christa was Carlos and Father Joseph, the priest.

"I'm pretty self-centered," Carlos said. "When Christa was working on something that I could illustrate, I paid a lot of attention. I deeply regret that I didn't insist on being with Christa all the time."

"She told her mother that Britta's disappearance, the proposed commission for the painting, and the cult were intertwined," I said. "I agree. I need to find that garden and the man who offered Britta the money. Christa never mentioned him?"

"Only that Britta thought he was very handsome and persuasive. He had a Latin name. Renaldo. No last name. And there are beautiful gardens all over southern Louisiana. Some along River Road by those old plantations are real showplaces . . ." Carlos drifted into silence. "I wish I could be more helpful. This is driving me insane. At first, I couldn't believe Christa was in any danger. She's so sure of herself at every turn. She's smart about people, a lot smarter than I am." He turned away. "I could kick myself."

He sounded so sincere, and he had been helpful, but he was also extremely slick, with polished manners and abundant charm.

"Will you send some of those photos to me so I can pass them along to Cece Dee Falcon at the newspaper in Zinnia? She'll publish a few, and I know she'll give you a photo credit. And pay, but at the newspaper rate, not fashion photography. The other pics I'll bet you can sell to Pouty. She probably has an entire photo gallery of herself, and I hate to think you worked this hard for little or nothing."

"If I can help find Christa, that's all I want. Believe me."

We stood at the back of Carlos's car, and he opened the hatch to put his cameras in. I noticed a beautiful earring in the corner of his trunk. New Orleans had an abundance of talented artists and jewelry-makers, and the earring incorporated the colors of Mardi Gras with a little skeleton, perfect for Halloween in the Big Easy—a holiday that was fast approaching and one I'd almost forgotten about in my intense focus on the case.

I was about to ask Carlos if it belonged to Christa, but he closed the hatch. "I hate to rush off, but I have a photo shoot for a restaurant. The excitement of shooting food." He rolled his eyes. "If you learn anything about Christa will you let me know?"

"Sure."

Carlos nodded and got behind the wheel. He drove off and I called an Uber. While I waited I put in a call to St. Lucy's Catholic church. I was in luck. Father Joseph Martin had time to meet with me.

On the ride to the church, which wasn't far away, I called Coleman, but it went straight to voicemail. I knew he was talking with the local police, and I simply asked him to call me when he got a chance. I was still full from breakfast, but Coleman had mentioned dinner at the Blue Moon, and I wondered if we needed reservations. I got Frankie's voicemail, too, when I called to let her know I was meeting the priest and would be back at the apartment afterward.

St. Lucy's was a small brick church sheltered among

a grove of live oaks. Lichen adorned the trees and the bricks, giving the church a sense of age and permanence. Reflection might be found sitting on a bench beside a statue of St. Francis, his hand outstretched to serve as a perch for a fat pigeon.

The heavy doors moved effortlessly as I entered, unsure where I might find Father Martin. I had barely stepped inside when a Sister met me and led me back to a suite of offices where a handsome man wearing a black suit and a white clerical collar sat at a desk.

"I'm Father Joseph," he said.

"Sarah Booth Delaney." I extended a hand and we shook.

"I understand you're helping Frankie search for her missing daughter." Father Joseph got right to the point.

"I am. Can you help me?" I could be equally direct.

"I don't know. I've known Christa since she moved to New Orleans, but the church really didn't hold a lot of interest for her. Don't get me wrong, she was a wonderful person, willing to help anyone. But religious study simply wasn't for her at this time in her life."

From all I'd heard about Christa, she was consumed with her desire to win that scholarship and begin a career as a hard-hitting journalist. I wasn't surprised that religion held little interest to her. Except the cult she wanted to investigate was a type of religion, as far as I could tell. I wondered if Joseph was trying to obscure this fact.

"If Christa wasn't interested in religion, why was she spending time here in the church?"

The question seemed to catch him unprepared. He pushed back from his desk. "Christa helped deliver food to the elderly and homeless. She and Carlos were dedicated to helping in that mission, and also to talking with some of the young people who had . . . issues. It shouldn't surprise you that not everyone in New Orleans is here legally. And teenagers, even those who are U.S. citizens, have difficulty relating to their parents at times. An older priest isn't always helpful."

Joseph was probably my age, which made me realize that the ten years or so between Christa and me was more than just a decade. It could prove to be a chasm. Then I had to wonder if I'd really matured much since college graduation. In many ways, I felt I'd lived two lifetimes, but my friends would say I was still the same impetuous daredevil of my youth.

"Father Joseph, did Christa ever mention a group of people who believed they had the secret to immortality, a kind of endless youth?"

"She did. I gave her some books about different sects, or cults, and their various beliefs. There was a group back in the eighties that preached immortality. It's a hard delusion to sustain, because death comes for everyone eventually."

I hadn't really done my due diligence on looking up cult groups, and this was helpful. "What did Christa tell you?"

"That a woman named Rhianna led the group. She claimed to be more than four hundred years old, and that she was once hanged as a witch."

"But she didn't die."

"Exactly. People who are desperate will believe almost anything, especially if the salesperson is attractive and charming. Rhianna, according to Christa, is both. But the other thing that Christa said is that she couldn't find any evidence of Rhianna being alive. No birth certificate. No social security number. No passport, though Rhianna claims to travel internationally."

"That would be impossible on a commercial flight without identification."

"Unless she has a private plane." He grinned. "Or spaceship. Christa said Rhianna implied that her immortality came from intermingled alien DNA."

"Do you know where the People of Eternity are located? The physical place?"

"A compound somewhere in this part of the state, from what Christa said."

"Had she found their location?"

He shook his head. "I don't think so. She was still searching."

"How did she hear about this group?"

He looked confused. "I thought it was from her friend Britta."

"Britta knew about the People of Eternity?"

Father Joseph frowned. "I could be mistaken, but I think so. I'm fairly certain Christa mentioned that Britta knew someone affiliated with the group. I hesitate to call them a cult even though they do seem to fit the description."

"What do you know about Rhianna?"

He signaled me to take a seat across from his desk. "Not much. Just a few things Christa mentioned. She was very caught up in the whole idea of this . . . group."

"Yes, she felt it would be a big break for her as a journalist. What did she say about Rhianna?"

He ran a hand through his dark hair, shot through with gray I now saw, and considered for a moment.

"She's very beautiful. She has the ability to help people transcend death and move on to the 'next phase' without suffering." He shrugged. "That's what I remember. I'm afraid I annoyed Christa because I was skeptical of such claims and urged her not to give them any oxygen with a big story. This Rhianna person isn't the first to make outlandish promises to people who soon lose their money."

"Yes, I've seen a number of false prophets promising everything from healing water to prayer clothes you buy for a hundred bucks to put on an ailing body part."

"Religion shouldn't be a scam," Father Joseph said. "Miracles happen through faith and through the generosity of God and Jesus. People like this Rhianna make a mockery of true phenomena."

"Were you opposed to Christa writing this story?"

He laughed. "Bad ideas don't need to be featured in the media, but I presumed that Christa would reveal this group for the fraud they are. On one hand, I looked forward to her exposé."

"And what role did Britta play?"

"You might ask her. I'm not certain."

I watched him closely. "Britta is also missing. She's been gone longer than Christa."

"I didn't know that. Now, I am worried. Christa and Britta were like two peas in a pod. It sometimes annoyed Carlos, the way they were so close and shared so much. I think he felt left out at times. Have you spoken with Carlos? He might have some ideas where the two women went."

"Thank you, Father Joseph." I was surprised that Christa hadn't approached Father Joseph in her quest to find Britta. "I appreciate all of your help. If you hear anything, would you contact me?" I gave him a business card with my cell phone number.

"Of course. And please, you do the same. When Britta and Christa return, ask them to stop by."

"I will."

# 9

Coleman was still talking with the local police officers when I finished with Father Joseph, so I went back to our apartment. I'd brought my laptop so I set up on the front porch in the fabulous fall sunshine and searched the internet for New Orleans gardens. There were thousands of private homes in Louisiana with notable gardens, and many in New Orleans. The lush and verdant patio gardens of even the small French Quarter apartments made me rue my lack of a green thumb. A skilled gardener knew how to work with the architecture, age, and climate of this great old city to create a sense of rich abundance and whimsy.

I called Cece and thanked her for doing the article on

Pouty. I let her know Carlos had taken some fabulous photos.

"He just emailed a file of the photos. He's very talented," Cece said. "His interest is more directed toward fashion or fine art than the daily grind of newspapers, which often are illustrative. But he could certainly work for a big-city paper if he chose to."

"I suspect he was a great partner to Christa for her work. I'm just surprised she didn't tell him more about this cult she was digging into. It's weird, Cece. They believe they can stay young for eternity and that they can also transcend death and ascend to paradise, as it were, in youthful bodies. Who wouldn't be willing to pay anything to do that? You could take your whole family. And your pets. You'd never have to suffer loss."

For a long moment, Cece was silent. "I think we experience loss and suffering for a reason," she said. "To eliminate that pain would remove the life lessons we need so that we become more aware, more compassionate human beings."

"You think suffering makes us better people?" The idea struck me as cruel.

"That's not what I said." Cece was treading carefully. She knew I was touchy. "I think some people become more compassionate after a terrible loss. You did. The thing we can't know is if you would have developed that much compassion without suffering."

"It's not a price I would willingly have paid." I was still a little angry at the idea that some grand design was in effect to make us suffer.

"I don't have the answers you want," she said quietly. "I can only tell you that I love you. That plenty of people do, including Coleman and Tinkie. You have lost much, but you've also been the recipient of plenty of good things. And perhaps those came to you because of who you are . . . because of your life experiences."

This was something I'd have to think about a lot more. "I'll have better answers when I've chewed on this for a bit. I just wanted to check in. Is Tinkie really okay with not working this case?"

"She's chafing about it. But the minute Maylin is in her arms, she doesn't think about anything else."

The idea that Tinkie would become a stay-at-home mom had never occurred to me—and I didn't like it at all. "She is intoxicated with Maylin."

"She's still your partner," Cece said, reading right through me. "Give it some time. You'll see. Tinkie worked too hard to be independent *and* a mother. She'll juggle both, I promise you."

And I chose to believe Cece, who was a lot wiser than I in many areas. "Hey, if you have any contacts in New Orleans who might know about an incredible garden, I'm looking for one that could be the location of the cult Christa was investigating."

"That's vague, way vague, Sarah Booth. Any details?"

"Statuary of gods and goddesses, beautiful fall flowers, a fountain. That's all I know. We hope to learn more."

"Still vague," Cece said. "But I'll ask around."

"Thanks, my friend."

"I have to go. Ed Oakes is glaring at me. I'm late with a story. Ed's already threatened to glue my butt to my chair. He might do it."

I had to laugh. Cece drove her boss nuts, but he adored her and recognized her talents. She pretty much had her way on everything at the paper, which is why she'd never been snapped up by bigger publications or even television. Not because they hadn't asked, but because she liked her current job too much to leave. "Ed puts up with a whole lot from you."

Cece ignored my last remark. "I'll ask Millie about the garden. If there's anything weird or supernatural going on in New Orleans, she'd know more than I would."

"Thank you."

We hung up and I thought about returning to the apartment and scouting out the old slave pens Christa's friends had mentioned. I didn't expect to find Christa or Britta there, but I was curious nonetheless. New Orleans, a port city, had been a hub of the slave trade. The city couldn't handle the large number of enslaved people brought in for sale, so many were held in pens on plantations outside the city limits. The grueling work in the sugarcane fields was some of the most dreaded because of the harsh conditions. Enslaved people had been sold on street corners in the Quarter. Many of the buildings had been built by them.

Instead of exploring, I walked over to Christa's apartment. Frankie wasn't there, and she hadn't left a note saying where she was going. While it was on my mind, I called the Blue Moon restaurant and made reservations for three people for eight o'clock. New Orleans had many things to offer visitors, and good food was at the top of my list. The better restaurants often had long reservation lists.

Frankie had left a key under the mat, and while I was waiting to hear from her or Coleman, I searched Christa's room again. Where had her laptop gone? Her notes? There was nothing that might indicate where she'd focused her research.

When an hour passed and Frankie didn't answer my texts, unease crept over me. She'd planned on hunting through Britta's things to find the photograph of the garden for which she'd been offered a commission. Now, so many things about Britta felt . . . wrong. Was the young woman really a blackmailer? Had she managed to draw Christa into some kind of scheme that put them both in danger and had nothing to do with the People of Eternity? What if Frankie, Coleman, and I were totally off base with the direction we'd taken?

I was about to walk back to the apartment I shared with Coleman when Tinkie called.

"Cece loved the photos Carlos took of Pouty. She's doing a full-page spread on Pouty's fall fashions and how a Delta gal has taken the New Orleans fashion scene by storm."

I didn't spoil it for her that I'd heard the good news about Pouty and Carlos. And Tinkie was absolutely correct—getting his photos published would lead to more work for Carlos, and Pouty would be thrilled by the attention. To my surprise, I'd come to view Pouty as a multidimensional person instead of just vanity in high heels, but she still had quite the ego. Being the center of attention was better than chocolate ice cream to her. Then again, she was recovering from a big rejection if she'd ever loved the flesh sculptor Leo LeMuse.

"How's Maylin?" I was tired of thinking about Pouty.

"She is the most perfect baby ever born."

"Without a doubt."

Tinkie sighed. "My parents aren't coming back to Zinnia right now. Mom just called and said since she'd already missed the birth, they'd stay in Greece for the winter. They'll be home in the spring."

"And Maylin will be twenty times cuter by then." I'd like to get my hands on Tinkie's mother and shake her until her teeth rattled. She had no idea how much she hurt Tinkie's feelings, and I didn't think she cared.

"You're probably right." Tinkie focused on the upside, but she couldn't hide the disappointment.

Maylin was Mrs. Bellcase's only grandchild. Likely the only one she'd ever have. I truly didn't understand her refusal to come home and acknowledge Tinkie's magnificent accomplishment. Maylin was a miracle baby and the fulfillment of Tinkie's biggest wish. She was the continuation of the Bellcase/Richmond line. Any normal grandmother would have been camped out in the spare bedroom sucking up every moment of time with her grandchild. Mrs. Bellcase was another kettle of fish.

"Hey, there's no telling what's going on with your parents. I wouldn't take it to heart. I'm sure there's a good reason."

"Yeah." I could almost see Tinkie's eyes filling, but I knew from experience she wouldn't cry. "I'm sure there's a good reason, like it doesn't mean a thing to Mother. I'm just surprised Daddy doesn't make her come home."

"You can't know what's going on. Let it go, Tinkie. You can break your heart a million times over and maybe for nothing."

She cleared her throat. "You're right about that. What have you found out about our missing Christa and that cult she was investigating?"

I gave her the skinny on what I'd unearthed, including my concerns that maybe I'd taken a wrong path, that perhaps the road that would lead to Christa involved Britta's past as a blackmailer and had nothing to do with a cult.

"I wish I could be with you in New Orleans," Tinkie said.

"Your job as food factory for Maylin is far more important. I'll find these young women. Coleman is on the job and so is Frankie." I didn't tell her both of my partners were out of pocket with no explanation. "We'll find those women and be home in no time."

"Halloween will be here soon," Tinkie said. "Don't forget. I got Maylin the cutest costume. She's a little ladybug. Red-and-black stockings and a round, red cushion suit. Chablis is going as a sunflower, like where a ladybug would be found." She laughed. "And I even got Sweetie Pie, Pluto, and Gumbo costumes. They're supposed to be butterflies, but Pluto isn't cooperating with his outfit. He keeps eating the wings." Chablis was Tinkie's pampered Yorkie, and Sweetie Pie was my red tick hound. Pluto was a black cat I'd inherited from a case, and Gumbo was a petite little calico cat Tinkie had recently taken in.

"Thank you for taking the animals over to Hilltop. DeWayne does a wonderful job with them, but they'll be happier with you and the baby." DeWayne was Coleman's number one deputy and he often babysat the pets for me. He was terrific with the cats and dogs, and especially the horses, but I'd heard a rumor DeWayne had a sweetheart. He needed to be free to pursue the flight of Cupid's arrow.

"I got DeWayne a costume, too." Tinkie laughed heartily. "He's not really cooperating. He and Pluto have a bad Halloween attitude."

"What kind of costume?" DeWayne was one of the most easygoing people I'd ever met. Tinkie must have picked out a doozy.

"A bumblebee. It's totally adorable. Black and yellow with a stinger on the butt."

"Good luck with that." DeWayne was good-natured but he'd never show up in public in that costume.

Movement in the kitchen of Christa's apartment made me freeze and lower my voice. "Gotta go. Someone's in the apartment." It was probably Frankie but I wasn't taking any chances.

"Should I call 911?" Tinkie asked.

"No." I crept around the front room and eased back toward the kitchen where yet again I saw the flicker of something green—and very quick—close to the floor. I did have a gun and I knew how to use it, but I didn't carry it around with me. It was in the trunk of the Roadster at the apartment next door. I didn't even have a can of mace with me, though Cece had bought me two tiny but deadly containers of it. One was also in the car and the other I'd given to Tinkie, who had the good sense to put it on her key chain. I should have been that smart.

"Can you see who it is?" Tinkie was still on the phone.

I could hear someone opening and closing cabinets. "Hang on. I'm almost there."

"Maybe you should run instead of going toward danger." Tinkie was never a coward, but she wasn't dumb either.

"Good plan." The shifting of things in the kitchen, opening and closing cabinet doors and the oven—it was either look and see who it was or run before they caught on to the fact I was there. Since I didn't have a weapon, withdrawal seemed the better choice. I could call Coleman and wait outside to see who exited.

"I've got to go. I'll call when I'm safe. Bye." I hung up so I could put the phone in my pocket in case I had to run fast. But before I could back out of the apartment, a giant lizard standing on his back legs came through the kitchen door. It carried a china cup of what looked like tea. We both jumped back a little, and some of the hot tea sloshed out of the cup and landed on the lizard's foot.

"Damn it to hell," the lizard said.

# 10

It took me a second to recover from hearing the lizard talk, but then I said, "They'll fire you from the Geico commercials if you cuss." The words were out of my mouth before I could stop them. The impossibility of this situation had stunned me into stupid remarks.

The lizard looked me dead in the eye and his little tongue slithered in and out. He seemed to have vertical pupils, and a chill traced over me. This was not a kindly Geico lizard or even a gecko. This was something else entirely. And somehow it was associated with Jitty. It had to be. There was no other possible explanation.

"Who are you and what do you want?"

"I might ask you the same."

I couldn't tell by the voice if the lizard was male or

female. I supposed it didn't matter. "Why are you pretending to be a lizard, Jitty?"

"Think about it, Sarah Booth."

Sweet relief. It really was Jitty. I walked up to the lizard and then walked all around it. "You'd make a lovely pair of shoes and a bag."

"Don't threaten me. You don't know who you're messing with."

Jitty's appearances generally held a message, but this was so far out of the realm of reality that I couldn't even attempt to make a connection. Most recently she'd been the grim reaper at Tinkie's house, and now she was in New Orleans as a human-size reptile that drank tea from china cups. A niggle of something almost came to me but it was gone. "Who are you?"

"I'm the source of all disease and pain. Evil actions originate with me, according to the Maori."

I grabbed onto Maori. I knew they were the indigenous people of New Zealand with a rich culture and their own language and mythology. But how that related to a lizard I had no idea. "You're going to have to be more specific. What do the Maori and lizards have to do with anything going on in my life?"

The lizard set the teacup on a table and put its tiny little T. rex arms on its sides, way above where its hips might be, if it had hips, which it didn't. The creature gave a whispery sigh, a sure sign of exasperation with me. "I am Whiro, the god of the dead. I inspire others to do evil deeds and I guard the entrance and exit to the underworld. I am very powerful."

"A lizard?"

This time when the lizard looked at me I took a step back. There was definitely something scary in those unblinking eyes. "Chill, Jitty. You've made your point. What are you doing here in that . . . personification?"

"In Maori culture, Whiro plays a crucial role. He tempts others into evil. He is a corruptor. A general badass. You have to watch out for people under his influence."

I snapped on it. "So, I'm looking for a corruptor." I had a sudden sick feeling for Christa and Britta. Had they been taken by someone who intended to corrupt them? "Are Britta and Christa in danger?" I asked, even though I knew Jitty wouldn't tell me. It was against the rules of the Great Beyond, and Jitty, for all of her sass and aggravation, was a rule follower. She did what she could to help me, which was symbolic and often more riddle than help.

"The world of the dead is a mystery." Jitty blinked those lizard eyes and slowly began to transform. The lizard disappeared and she took on the form of a woman. In this incarnation I could see the Polynesian heritage of the Maori people she'd come to represent. From that she shifted again to the Jitty I knew, loved, and relied on.

And I had questions. "Twice you've come as a representative of the dead—once as a gatherer of souls and now as a corruptor and the guardian of the underworld. Are Christa and Britta in danger? Are they dead? Just answer me that."

"Halloween approaches, Sarah Booth. It's the moment when the veil between the living and the dead is thinnest. It's a rare opportunity."

I knew the old stories told to me as a child to scare me, about times when the spirits walked the Earth, crossing from one world to the other. Demons and unhappy souls were free to roam along with loved ones.

Aunt Loulane had never held with trying to frighten me into obedience and compliance, but some of my Baker relatives were always good for a spine-tingling ghostly tale. I thought about Jitty's comment. "If Christa was taken by a cult seeking and worshiping eternal life, Halloween would be the moment when this transition from one sphere to the next would be easiest. If there is to be no pain in the transition from life to death and eternal life, Halloween would be the fulcrum."

"You're smarter than I gave you credit for being." Jitty was growing thin and wispy, fading into the ghostly light herself.

"Wait! Does Whiro really look like a giant insurance-selling lizard?"

"That's gecko to you." Jitty was fully back to her sassy self, though still a bit translucent, wearing my favorite pair of black jeans and the teal sweater Pouty had dissed. She continued bantering. "There's not a lot of Whiro art lying about for me to draw inspiration from. That's the wonderful thing about the Great Beyond. Freedom to interpret. Just be on the alert and watch out for liars and shysters."

She disappeared just as Coleman opened the front door and came inside.

Coleman's time with the NOPD had been well spent. He'd discovered CCTV footage of the section of Jackson Square where Britta had her art stand. He'd managed to get the NOPD to give him a copy of the footage that was intermittent, but still showed Britta setting up her stall, painting, talking to some of the other artists, and meeting with a dark-haired man who was savvy enough to avoid the camera. They had a conversation and he handed her what looked to be a photograph.

"I think that's the man who was trying to hire Britta. Carlos thinks his name is Renaldo. I wish we could see his face."

"He's smart and has the instincts of a criminal to avoid identification," Coleman said.

"That could be the garden he wanted to commission her to paint. Frankie was looking for the picture, but I don't know what she found." I checked my watch. My concern for my mother's friend was growing. She didn't seem to be the sort of person who'd disappear without leaving a note or a phone call—if she was able to do either.

As if he read my mind, Coleman said, "I wonder why we haven't heard from her?"

"Me, too. I honestly don't know her well enough to say what her normal behavior is, but I wouldn't have suspected she'd take off without leaving a message of some kind."

"Did she happen to mention anyone she stays in touch with?"

Coleman asked the practical question and I had no answer. I'd failed to ask Frankie the simple, basic question about whom to contact if we needed to. I only knew she lived in Ocean Springs, and I gave Coleman that information.

"I'll make a call," he said, walking out onto the front porch. "Maybe she went home to get something. The OSPD might do a ride-by or welfare check for me."

"Thank you." I texted Frankie a simple message telling her I was worried and to please make contact. Then Coleman signaled me out onto the porch and pointed to the neutral ground between the lanes of Esplanade.

Burt Steele, Leitha, and Frankie were crossing the street, headed our way.

"Thanks, but I see the person I was worried about. I appreciate your help," Coleman said into the phone and hung up. I also put my phone away. Frankie kept pace with Burt and Leitha, but she looked glum. As she drew closer, I was fairly certain she'd been crying. When she saw Coleman and me, she looked relieved and waved, redoubling her pace. Burt and Leitha peeled off and went toward the fourplex they lived in.

"I didn't mean to be gone so long," Frankie said. "I should have left a note. And my phone is dead. Sorry. I was positive I had a full charge this morning, but obviously not."

She had been crying, and I wasn't about to fuss because I'd been worried. "Did you learn something?"

"I visited with Britta's parents in their hotel."

I could tell by her expression and tone that things had not gone well. "What happened?"

"Britta isn't the young woman I thought she was. Her parents are . . . not what I expected."

"Did they know anything?"

She shook her head and again her eyes filled with tears, but she didn't cry. "They weren't shocked that Britta used her looks and artistic talent to meet people she later blackmailed. They didn't seem to disapprove at all. It was more like they felt the people she blackmailed got what they deserved by trying to 'take advantage' of Britta." She used air quotes to offset 'take advantage.' "They didn't seem to see that what Britta was doing was as bad or worse."

Frankie wasn't judging anyone, but she was worried about Christa. She'd discovered that Christa's friend had behavioral habits that could easily put Christa in danger if someone sought revenge. The two women lived together and spent much of their free time together.

"Did Mr. and Mrs. Wagner have any idea where Britta might be? Or Christa?"

"They weren't very helpful. They got the idea I was blaming Britta for Christa's disappearance, but I wasn't. I only wanted information. I tried to see if Britta had mentioned anything about the garden painting commission to them, but they said she hadn't."

Coleman gave me a look and I could read his thoughts—this was something the NOPD would ask the Wagners. They might not tell Frankie anything, but they'd talk to the law or find themselves in big trouble.

"Where are they staying?"

"DoubleTree."

"And did Burt and Leitha go with you to meet them?" I was just curious.

"No, they met me afterward and took me to the little café that Christa loved. Leitha gave me a photo of Christa. She took it just before Christa disappeared." She pulled up the picture on her phone. "She looks so happy. And confident."

Christa's smile was wide and welcoming, as if she had no indication trouble was headed her way. But it wasn't the pretty girl I took notice of. It was the earrings. Unique design. I tried to freeze my features, because one of those earrings was in the back of Carlos's car, even though he said he hadn't seen Christa the day she'd disappeared.

"And this was taken just before she went missing?"

"Yes, maybe an hour before. Why?" Frankie asked. Coleman, too, was curious but he didn't say anything.

"I wanted to have an idea what she was wearing the day she disappeared. The sweatshirt hoodie has a distinctive logo on it. That's a football team logo, right?" I was floundering a little because I didn't want to upset Frankie.

"Oh, that. Christa was a big New Orleans Saints supporter. The fleur-de-lis is their team symbol, so not so unique," Frankie said. "Everyone in the Quarter probably has clothes with that emblem on them."

Frankie was right, but I'd covered the awkward moment where I might have told her about the earrings. I would tell her—I didn't hide information from my clients—but not yet. I needed a cordial relationship with Carlos because I intended to find out exactly what he knew about Christa's disappearance. He'd lied to me.

"Sarah Booth said you were searching for the photo of the garden," Coleman said. "Did you find anything?"

Frankie's face lit up. "I did. But I don't know if this is the place." She went to Britta's bedroom and came back with a photo that looked as if it had been printed several years earlier. It was a little worn and the surface was dirty.

Coleman and I drew together to study the landscape, which was incredibly beautiful. The flowers were stacked in bronze, orange, yellow, and red waves, with trees and shrubs also showing color. There were statues scattered among the green hedges. The whole place held the lushness of the subtropics that marked New Orleans and the Gulf Coast area.

Coleman checked the back of the photo but there was no location or date. I could see why someone would want a large painting of this, though. There was a sense of both timelessness and an endless peace. Eternity. "Any idea where this might be?"

"I truly don't have a clue," Frankie said. "I didn't show the photo to Leitha or Burt. Should I?"

"Maybe later." Since I'd learned that Carlos had lied, I was less than willing to trust any of Christa's so-called friends. "I think I'll talk to Leitha and Burt before we go to dinner, if that's okay. I made reservations at the Blue Moon for eight."

"Good," Frankie said, her worry revealed clearly in her expression. "I remembered something else Christa said. It was about Halloween. She said she had to find her answers before Halloween."

"Why?" Coleman asked.

I knew the answer. "Because the veil between the living and the dead is thinnest at midnight, Halloween night. If you're going to step into eternity, that would be the hour to do it."

"If there was going to be a ritual, it would be then." Frankie swallowed. "I don't know what this cult believes, but if they have Britta and Christa, why are they holding them? That's the question that's eating at me. What will these people, who are foolish enough to believe in eternal life or permanent youth, do to attain it?"

That was the dark question at the bottom of my fears, too.

# 11

I took the photograph Frankie had discovered in Britta's room over to the fourplex, where I found the young people sitting on the balcony. A flight of exterior stairs led up to the balcony, and I used that so I didn't have to go through any of the apartments. The buildings were perfectly designed for friends to gather on the screened balconies. The group had drinks and some were smoking cigarettes. I gladly accepted the offer of a Lynchburg Lemonade.

"How's Frankie?" Burt asked. "She was upset, but doing her best to hide it."

"She is upset. We have to find Christa and Britta." I tried to back into this conversation, but it was going to be touchy. "How well do y'all know Britta?"

They looked at each other and Leitha spoke. "She's quiet. We like her a lot, but she never talks about herself. She's always painting. She's so dedicated. And she's developing a following. People are seeking her out for commission work."

Addie had joined the group and she came out of the apartment wearing an apron and holding a wooden cooking spoon. "Hi, Miss Delaney. You must be talking about Britta and her painting. She's obsessed."

I handed the photo of the gardens to Addie. "Do you recognize this?"

"It's beautiful, but I've never been there. Is it local?"

"I presume it is. I'm trying to find out what gardens Britta was being commissioned to paint. Any ideas?"

"Britta played everything close to the vest," Addie said. "She was smart and friendly, but I don't think I really know anything about her or her family." She looked at her friends. "Do any of you? I mean, she's from Düsseldorf, and she had an art scholarship to some German university. Her folks apparently have money to fund all of her travels." She shrugged. "But I don't know much else. I'd never given it much thought, but that's kind of strange."

"She didn't talk about the past. She lived in the moment. She said it was part of her belief system," Leitha said. "I kind of admired that. Most of us are mired in the past and terrified of the future."

That was interesting coming from such young people. Normally, the young were believers in their invincibility. Never suspecting that arthritis would catch up to them or that bad food and hard drink would damage their internal organs, they raced toward the future, tumbling, falling, and going splat without any worries.

"What do you have to be afraid of?" I asked the question good-naturedly, more as a tease than a serious query, but Leitha blanched.

"Every day now is another inch toward decay and dying." She physically backed away from me.

I was prepared to laugh at the bleakness of her statement, but she was serious. My humor fell away. "You're only what, twenty-two, and you're worried about decay?"

"You can't deny the physics. When you're a growing child, you renew your cells. At twenty-one, it's only downhill. I've peaked out. Now things start going wrong. The body stops producing the hormones that keep you young and fit. Your metabolic system begins to fail. I'll get fat and wrinkled and diseased."

Leitha was a long way from having to worry about any of those issues, but they preyed on her mind. Her attitude seemed really unhealthy to me. "Why are you even thinking about that?" I asked her, and I looked at Burt and Addie. They were her friends. Surely they could see how self-destructive her thoughts were.

Burt shrugged. "Leitha talked to Christa a lot about some of this stuff."

"And Christa believed this—that she was decaying?"

Leitha nodded. "She said that's why she wanted to find the people who believed in eternal youth and immortality without death."

So they *did* know about the People of Eternity. They'd lied to me.

"Why didn't you tell me this yesterday?" I asked.

Again the three exchanged glances. Finally, Addie spoke. "Until we knew you were really a friend of Christa and Britta, we didn't want to say anything. I mean, Christa talked about her mom and they seemed genuinely close, but we'd never seen a picture of her. We couldn't ask her for a photo ID. And we didn't know you from Adam's house cat."

She had a point that actually lifted my spirits. If these young people were that cautious, then perhaps Christa had been also. Maybe she was on Britta's trail but didn't have the privacy to check in with her mom. It was a long shot, but I so wanted it to be true.

"Look, Christa may be in serious trouble. Britta, too. If you know something, tell me."

"All of the information should be in Christa's journal," Addie said. "She made meticulous notes. It's the thing that gave her a leg up on the rest of us vying for big stories and national publications. And she had a memory like an elephant."

"We can't find her laptop or any journals."

"That doesn't make sense. She was careful to write everything down. Maybe Carlos has her notebooks and computer. Sometimes she stayed at his place."

That was not good, but I kept my face blank. "I'll check that out with him."

"Father Joseph was helping her find sources," Leitha offered. "Frankie said you were talking to him, but he knows a lot of wealthy people in New Orleans. He told Christa hobnobbing with them was part of his job description. Those were exactly the kind of people attracted to the idea of eternal youth. They all had money for plastic surgeons and for buying youth. Christa mentioned that some of the cult people would hang out around one particular plastic surgeon's office. She took some photos. Have you found her phone?"

"No." I hadn't found a single thing of Christa's that might have information on it. "Do you remember his name?"

"I do!" Leitha was excited. "Christa made fun of the wife's name. Pouty. But his name was Leo. Leo LeMuse. Christa said he made it up. Like his last name was really Sowbreath or something awful and he just had to change it."

Oh, a couple of puzzle pieces had just snapped together with a vengeance. Pouty was not the unhappy doctor's wife she presented herself to be. She was more like his partner in . . . what? Crime? Bilking rich women out of money for surgery they didn't need? There was no law against any of that. But she hadn't been truthful. In fact, I wasn't certain anyone I'd spoken to in New Orleans had actually told me the truth.

Pouty had told me exactly what she wanted me to know. Going into detail about her pending divorce was an interesting ploy. Allegedly pending. I didn't trust that, either. She'd concocted a web of lies and I'd flown right into the center of it. But why? Why were all of these people either hedging the truth or outright lying?

"No one has heard from Christa or Britta?" I gave them pointed looks.

They all shook their heads. "We swear."

Even on a stack of Bibles I wouldn't trust them now.

"If you hear from either woman, please call me or Frankie."

They nodded again, but I had little faith they'd follow through.

# 12

The Blue Moon was the perfect place to sip a glass of excellent wine and let Frankie talk. She was scared, and she grew more so every day. I couldn't blame her. It was common knowledge that after forty-eight hours the chances of finding missing people began to go down.

Coleman put a hand on Frankie's, giving her fingers a squeeze. "I don't have a lot to report, but I called some friends in Interpol to check on Britta Wagner."

I could have kissed Coleman right there in the restaurant. "Did you find out anything?"

"Only that she doesn't have a record with them. Whatever she's done, the crimes weren't big enough to get international notice. That's likely how she traveled about so freely."

That was good news. It limited our search. If Britta had been abducted by someone she was trying to blackmail, there was a good chance that it was a local person. Both women might still be in New Orleans.

"Tomorrow, I'm going to talk to the Wagners," Coleman said. "They might be more forthcoming with me. I don't have any authority here in New Orleans, but I am a sheriff. That might rattle them into talking."

"Good plan." I relayed the information I'd gathered, including the meeting with Pouty and the information she'd divulged on the People of Eternity and their cockamamie ideas.

"Who are these people?" Frankie asked.

"No one you want to know," Coleman said. "Honestly, people will believe the most outlandish things if they are desperate."

"Do you think this Rhianna believes she can grant eternal youth?" I asked.

"Hard to know. Some people can get swept up in their own fantasies, but my suspicion is that this is a scam and they are bilking money from wealthy clients."

We'd finished a delicious meal and Coleman had the floor. I looked at him and felt a thud in the region of my heart. He was a good man, and I loved him. His kindness to Frankie made me love him even more.

"I did a little research at the police department," he continued. "There are other groups that have come and gone that believe human life can be extended to long periods of time. Some believe immortality is possible. Humans may be the only species that are born knowing they will eventually die, and it's this knowledge that immortality organizations try to dissolve. From my research, it seems most of these forever-young groups feel that the human acceptance of death, or the 'death cult' as some call it, is a self-fulfilling prophecy."

"What happens when the leader dies?" I asked.

"I guess that pretty much kills the organization," Frankie said.

"Yes and no," Coleman said. "Sometimes others step in."

"Is there any evidence these groups actually extend life?" I asked.

Coleman shook his head. "That I can't answer. Based on what I know of the world, I'm skeptical."

"Wouldn't it be something if we could attain immortality?" Frankie said. "What a world it would be if the presence of death could be diminished."

The minute she said it, I understood the allure. "I guess Rhianna's claims of alien DNA aren't so far out there, then. It would take an infusion of something other than the regular human elements of a body to stop the aging process."

"And I'd be willing to bet that Rhianna has already claimed that any DNA check of her body won't show anything unusual—that the alien DNA is not traceable. So there is no evidence. There's no way to prove if she's able to transmit this new DNA to her followers or not. Only time will tell."

"And that's not the best scenario for the followers," Frankie said. "By the time they realize they're aging at a normal rate . . ."

"I'm not sure that would dissuade the dedicated followers," Coleman said. "If you track these People of Eternity down, Sarah Booth, it will be interesting to see what evidence they present. And how they explain death, because in every group someone is going to die."

He made some really good points, and it only made me more eager to find the People of Eternity and see what they were espousing. "Did you find anything on Rhianna, the four-hundred-year-old former witch?"

"Not yet," Coleman said. "She's unknown to the police department so whatever she's doing, she's keeping it very quiet."

"Might any of the police officers know about the garden Britta was commissioned to paint?"

"I'll copy the photo and take it down there tomorrow and ask. Police officers aren't normally invited to magnificent gardens on social calls, but it never hurts to ask."

He had a point, and the People of Eternity were private and secretive. Our only lead into the group so far was Pouty. Tomorrow I'd follow up with her. Or maybe Cece could come interview her. That would be even better, in some ways.

"I found a place with a unique fence." I described the wrought iron fencing with the spears and Cerberus's heads.

"Guard dog of the underworld," Frankie said. "Christa loved mythology. That does sound intriguing. Maybe Rhianna is there. We can at least look."

It was a bold move, and perhaps the only one that we could play if we wanted to see what was behind the sturdy fence.

"Only if I know when you go there," Coleman said.

"For sure," I promised. "One of us needs to find this Rhianna and talk to her." I really could use Tinkie's help right now, but I didn't say that. Maylin was the top priority, and I completely agreed with that decision. It was just that Tinkie had social power moves that I didn't.

"I say we adjourn for tonight," Frankie said. "I'm exhausted, and I know both of you are, too."

We took a taxi back to the apartment where we were staying. Enjoying the crisp night, we walked Frankie to Christa's place. As she started to unlock the door, she hesitated. "I'm good. You two go on over and get some rest. Tomorrow will be busy."

She was giving Coleman and me license to have some privacy. I gave her a hug. "We'll be just across the lawn if you need us."

Arm in arm, Coleman and I walked to our quarters. When the door closed behind us, Coleman swept me into his arms with a big kiss. "That was one of the finest meals I've ever had, but I'd rather be in the kitchen at Dahlia House eating grilled cheese."

I had to laugh, but I understood what he was saying. Christa was missing, and each minute made it more serious. Neither of us wanted to see Frankie hurt, but we couldn't stop it. I wanted to ask Coleman if he thought Christa and Britta were okay. I wanted his gut reaction, because we really had no evidence to indicate one way or the other. But I didn't ask. Not now. There was time in the morning, when we were both rested, and when we'd had a chance simply to be together.

# 13

We'd left the balcony door open, welcoming the October night. Often humidity made it impossible to enjoy an open door or window, but this night was perfection. I awoke snuggled against Coleman, who slipped out of bed to make coffee. The sky was a fabulous mauve with a few lavender clouds on the run from the sun. These were days made for walking, laughing, and playing.

It was also the perfect day to track down Rhianna. If there was a cult of people who believed they were immortal, there should be some way to find them. Want ads, internet, occult shops. There were plenty of venues in New Orleans and one of them would lead me to Rhianna.

I stretched and accepted the black coffee Coleman

served me in bed. He was framed in golden light from the open door, and I took a moment to appreciate the view.

"You're in your prime, Coleman Peters, and I am lucky to share this time with you."

"I feel the same about you." He sat on the foot of the bed, his cup of coffee in his hand.

I didn't argue, though I didn't really believe it. At thirty-four, as Jitty reminded me every chance she got, doors of opportunity were closing. The female body aged much differently than the male. Some women had viable eggs until they were fifty, but the Delaney women had always suffered from bizarre and unusual womb disorders. I could still remember Aunt Loulane whispering with her friends about Cousin Martha's tilted womb, or Great-aunt Jacqueline's scarred Fallopian tubes.

There were horror stories of ectopic pregnancies, miscarriages, pregnancies that went for eleven months resulting in the birth of babies with twenty-four-inch heads and a full set of teeth. The Delaney women did not have an easy time of childbirth, according to the family stories.

"Hey, what's wrong?" Coleman put a hand on my knee.

"Tinkie is so happy with Maylin. It makes me think about . . ." I wasn't actually thinking about having a baby. I was thinking about gynecological disasters. And I didn't want to tell Coleman that. What man wanted to hear about pica cravings where desperate Delaney women ate burnt matches, clay from a local gully, coffee grounds, or charcoal?

"Are you thinking you want to have a baby?" Coleman asked.

I couldn't read a thing on his face. He was totally deadpan. I had a moment to decide how to play this hand. I decided on total honesty. "No. I'm not ready for a child yet. Are you?"

The relief was clear to see. "Not yet, Sarah Booth. I admit that I've spent some time daydreaming about a little boy and girl, our children, and the things we'd all do together. Sometimes Dahlia House seems so empty with just the two of us there."

If he knew about Jitty he wouldn't think it was so empty, but he was right. I'd grown up in a house filled with music and dancing and flower arrangements snatched from roadside ditches, the smell of apple pies baking, or my father's laugh as he recounted some of his legal peccadillos to Mama. That was the kind of home I wanted to bring my child up in, if I ever had a child.

"There's still time to wait." I wasn't going to let Jitty or my ovaries rush me into a lifetime commitment until I was ready. As far as I was concerned, we could adopt.

"I'm glad you feel that way," Coleman said. "Takes the pressure off. And watching Frankie tortured by worry for Christa, I don't know if my heart could take it."

"There is that." I'd lost everyone in my family. Could I risk loving a child with the possibility of losing it? I wasn't certain I could recover from that. "But we don't have to decide today." I threw the covers back and bounced out of bed. "First dibs on the shower."

Call me a coward, but I was ready to leave that conversation and get back on the job. Laying out plans for the future seemed the most dangerous thing anyone could do and I wanted to run from it. So I did.

By the time I'd showered, dressed, and put on a little makeup, Coleman had fresh beignets that someone on a bicycle delivered. We sat on the porch consuming the sugary goodness with black coffee. Coleman's powdered sugar mustache made me laugh. The gloom and fear had dissipated. Today would be a good day. We would find a real lead.

When we were dressed for the day, I said goodbye to Coleman, who was taking the garden photo to the NOPD. I walked over to the next building and picked up my client. Frankie and I drove to the Garden District to check out the place hidden behind the barricade of a wrought iron fence featuring the guard dog of Hades. I parked in front of the property and got out. Frankie had been extremely quiet. When she saw the fearsome Cerberus adorning the fence, she stepped back, her face ashen.

"This looks like some bad mojo," she said. "If Christa is in there . . ." She faded to silence, but I knew what she was thinking. If her daughter was in there she feared she was in real danger.

I found the gate latch and, with a lot of elbow grease, it opened. It was almost as if the gate had nearly rusted shut. Creepy. The fact that the sidewalk was mostly covered with weeds and grass, and that the trees and shrubs had almost crowded out the path didn't help. With Frankie at my side, we marched down the narrow concrete strip and into the thicket of plants. They were beautiful, and I was assaulted with rich floral perfumes as we brushed against blossoms. But after two or three minutes, we found ourselves at an empty lot. What once had been a large home was gone. The charred timbers spoke of a fire or lightning strike. All that remained were the sweeping front steps where Christa had been photographed by Frankie.

Frankie sighed. "I'm relieved, and I'm not ashamed to admit it," she said. "That fence is unnerving."

I had stepped away from Frankie, closer to the foundation of the house, then stopped in my tracks. There were black candles burned to nubs. Strange designs that I associated with the occult had been etched into the cement or painted with red paint. The scene was upsetting, and though I tried to keep Frankie from looking, I couldn't.

"Is that witchcraft or voodoo?" She looked at me, unable to hide her raw emotions.

"Probably kids fooling around," I offered, but Frankie wasn't having any of that.

"I've come to accept that there is great evil in the world, Sarah Booth. Supernatural, spiritual, or just in the hearts of men. Whoever was here"—she pointed at the ritual area—"is a very bad person. They were creating energy for evil purposes. I don't know if these are the people who think they can live forever or someone else, but this has the stench of selfish power all around it. Let's hurry and look because I don't think Christa is here and I have a feeling something bad is on this property."

I wasn't ready to leave yet. The property around this ruin of a house was large and hidden by overgrown foliage. The subtropics of the coastal South was the perfect incubator for seeds blown by wind or dropped by birds. Volunteer oaks, tallow, locust, or a thousand other varieties of trees could take root and grow in one season of gardening neglect. The grounds of Cerberus House, as I'd dubbed this place, looked as if at least two decades of neglect had resulted in a jungle. Anything could be hidden on the back of the property. I wanted to explore, but Frankie looked like she was about to implode. I could come back later.

As I turned to leave, I saw a flash of glitter on the ground just outside the circle of candles and sigils in a clump of dewberry brambles, weeds, and volunteer privet. I stepped toward it, but before I could reach out my hand, something large and vicious snapped at the toe of my boot.

"Holy crap!" Frankie cried out.

I didn't say anything. I was too busy scrabbling back to safety. A large spring-loaded trap, hidden in the vegetation, had almost caught me. The powerful jaws, complete with ragged, sharp blades, could have broken my foot or worse. If the trap had closed on a soft tennis shoe or a sandal, it might have severed an artery.

"Damn." A cold sweat had broken over my skin, and my heart was pounding.

"Come away from that," Frankie insisted.

"Just a minute." I had to calm my breathing and heart rate before I investigated the trap further. When I'd inhaled several times and my hands were no longer shaking, I eased over to the wicked metal vice and bent down. It was harmless now, but it was still a ghastly and cruel means of catching something. I'd never understood people who could bait these horrible devices and hope to catch anything with such cruel force.

"Get away from that thing," Frankie said. "There could be another nearby."

I picked up a stick and poked into the tall grass, weeds, and bushes. She was right. It never hurt to be safe.

"Sarah Booth, if you get your hand caught in one of those traps, you'll be maimed for life."

She was also right about that, but I used my stick to pull the trap toward me. When it was clear of the weeds, I snapped some photos with my phone. Even though I suspected this was a serious attempt at real harm, I was still appalled when I realized the trap was chained and bolted into the concrete foundation of the house. It had been deliberately set, and it was meant to hold whatever it caught until someone came to release it. No telling how many others were on the property. Or how many roving cats or dogs might fall into one of these. Surely they were illegal within the city limits. I'd have to check.

In the excitement of finding the trap, I'd almost forgotten about the sparkly item that had first drawn my attention. Using my stick, I parted the weeds and grass. Something bright and shiny winked at me. I picked up the earring, ignoring the roaring sound in my ears. Before Frankie could see it, I tucked it into my jeans pocket and beat around the weeds more with my stick.

"We should go." Frankie was eyeing the narrow strip of concrete that served as our walkway onto the property.

"Okay." I climbed on top of clumps of bricks that had once been a fireplace. The height gave me the advantage to look over the tops of the densest weeds and plants. The land, dotted with incredible oak trees that were being choked out by underbrush, sloped gradually to what looked like a small stream or runoff. I couldn't be certain, and I wasn't going to investigate until I had a stout stick and someone with medical skills to help me. It was a very unusual property in a dense city.

My fingers went instinctively to the pocket where the earring was stored, and when I noticed that Frankie was moving around the rubble of the house to go to the sidewalk, I pulled it out to check it again.

Dread touched me with a cold hand. This looked exactly like the earrings Christa had been wearing in the photograph Addie had taken of her, and like the one I'd found in Carlos's car.

"Did you find something?" Frankie called out. She was too far away to see that I had anything in my hand.

"Nope. I'm just trying to figure out how large this property is. Someone needs to check it for additional traps."

"I agree, but good luck getting that done. I doubt it'll be a high priority."

"When I make the city understand that since they are now aware of the issue, they are responsible for anyone who is injured—that will get them on the job."

Frankie's smile was bleak. "You sound exactly like your mama. I miss her so much."

"That makes two of us."

# 14

By the time we got back to my car, it was clear Frankie had a migraine. Every time I turned a corner I was afraid she'd be sick, but we managed to make it back to Christa's apartment without an unpleasant incident. I helped her inside, put a cool cloth over her eyes, and shut out as much light as I could in the bedroom. She had migraine medicine, which she took, saying she hated to abandon me, and she'd probably sleep for several hours. Our plans to talk more with Father Joseph and Carlos were thwarted, but I could do those things by myself or with Coleman.

Besides, the earring in my pocket had put me on another track entirely.

If it belonged to Christa, then she'd been at the empty

lot location. And she'd also been in or around Carlos's vehicle on the day she went missing.

I took a seat on the front porch of Christa's apartment to make a few phone calls before I chose a plan of action. Tinkie answered on the second ring.

"You need me, don't you?" she asked.

"Always, but I'm doing okay." I might be able to move faster if she were working with me, but after the incident with the trap, there was no way in hell I would put my partner in that kind of danger, especially at this time in her life.

"Where's that lawman? Isn't he carrying his weight?" She chuckled.

"He is. But he has a different set of skills, Tink. You know you're the best at what you do."

"You don't have to say that, Sarah Booth, but I needed to hear it." She sighed. "I would rather be with Maylin and Oscar than anywhere else on Earth. But I want to be with you, too. I feel really left out, and like I'm shirking my duties."

"Only for the short term." I understood her feelings, and I wouldn't lie to her. Only one lie stood between the total honesty that Tinkie and I shared. "You'll be back in action before you know it. We'll get one of those papoose carriers and take turns hauling Maylin around to crime scenes."

Tinkie laughed. "She'll be warped, you know."

"In a good way. Like us." I needed to ask a favor. "Can you call Pouty and set up a meeting with Rhianna?" I'd filled Tinkie in on what we'd discovered and I knew that she had the bankroll to make Pouty sit up and take notice. "I need to get a reading on her and this might be the quickest way."

"Are you sure that's a good idea?" Tinkie was worried. "That bear trap sounds like someone has some violence issues. Did you call the city to get the property checked for more traps?"

"No. I'm waiting until Coleman and I can go over the area ourselves. I sent him a photo of the trap and told him about it, but I don't want any evidence disturbed or destroyed. After that, I'll make sure someone checks out the grounds. Humans or animals could be hurt if there are more of those traps set." I went back to my request. "I really have to meet this Rhianna woman in the quickest way possible. Time is running out for us, Tinkie. If these people are part of some kind of cult and they're holding these two young women for some reason, my gut tells me it's going to be a bloody reason." The black candles and sigils had really gotten to me. The earring had confirmed my worst suspicions.

"I'll give Pouty a call as soon as we hang up. In fact, Cece mentioned she might drive me and Maylin to the Big Easy for lunch tomorrow. Maybe I could meet with Pouty and wave a check under her nose. Motivate her to help you out."

"That would be perfect. Thank you."

"Pick a lunch place, make reservations, and let me know. We'll be there at high noon and I'll have Pouty in tow."

"Perfect."

"Sarah Booth, Halloween will be here in three days."

I inhaled sharply. The candles, sigils, and ultimately the dangerous trap had reminded me that if these people truly believed they were going to ascend or gain eternal youth or immortality, there was a big possibility of some kind of sacrifice. The death of an innocent was often the price to be paid for some special gift from the dark forces. It didn't matter that such beliefs were insane. And if this was some kind of cult that intended to gain immortality through sacrifice, the ritual would likely take place at midnight on October 31. The sands were draining through the hourglass. Like Dorothy, I had to make every minute count.

I checked in with Coleman, who had set a land-speed record and come up with a name, Abe Addon, and a promising lead on the purchase of five steel-jawed traps. Not exactly a common order in New Orleans proper. Coleman had tracked the purchase down to a man at an address in the French Quarter. He was checking it out now. I had to admit I had a twinge of worry. A person who would use a trap like that for any reason was not a good person, in my book.

"Coleman is on a lead right now. It's slow, but we are making progress."

"What kind of lead?" Tinkie sounded a little wistful.

I told her about the five traps and the man Coleman was looking for.

Her reaction was instantaneous. "Sarah Booth! Stop him."

"What?" I was concerned for Coleman's safety, but Tinkie was downright panicked.

"Abe Addon. Say it fast. Say it!"

When I did, I felt my heart clinch. "Abaddon. The destroying angel." Tinkie and I were both fans of scary movies and Abaddon was often featured as a prime figure of evil. This was too much. We were researching a cult and one lead was for a man named after the chief demon. "Gotta go, Tinkie. I have to find Coleman before he rushes into something."

"Hurry. I'll see you tomorrow."

I hung up and called Coleman. The phone went to voicemail, and I left a desperate message as I was running to the car. Coleman had given an address in the French Quarter that wasn't far from Barracks Street, where Carlos lived. I knew exactly how to get there.

"Ms. Delaney!"

I turned around to see Addie Graham coming after me. "Addie, I can't talk. Emergency," I said.

"I'm coming along."

I didn't have time to argue and, actually, I was glad to have her with me. She could call the law if things got too dicey.

Bringing Addie had another benefit because she knew a shortcut to the street where I'd find Coleman. When we pulled up in front of the address, behind Frankie's car, which Coleman was still driving, I warned Addie to stay in the Roadster. "If you see or hear anything, call the police right away."

"What are you doing?" she asked, confusion on her face. "Just stay here with me and wait."

"I can't." I slammed the car door as I made a beeline for the patio gate. A ten-foot privacy fence, thick and solid, enclosed the side and backyard. There was no sign of Coleman anywhere, and I felt light-headed from the panic.

To my surprise the gate latch responded to my slightest touch. The heavy wooden gate swung open, and I stepped into a courtyard filled with beautiful plants, flagstones, and a fountain that tinkled. Near the back of the house I saw movement. Coleman!

"Psssst!" I tried to get his attention, but he was focused on the door, as in using a lock-pick device to open it.

Coleman was a real law-and-order man. This was out of line for him.

"Stop." I loud-whispered the command.

He glanced over at me and his expression went from confusion to concern. "What are you doing here?"

"Saving you from a demon. Did you bring your gun?" I asked Coleman.

He shook his head and returned to work on the lock. A moment later, the door clicked open.

Coleman was off duty, so he wasn't armed. I hurried back out of the gate to the car, retrieved my gun from the trunk, and took it to him. Addie wasn't in the car but I didn't have time to track her down. He motioned me behind him. The house was still preternaturally quiet. We stepped through the doorway.

Step by step we eased into the elegantly decorated house. Art covered the walls and a thick Turkish carpet was on the hardwood floor. Comfortable, modern furniture filled the small dwelling composed of old reconditioned brick walls. It was a beautiful space and eerily quiet. Somewhere I could hear the ticking of a clock, a sound warning me that action was immediately required to save Christa and Britta.

I stayed in Coleman's footprints, as he'd taught me, as we moved deeper into the house, which was a basic shotgun design. The building itself was old. The bricks looked handmade, probably by slaves.

We made it to the kitchen without incident. Coleman signaled me close so he could whisper in my ear. "Stay here." He nodded toward a closed door that could be a bathroom or utility closet.

I nodded.

He stepped forward and threw the door open. Instead

of entering, he stepped back from the pool of blood that was oozing toward the door.

He didn't have to tell me. I pulled out my phone and called the police. I gave them the address and said there'd been a murder. Coleman would have to explain how and why we were in this apartment, but that would come second to reporting what looked to be the murder of an older man.

"Who is he?" I asked, no longer finding it necessary to be quiet.

"The house belongs to Abe Addon," Coleman said. "Or at least that's who supposedly bought the traps." He looked at me. "Why are you here?"

"Because Abe Addon is a mythic demon, Abaddon."

"What?"

"Tinkie realized it before I did. We both watch a lot of the same TV shows and movies. Abaddon is a demon of destruction. I came to save you."

He put his arm around me, gently shielding me from the dead body on the floor.

"How did he die?" I could have walked over to look, but I didn't.

"Shot. In the temple."

"Suicide?" I asked.

"I don't think so. There's no gun beside the body."

Coleman always got the details at first glance. I'd been so shocked by the body, I hadn't noticed.

"This man hasn't been dead long," Coleman said.

I'd take his word for it. I'd come in the door of this house expecting to find a demon—or at least someone impersonating a demon. Instead, I'd found a dead man brutally murdered.

The ante on finding Christa and Britta just went up exponentially. I put a hand on Coleman's shoulder. "Okay if I sneak out before the cops arrive? I have some things I really must do."

"Go ahead," he said. "That'll actually make it easier." He handed me my gun. "Don't touch anything on the way out."

# 15

I'd left the keys to the Roadster with Addie in case things got too dicey. She was back in the car and seated behind the wheel. I jumped into the passenger seat. "Drive! Fast!"

She peeled away from the curb but cast a strange look at me. "What happened?"

"There's a dead man in that house."

"You got in?"

I'd forgotten she couldn't see over the privacy fence. "Yeah, Coleman was there and he let me in."

She hit the brake. "You left the sheriff person there?"

Addie was finding my actions hard to accept, but there wasn't time to explain. A phalanx of police cars came screaming around the corner.

"Go!" If I were caught near the scene, I might end up

in an interrogation room for hours. I didn't have hours to waste. "Go, Addie, or get out of the car."

She hit the gas and we merged into traffic. I turned and watched patrol units park in front of Abe Addon's house. Police officers jumped out of the vehicles and quickly surrounded the house. Addie put her foot on the gas and kept going. I kept an eye on the action at the house until I couldn't see any longer. My thoughts were as jittery as my nerves.

"Should I drive home?" Addie asked.

"I'll drop you there. Unless there's someplace you'd rather be?"

"Jackson Square."

I indicated that she should turn around and head back the way we'd come.

We rode in silence for a moment, but I could see Addie wanted to ask me something. "What is it?"

"That man who was dead. What happened?"

I had to remember that even though Addie was on her own and working, she was still something of a kid. Normal people didn't stumble over dead bodies and flee a crime scene with the cops arriving. "I don't know. Coleman will find out and tell me."

"Someone shot him?"

The bloody scene came back to me. "Yeah. They did." And in a pantry at that. Such an unfortunate place to die.

"Who was he?" Addie kept her eyes on the road, but she cut a quick glance at me. "I mean, why were you going to his house?"

"I don't know who he really is. We thought they might know something about Christa or Britta."

"Why? I mean, why would that guy know anything?"

Abbie was a virtual Sam Spade with all the questions.

I was going to turn the tables. "What do you know about rituals, magic, and voodoo in New Orleans?"

That stemmed the tide of her questions. She was silent until she pulled over in a space to unload trucks in front of a praline shop on Jackson Square. "I'll jump out here. Thanks for the ride."

"Addie, do you know anything about the magic community?"

"Only that Christa thought the story she was pursuing involved magic rituals. Maybe dark magic, like voodoo. Some kind of worship, maybe Satanic."

"Does the name 'Abaddon' mean anything to you?"

She shrugged. "Not really. It's some kind of major bad guy in the dark magic world. I watch a lot of horror flicks. We all do. And there's always the undercurrent of voodoo around here. Marie Laveau is still an icon here." She bit her bottom lip. "Some people say she's still alive. They see her in St. Louis Cemetery No. 1 where she's buried. They say she drifts among the crypts on clear, moonlit nights and that she helps people in need if they ask her."

Goose bumps ran up my arms, but I got out of the car and walked around to the driver's side. Addie got out and handed me the keys. "You might talk to some of the tarot card readers around the Square. Some of them may know more than I do. And I've heard there are several covens of witches who convene in the Quarter, but I don't know any of them. Want me to ask around?"

"That would be a big help. And, thanks, Addie." I was about to get in the car when I remembered the earring I had in my pocket. "Hey, just a minute." I pulled out the earring. "Do you recognize this?"

She frowned and took it into her palm. "It looks familiar. Where did you get it?"

"I found it."

"Where?"

I decided not to tell her the truth. Or at least not the whole truth. "In the dirt. If a local artist made it, I was hoping they could make another so I'd have a pair. One earring is kind of sad."

"Yes, it is." She handed it back. "I'll keep an eye out for someone who does that kind of craftsmanship." She pointed to a delivery truck headed right for her. "You'd better get out of that unloading zone or they'll arrest you and tow your car."

She was right about that. New Orleans had limited parking space and they enforced the laws with vigor. "Thanks." I started the car and drove straight to St. Lucy's church. I needed another word with Father Joseph.

On the way to St. Lucy's, I detoured near Abe Addon's house to see what was happening. The police had that portion of the road blocked off, and I saw Coleman leaning against the back of a patrol car, talking with three city officers. He looked at ease. Hopefully, they were believing whatever story he'd come up with to tell them.

Coleman wouldn't enjoy fibbing to other officers, and he would be as honest as he could. The sticky wicket in that conversation would be how he got into the house. I was glad it was him and not me doing the explaining.

In twenty minutes I arrived at St. Lucy's. Traffic clogged the streets, making the short distance a slow journey. Before I went inside, I texted Frankie to let her know where I was. I could only hope she was sleeping her migraine away. I wished Tinkie was with me, to observe reactions, but I would handle it on my own. I smiled at the realization of how many things I'd come to rely on her for.

When I entered the church, it was still and quiet. I wasn't a churchgoer, but I found solace in the still beauty of the small sanctuary. The stained glass windows were works of art and I took a moment, examining all of them and the carved stations of the cross placed along the interior walls. New Orleans had unique and wonderful artists. The sculptor who'd done this work was exquisite, as was the glazier who'd created the depiction of angelic warfare against demons in the windows.

The windows contained a more action-based theme, different than the honoring of the Virgin Mary, Jesus, the saints, disciples, or prophets I more often saw. My particular love was the ones that demonstrated the parables that Jesus taught. These, though, were terribly compelling.

"May I help you?"

The voice behind me made me jump at least two feet forward. I turned around to confront a middle-aged nun. "I was just admiring the stained glass."

"Yes, it's lovely." She stared past me, toward one of the windows. "We were lucky to have a donor pay for the windows."

"Did the donor select the artist and themes?" Often a donor held great sway.

"Yes. The windows have elicited a lot of other donations to the church, too. I know the bishop worried that the windows were too . . . violent, but they've brought only positive attention. We've been blessed." She smiled. "The Bible is a rather violent book, if you think about it."

She was right about that. "Is Father Joseph in?"

"He is. In his office. I can announce you or you can just

tap on his door. He always welcomes anyone who needs to see him."

"I'll just knock on the door. Thank you, Sister."

I headed toward the office area, but I turned back to ask the Sister who the window donor had been. The sanctuary was empty; she was gone. She'd disappeared so quietly I felt a ripple of unease. I forced a grim laugh and knocked at Father Joseph's door.

"Come in."

I stepped inside the warmly lit room with a sigh of relief.

"Sarah Booth, what brings you here?"

"I'm no closer to finding the missing women, but I do have some questions about voodoo or Satanic rituals."

He frowned. "What did you hear about Carlos?"

"What do you mean?"

He looked down at his desk and I accepted that he hadn't been totally forthcoming about any of this. Anger shot up my spine and nearly blew off the top of my head. "Tell me everything you know about Carlos. All of it. Not just the superficial family stuff." I pulled the earring from my pocket and put it on his desk. "Christa was wearing these earrings the day she disappeared. I saw one of them in Carlos's car, even though he said he hadn't seen her that day. This one I found at a site where some sort of rituals were being performed. Now Christa is missing for three days; Britta longer. This isn't a game, it's serious. I need to know everything."

"There are things told in the confessional I can't share. You know that."

So, he did know more. "I'm not asking you to break a confidence, but these two girls' lives are at stake. If you know something that can help me find them, you have to tell me."

He finally met my gaze. "One of Carlos's cousins joined the People of Eternity cult. He's the one who really told Christa about it. Or at least that's what Addie told me. Addie said she was interested in pursuing the story—she's a journalist, too—but that Carlos said he'd mentioned it to Christa first."

"What did Carlos know about the cult?"

"I don't really know the details. He said they were into some strange god or goddess worship and that only rich people could join. The leader, Rhianna, promises eternal youth and access to the afterlife without dying." He frowned. "It's bullshit, if you'll pardon my language. There is only one route to the afterlife and that is through Jesus."

"Did Carlos mention a location?"

"He may know the address where they meet. Christa wanted him to photograph the meetings to go with her story."

I'd wasted two days in New Orleans when I could have been a lot closer to finding Christa if only her "friends" had told me the truth.

"Do you have any idea where Carlos is right now?"

"He said he had some assignment to photograph. Over by Jax Brewery. I swear to you, he is working on finding Christa. He loves her."

"Only not enough to tell the truth to the people her mother hired to look for her. Doesn't sound like love to me." I was loaded for bear with Carlos and the priest. "This delay—just hope it hasn't cost Christa or Britta their life." I stood up, too angry to stay seated. I'd look for Carlos and as a second measure I'd find Addie. If she knew anything about POE, I'd drag it out of her.

"I'm sorry, Sarah Booth. I didn't mean to deceive you, but there are rules and boundaries."

"And there are consequences. Now I have to find Carlos."

# 16

With Coleman at the NOPD and Frankie laid low with a migraine, I called Carlos repeatedly and left a dozen messages. No response. Finding myself stalled, I used the time to drive to the city library and look up the address on Third Street in the crisscross directory to see who owned it. The reverse directory was old school but still very helpful.

The property was owned by Rebus Mitchem. There was a phone number listed, so I put the number in my phone to call when I left the library. I also looked up the property in the Quarter where Abe Addon was supposed to live. No big shock, the property was also owned by Rebus Mitchem. No mention of an Abe Addon. It seemed Abe and Rebus were one and the same. Rebus Mitchem was a man who owned several very valuable properties and had deliberately tied himself to a demon's name. Interesting.

I took down all the information I could find, realizing that Coleman could get the same info in a blink from the NOPD, but it made me feel productive to work on filling my notepad. I also got the research librarian to help me look into the history of both properties.

When I showed the librarian a picture I'd taken of the unusual fence, he nodded. "Oh, yes, that's the old Riley place. Once upon a time, it was a grand home. The cream of society gathered there for balls and cotillions. I think there are some photos of the house when it was maintained. The grounds were patterned after formal French gardens. During the seventies and eighties, many weddings were hosted there because of the beautiful flowers and plants. When the Riley family owned the place, they maintained exotic blooms that flourished. My mother, who followed society news, said different segments of the gardens lent themselves to themes, like Arabian Nights or Hollywood or historic settings. Folks loved going there to see the creativity of each event."

"There's nothing of that left now. It's a jungle." I sounded grimmer than I intended, but the place haunted me. "Tell me the juicy gossip about the old place. There's bound to be a downside."

His quick grin rewarded me. "You're very astute. In recent years, there's been talk of dark happenings on the grounds. New Orleans is a big city, but in some ways, the various districts are like small towns. When the author Anne Rice moved here, there was an upsurge in stories about witches and covens and black magic. Folks went nuts talking about the old Riley place and the ceremonies held there."

"Details?" I asked.

"You know, the usual. People in robes or cloaks, fires, dancing and chanting. Very pagan. Witchy, even. Police raids yielded nothing, as far as I know."

"Are there any written accounts of those activities?"

"When the newspaper was still published daily, I'm sure there were articles written. It's too delicious not to report on. And the *Times-Picayune* always loved portraying New Orleans as a city linked to supernatural forces. The tourist trade ate it up."

"And in recent years?"

"That's all in the past now. A couple of years ago the house was struck by lightning and burned to the ground."

At least that gave me a timeline. "These dark happenings, was anyone ever hurt?"

He motioned me to step outside the library, where he lit up a cigarette.

He drew in, exhaled, and began to talk. "I'm trying to remember. You might want to check back issues of the paper. Especially around Halloween. There was always something going on. New Orleans has a very healthy supernatural underground. You have no idea of the tourists who come here specifically to see Marie Laveau's grave. They come in droves to see where *The Originals,* that vampire show, was filmed." He flicked his ash. "Only problem is that television show was mostly filmed in Georgia. Some scenes were filmed in the French Quarter and wannabe vampires come seeking that connection to a world where some live forever."

His words were a grim echo of my own thoughts. "That's true. Vampires live forever. I suppose to some, the allure of immortality is great."

"The vampire legends don't portray that as such a great

gift. Imagine living endlessly while those you loved perished unless you made them a vampire, too."

"Have you heard anything about a group called the People of Eternity?"

He stared into the distance. "I can't say that I have. At least I don't recall anyone asking for research or information about them. What do they do?"

"Eternal youth. Immortality."

"There is a youth cult here, but it isn't supernatural. It's all about the scalpel. New Orleans is certainly a haven for plastic surgeons. A lot of celebrities who want surgery but want to escape the scrutiny of the paparazzi come here. That's the only youth cult I know anything about."

"Have you ever heard of Leo LeMuse?"

He laughed. "Oh, he's the most sought after of the 'reconstructionists.'" He used air quotes around the last word. "He runs ads in every upscale magazine in the nation. They say his work is perfection. His clients are all very wealthy and the fact that insurance doesn't often cover his services means nothing to them."

"I've heard he's highly sought after."

"I, on the other hand, am courting death with these cigarettes and they're terrible for my skin." The librarian finished his cigarette and signaled that he had to go back inside. "The library administration doesn't bother me about smoking and I try not to take advantage of their lenience with my breaks. Smokers are the new lepers, you know."

I did know and was glad I'd quit. "Thanks for all your help." I followed him inside and went straight to the archives to do exactly as he'd suggested.

I had digital and paper files to read through when I finally looked at my watch. I was shocked to see it was midafternoon. I'd forgotten about lunch and everything else. The fact that I hadn't heard from Coleman was suddenly concerning. Had he actually been arrested? I'd never really considered that as a possibility, but maybe I should have.

I texted him to see if he would—or could—respond. To my relief I got a brief text back. "All okay. Talk soon."

I tried Carlos again, with no result, so I gathered up my notes and stopped by the desk to say thank you to my helper. Then I was on the way to Esplanade Street and Frankie. I'd neglected her for the afternoon, too, but I'd found a lot of interesting information and a possible lead on how to locate the People of Eternity.

When I arrived back at Christa's apartment, I found Frankie and Burt drinking coffee. She looked much improved. "How's the headache?" I asked.

"Gone, thank heavens."

That was good news. I turned to Burt. "Any idea where I can find Addie?"

"She came through about an hour ago, packed some clothes, and said she had a line on a big story. She said to tell Leitha not to worry, that she'd be back in a few days."

Convenient. I'd talk to Leitha later and see if Addie had left a means of communication. I wanted to have a word with her. Pronto.

"Did you find any clues about Christa?" Frankie asked. There was such hope in her eyes, I hated to disappoint her, so I was careful with my response.

"I found some information on occult practices in New Orleans that may lead me to the People of Eternity. And I learned a lot about some locations I think will yield promising information." Frankie would have no clue about the dead man we'd found in the Quarter, so I kept my lips zipped. It was a difficult subject to broach since I didn't know what role he might play in Christa's life, if he played any at all. "Coleman will have some news when he gets here." Okay, so I was a bit of a coward and would push it off on Coleman to reveal the necessary facts. But he would also know what he wanted to reveal and what he wanted to withhold.

My phone chimed again, and I read another text from Coleman. "I'm on my way."

"What did you find about occult practices?" Burt asked. "We live in a city with tarot readers, covens, and voodoo shops on every corner. I guess we don't pay as much attention as we should. That whole supernatural thing is part of the charm of the city, and I guess we just take it for granted."

I told Burt about the property on Third Street and let Frankie know the place was owned by a man named Rebus Mitchem. I'd also discovered some tidbits about him.

"Rebus claimed to be a warlock, and when the house was there, he held numerous rituals seeking help from the dark side. Or at least those were the rumors. The NOPD was called several times to investigate wild parties. Orgies, plentiful drugs, that kind of thing. There was a lot of talk but not a lot of action on the part of the police."

"I've heard stories of people who worshiped Satan," Burt said. "I know some people who say they're witches, but they're white witches. They don't consort with the dark side of things."

"I don't know how Rebus affiliated, dark or white, but he had a reputation for being dangerous. It was said he could curse or hex anyone who offended him."

"Where'd you get all of this?" Burt asked.

"Library. It makes for some interesting reading."

"Is Rebus Mitchem still alive?" Frankie asked.

I hesitated. I could tell her about what Coleman and I had encountered now, but again I chose to wait, taking my lead from what Coleman wanted to reveal. "I don't know. The articles didn't say. The house was struck by lightning and burned down a couple of years ago. He also owns some property in the French Quarter." I wondered if his property ownership had anything to do with what happened to him—if he was indeed the dead man.

Burt stood up. "I promised Leitha I'd make some dinner. I sure wish Christa and Britta would return. They're the best cooks. I struggle."

"I'll throw together a meal for you guys," Frankie said. "Maybe our wayward girls will be home soon and they can resume cooking duties."

"Absolutely." Burt gave Frankie a quick hug and headed down the stairs to his own apartment. I was standing at the railing when I saw Coleman pull up in Frankie's car. He got out and waved, his face giving nothing away.

"Can I make you a drink?" I called down to him.

"Sure. Whatever is convenient."

Coleman was easy that way. I went inside and poured some bourbon, neat. I made one for me and for Frankie, too. It had been a long, grinding day. He was in the swing when I got back to the porch and he signaled me with his eyes. He was about to fill Frankie in on his day.

"I was telling Frankie about Rebus Mitchem. The man who owns both the property in the French Quarter and the one on Third Street." I gave him the opening.

"So you found out his name. Did you tell Frankie he's dead?" Coleman asked.

I shook my head. "I wasn't certain. Is it really him?"

"The police identified him." Coleman sipped his drink.

"They weren't all that happy to find me in his home with the dead body."

"You found a dead man? What happened to him?" Frankie asked.

Coleman looked at me and I nodded. Frankie was tough enough to handle whatever he'd discovered. "He was murdered. The police are still investigating, but there was talk he was involved in occult happenings. That property has quite a reputation."

"And you both saw the body?" Frankie looked as if her migraine might return.

"Yes," I said. "Coleman and I intended to ask him some questions, but someone beat us to him." I turned to Coleman, who looked tired. "Do you think he was killed so he couldn't talk to us?" I asked.

"I don't know enough about him to hazard a guess as to motive. Our more urgent need is to find the People of Eternity and talk to them." Coleman's deadly serious expression made me itch for action. Time was not on our side, and with each passing hour, the likelihood of finding the missing women decreased. We all knew this fact so there was no need to mention it.

"We can set up outside the Third Street property tonight," I said, "but what I learned at the library indicated the property isn't being used that much now."

"I suspect you're right, but that trap says there's something there worth hiding. There are a couple of off-duty police officers who said they'd set up surveillance on Third Street tonight. They've been eyeing Rebus Mitchem for a while now," Coleman said. "You and I—we need to talk to this Rhianna woman or some representative of this cult. We have to do that now. Our goal is to find her as soon as we can."

"Does the NOPD know anything about her?" Frankie asked.

Coleman nodded. "A little. The group has only recently come up on their radar, and the chief said they thought the leader, Rhianna, was committing fraud, embezzlement, and financial crimes. They've only had two complaints, both recent and both about money. The People of Eternity aren't a big priority, but they are definitely on the NOPD's watch list."

"Do you know who complained?" I asked.

"I do, and you're going to find this very interesting. Dr. Leo LeMuse filed both complaints."

"Pouty's plastic surgeon husband?"

Coleman nodded. "He claimed that the People of Eternity are bilking his wife out of tens of thousands of dollars using fraud and possibly blackmail."

"This is likely why he and Pouty are divorcing."

"Dr. LeMuse claims Pouty is under the influence of this group and can't be trusted to make decisions in her own best interest. He's trying to get her committed."

Oh, baby, Pouty was not going to like that. If the men in white coats came to grab her up, she was going to fight nasty. "Pouty had some interesting things to say about Leo, too. She said he was cheating on her with a younger woman. Someone in her twenties." The little puzzle pieces clicked into place. "Someone Britta or Christa's age."

Frankie leaned forward. "I don't think Christa would involve herself with a married man, and certainly not a plastic surgeon. She's not really into all of that."

"But Britta had a thing for men with money," I said. "And even if she wasn't interested in him romantically, she might be financially. For blackmail purposes if nothing else."

"We need to have a word with Leo LeMuse," I said, checking my watch. "Frankie, will you be okay here alone if we track him down?"

"Of course." Frankie lifted her chin, and that gesture reminded me of my mother so much it was like a little stab in the heart. "I'll make some chicken and dumplings for Leitha and Burt. I'll stay busy and I won't be alone."

# 17

Coleman and I were barely ahead of the five o'clock traffic, and I wondered if Leo LeMuse would still be in his office. Coleman didn't want to call and alert him that we were coming. I understood why; we had no jurisdiction to hold LeMuse. We had to catch him before he could hide. If he knew we were coming to talk to him he could simply go on vacation and avoid us.

We arrived at his beautiful art deco building on Canal Street just as his staff came out the back door. Coleman walked up to one of the women and talked with her for a few minutes. She glanced over at me, still in the Roadster, as Coleman had requested, and then she took Coleman inside. I sat up, ready to jump through the door with them, but I stopped myself. If Coleman could get inside, he could do the interview as well as I could. I didn't want to squelch his chances of getting LeMuse to talk by demanding that I be let in. Coleman didn't need me. I just didn't like being left out.

After a few moments, the woman came out and walked toward me. "Sheriff Peters has asked me to let you in."

That Coleman! I owed him. He knew how hard it was for me to be out of the action. "Thanks." I scrambled out of the car and followed her to the door.

Before she unlocked the door she faced me. "Dr. Le-Muse is a wonderful surgeon. He's an artist. His patients adore him. Don't make trouble for him. He's got enough on his hands with that crazy wife of his."

Golden opportunity knocking at my door! "How crazy is Pouty?" It was always good to get another perspective.

"She's desperate to be someone special. Nothing satisfies her. She's empty inside, which is why I think she's gone over the deep end with this religious group she's hooked up with."

Interesting that LeMuse's staff knew all about Pouty's business. I wondered who the leak might be, him or her, or both. "You think the People of Eternity are a religious group?"

She shrugged. "I don't know what to call them except hucksters and deceivers. They promise things they can't deliver. From what Leo says, Pouty has lost the ability to think rationally. She *believes* she can find eternal youth and immortality by believing in whatever Rhianna says. Faith alone, as they say. Right," she scoffed. "Faith and about eight grand a week into the POE coffers. It's really very sad, you know. And dangerous. Someone needs to step in and stop Pouty before she hurts herself or sends Dr. Leo to the poorhouse."

"Thank you for the insight." Someone was very loyal to Dr. Leo. I stepped inside and she closed and locked the door from the outside. I was in the belly of the plastic surgery beast. Coleman's voice came to me from down the impossibly sterile white hallway. Beveled mirrors adorned the walls, creating a kind of fun-house sensation that wasn't fun at all. Everywhere I looked, I stared back at myself. If I'd been a person looking for physical flaws, I would have found plenty to moan about.

I came to an open door and looked inside to see Coleman seated in front of a huge, empty desk. The man behind the desk made me stop and catch my breath. He was an Adonis. Golden-haired, blue-eyed, handsome. Criminally handsome. I could see the dangerous appeal of a physically perfect surgeon and the siren call of lasting beauty. I had no doubt Dr. Leo was raking in the money as fast as he could.

"Ms. Delaney," he said, waving me inside. "Please take a seat. I understand you know my wife."

"We grew up in the same area," I said. "Pouty and I weren't really friends. My partner knows her, and I met with her yesterday for a fashion interview and shoot."

"Yes, she told me all about it. You couldn't have given her anything she wanted more than that. Fame in her hometown newspaper. What every girl craves."

I couldn't tell if he was being sarcastic or sincere. "Yes, Pouty loves the camera and it loves her. She's very photogenic."

"Yes, she is. Before you ask, she's only had a little work. Light touches to turn back the clock. Of course, now she doesn't need my talents. She's signed up to be forever young through the magical practices of her new best friend, this Rhianna creature." He snorted. "And people think I charge a lot for my surgeries. This woman doesn't do a damn thing and Pouty has siphoned off at least sixty thousand dollars—that I've found. I'm sure it will be over a hundred thousand by the time my accountant finishes tracking it. One thing about Pouty, she knows how to hide her financial crimes."

"I gather you don't approve of Rhianna and the People of Eternity," Coleman said.

"It's a scam. They're a bunch of grifters playing on the stupidity of desperate people who truly think they can live forever or ascend to paradise"—he waved his hands up, imitating departing souls—"without the indignities of death." His voice got all woo-woo. "They will transition to paradise without suffering death and they'll retain their physical bodies at the peak of perfection." He dropped back into his normal tone. "Right. What total hogwash. Only an imbecile would buy into this horseshit. I didn't marry Pouty for her intelligence, but I thought she had at least three working brain cells. Apparently not."

Leo LeMuse had no problem letting anyone know exactly how superior he felt to everyone around him.

"Have you attended any of the meetings with Pouty?" Coleman asked. He was lounging back in a club chair, taking it easy. Leo had focused his ire at me. Funny that his patients were mostly female, the women he convinced that they needed surgery. The women he "practiced" medicine on. Pot calling the kettle black, some?

"I wouldn't be caught dead at a meeting." Leo drilled me with an angry gaze. "But I did meet up with the harridan of the cult for a drink *once*. That was plenty for me. You should have seen the dollar signs pop in her eyes when she realized who I was. I never should have gone. I'll never be able to extract Pouty from that cult, and now I'm tired of trying. She's on her own."

"You've washed your hands of your wife?" Coleman's eyebrows said it all.

"Not for long. Meaning she won't be my wife for long. My lawyer is drawing up the divorce papers."

"When you met Rhianna, what was the physical location?" I was bummed he hadn't gone to a gathering or service or whatever, but maybe I could get a useful name.

"Court of Two Sisters. I insisted on a public place."

Damn. That wasn't helpful. "But Pouty goes to the meetings, right?" I asked.

"Oh, she goes. Every time she puts her foot near Rhianna it costs me five grand. There are charges to attend the daily spiritual sessions, charges for energy realignment, charges for herbs and vitamins, charges for conferences and healing sessions. If I could use this model for my practice, I'd only need five wealthy clients to stay in business. I wasn't about to attend any meeting or session and pay for the privilege of being bilked. We met for Bloody Marys. I was in and out in thirty minutes. It doesn't take me long to figure out when a hungry shark is about to snap off my legs."

In that regard, perhaps Leo was smart.

"Did Pouty ever tell you where they held these meetings?"

He frowned. "Maybe. But I wasn't paying attention." He snapped his fingers. "Wait a minute. There's some garden. I remember Pouty complaining about the humidity back in August. She said something about how Rhianna should suspend outdoor events until the weather cooled."

"Can you remember anything else?" Coleman pressed.

"Yes, Pouty always had wax on her shoes when she came back from an evening event. Very expensive leather shoes, and she'd just let the wax cake up on them. That's Pouty's problem. She's always had too much. No appreciation."

The wax was interesting because it indicated some type of ritual was being conducted, but the information wasn't really helpful in finding a location. Candles could be burned anywhere from a church to a basement or clearing in the woods.

"Does Pouty have a GPS in her car?" Coleman asked.

The brilliance of his question made me open my mouth like a breathless guppy. Leo looked at me.

"Adenoids?" he asked. "We can do a procedure to take care of that, deviated septum, sinus issues, and bob that nose at the same time. Free nose job, if you get my drift. I can write it so your insurance will cover it."

I put my hand to my nose and squeezed. My nose was perfectly fine. Not too big. Not too small. It was just right. I froze. Leo was working on me with his crazy Mr. Fix-It routine. "My nose and adenoids are just fine. My septum isn't deviated."

Leo gave an eye roll. "Denial is the first step to enlightenment."

"That sounds an awful lot like something a spiritual leader would say. Maybe a cult leader." I was annoyed and I let it show.

Leo only laughed. "You'll come around. Another five years, you'll be discreetly googling the best plastic surgeons in the region. Give me a call. I'll give you an ex-wife's friend discount."

"Leo!" Coleman got his attention and repeated his question about Pouty's GPS.

"Yes, her car has GPS."

"May I see it?" Coleman asked.

"Do you have a warrant?"

"You know I don't. I told you I don't have jurisdiction in New Orleans." Even Coleman was about to lose patience. "I'm asking for your help. It might lead to you getting some of your money back."

"Sure." He checked his watch. "Pouty should be home now. She's making the first pitcher of martinis." He reached in his desk drawer, withdrew a key, and tossed it to Coleman. "Just tell her I gave the okay for you to look in the car." He held up a hand. "The car is in my name, not hers. Don't worry."

At last it felt as if we might be able to find Rhianna's location. Time was wasting. I stood up and edged to the door. I couldn't get out of that place fast enough.

# 18

Pouty's home was something to behold. It had to be at least ten thousand square feet. The gray brick rose out of a perfect lawn surrounded by palm trees. There was a distinctive Hollywood vibe to the place. Beverly Hills with a 90210 zip. I wondered if Pouty's taste was on display or if Dr. Leo had created a nod to his celebrity patients.

I went to the front door and knocked, as Coleman requested. He followed the driveway to the back of the house, hoping Pouty's car would be easily accessible. In this scenario, I was the diversion.

I knocked again and rang the doorbell twelve times straight in a row. Why not? If I was supposed to be an annoyance, why not go whole hog?

A maid answered the door and informed me Mrs. Le-Muse was unable to entertain visitors at this time.

"I'm not a visitor. I'm working on a big story for a magazine," I said. "Pouty needs to talk to me. It's important."

The maid was perfectly deadpan. "She's exercising. She never deviates from her schedule. You can make an appointment and come back."

"Her husband said she'd be making a pitcher of martinis right now, and I could sure use a drink."

My personal knowledge made her shift back from the door and I pushed inside. Capitalize on the moment—good detectives knew this rule.

"Stop! You can't come in." She tried to wedge herself between me and the hallway, but it was truly only a half-hearted attempt.

"It's okay. Dr. Leo sent me," I said. "But I do need to speak with Pouty. Would you tell her Sarah Booth Delaney is here? I'm not leaving until I talk to her."

She fled the hallway and didn't look back. I was left on my own to wander into the living room and den, both of which were empty. I could hear music coming from upstairs so I headed that way. The house was big, and even though I was looking for a window that faced the back of the house, so far I hadn't found one. I couldn't even guess where the back of the house might be. I could only hope Coleman was getting the info he needed from the GPS.

"Pouty! Pouty!" I called for my hostess, following the sound of dance music along the second floor toward a closed door. I tapped lightly at the door. The throbbing base vibrated in the wood. "Pouty!" I knocked harder.

When no one came to the door, I turned the knob and pressed it open. The wall of music made me hesitate, but I persisted. I eased into the room and took my bearings.

The suite was enormous and filled with beautiful furniture. I was in a type of foyer that opened into a full bath on my right and a honking big closet on my left. I took a moment to appreciate an entire wall of shoes, all in boxes, and organized by color. Pouty had a shoe fetish.

I heard labored breathing and strenuous puffing, and I walked into the bedroom. Pouty was in front of a wall of mirrors as she jumped and stretched and twisted away to the music and some instruction coming from one mirror that held the image of a finely sculpted exercise instructor. She was performing the routine as she talked Pouty through it. I watched a minute, impressed with Pouty's hard work and toned body. If the doctor's wife was paying for youth and an afterlife, she was doing her part to keep her body in shape to enjoy it. She made me feel like a slug.

"Hi, Pouty!"

She screamed and faced me. "What are you doing here?"

"Looking for you. I wanted to confirm our meeting tomorrow with Tinkie and Cece."

"You came out here to my house to ambush me so you could confirm an appointment I have with your friends?"

I shrugged. "I was curious, I guess. Beautiful home."

Pouty turned off the music and the mirror. "You've disrupted my exercise."

"Leo sent me. He said you'd be making martinis. I thought maybe if you told me where the People of Eternity are meeting, I could arrange some dynamite publicity. I have connections with some television stations. Maybe I could even help you convince Dr. Leo he should give Rhianna a chance."

"He is such a jackass." She picked up a towel and wiped

the sweat from her forehead. "But it is the perfect time for a martini. Follow me."

By the time I had a martini in hand, Pouty made it clear she wasn't going to tell me a location—or anything else helpful. But she waxed eloquent about Rhianna and POE. The only thing she gave away was that the meetings were held in isolated places where singing, chanting, dancing wouldn't disturb neighbors. Pouty was enthused about the ceremonies, as she called them, and she let it slip that she was actually a new member. She needed to bring in two more members as part of her agreement with POE. Hence her interest in Tinkie.

Coleman texted my phone. He was finished. It was time to go. I sipped half of my drink—gulped really—and made my excuses to leave. As I stopped for her to open the front door for me, she put a hand on my arm.

"What are you really doing here, Sarah Booth?"

Pouty was nobody's fool, but I'd prepared and had an answer that best served my purposes. "I'm interested in the eternal youth. But I'm more interested in ascension without death. Would I still be able to be with my family if I did that?"

Pouty was taken aback. "I don't know. But I will ask Rhianna when I see her next. I will get that answer for you."

"You really believe in Rhianna, don't you?"

"Rhianna and her assistant, Renaldo, are the best thing that ever happened to me, Sarah Booth. I'm eager to talk to Tinkie about it. If she decides to join us, I'll put in a word with Rhianna to allow you to be part of it, too. You have a lot of property. If you sold that, you could afford it."

"Thanks, Pouty. I'll see you soon."

I walked down the winding sidewalk to the car parked in the drive. When the front door closed, Coleman slipped around the side of the house and joined me.

I hopped in the passenger seat and gave Coleman the key. The minute we were in the car, Coleman turned to me. "I think we have a location."

"How are we going to play this?" I asked him.

"I'm going to investigate tonight. The more we know, the more effective you can be when you finally meet up with Rhianna. Tomorrow, you're going to go with Tinkie and Cece to meet with Pouty and see if you can't get an invitation to one of the sessions."

I'd already set the stage for that meeting, but I had other worries. "You aren't going to do this alone tonight," I said, meaning every word.

"No, a couple of the off-duty NOPD officers will back me up. Sarah Booth, after that steel-jawed trap you found, I can't let you go with me in the dark to a place that may be booby-trapped. These men are trained in detecting snares and traps. If I have to worry about you, it will put me at risk of getting injured myself."

This was an old script between us. "Coleman, this is my case. You're helping me. I can't ask you to risk this without me." I could feel my chin jutting out in stubbornness.

"This isn't up for debate. You stay with Frankie. And don't come out to Third Street. Tomorrow, you can do what I can't do. We're a team. Let me be a real team member."

As he talked, he was driving fast toward Esplanade. Coleman had learned his way around New Orleans in record time. I could still get lost walking two blocks over. I wasn't going to argue with him, but I also wasn't giving up. I'd follow him. I knew where he was going and I'd simply drive there on my own.

"Why don't you and Frankie grab some po'boys for us for later. I'll be back before you know it." He turned in front of Christa's apartment and stopped the car. "Please, just cooperate."

It was the "please" that finally did me in. "Text me every twenty minutes."

"Okay."

"If you don't, I'll come after you."

I got out of the car but before he could pull away, I walked around and put my hand on his arm. "What did you find out? You never told me."

"I got more than a GPS reading. I found a note. There's something scheduled at Third Street tonight. Pouty has been in or near that location. I don't know what's going on, but I intend to be there to find out."

"The People of Eternity are meeting there?"

"I'm not sure exactly who it is. The note didn't mention specifics, just the location. The two officers I asked to check over the property have agreed to go with me."

I really wanted to go. Badly. But I had to let Coleman be my partner. I understood that even if I didn't like it. Besides, I had other fish to fry. I might not be able to wade around in high weeds with Coleman and the cultists, but I could make progress on my case. I needed to talk to Carlos again. And find out when Addie would be home.

# 19

Instead of going to the apartment where Coleman and I were staying, I went to Christa's place. Frankie's car was there, so I figured she was home. As I started up the steps, I saw a figure in a red hooded cloak standing at the base of the beautiful oak trees that lined Esplanade Avenue. The figure was the size of a child, but when it realized I saw it, it moved very fast toward me. I'd never seen a child run so nimbly—or quickly.

The speed of the small person startled me and also frightened me. I knew it could not be a creature of this world, which made it even more menacing. It neared the foot of the steps and looked up at me with red, glowing eyes in the face of an old and wizened man. Black fur surrounded the ugly little face.

A low growl came from its throat. New Orleans was a city of magic, both dark and light, and I knew the legend of this wicked creature.

"The *Nain Rouge*." I whispered the words I'd learned from my great uncle Alton Crabtree. This was a living depiction of the creature Uncle Alton had told me about in stories designed to chill my child's soul. My uncle was a helluva storyteller who'd given even my mother the shivers. Uncle Alton had collected a series of Native American legends and folklore in his travels through the heartland of America, and he could deliver those stories with an authenticity that made the most gruesome aspects come alive. My mother and I loved to sit in front of a blazing fire and listen to his tales, though sometimes he petrified me with fear.

I was not prepared to deal with the *Nain Rouge* without Uncle Alton's help. "Get away from me now!"

The creature looked up at me, as if waiting for some sign.

"Go away." I pointed toward the street.

It merely laughed.

"Go!" I eased up the steps, praying that Frankie hadn't locked the door and that I could get inside. The *Nain Rouge* was a harbinger of bad things to come. The literal translation of the Ottawa language was "red dwarf." My uncle said if one saw the *Nain Rouge* that death was imminent. "Get away from me."

The impish creature lunged toward the steps and I scrambled higher. Coleman had returned my gun to the trunk of the Roadster and I had no weapon. Maybe there was something inside Christa's apartment I could use. I wasn't handy with a knife, but maybe a fireplace poker? "Stay back," I warned it, knowing my words were an empty threat. What was I going to do, smack it in the face with a verb?

"Sarah Booth. I'm gonna gitcha."

Except the threat was delivered not in the growl of the red dwarf, but in the soft drawl of someone I knew quite well. That was the final straw. Awareness and anger washed over me in equal waves. "Dammit to hell, Jitty, I'm going to skin you alive."

The ugly red creature began to shift and morph as I watched. In a matter of seconds, Jitty stood before me, wearing a revealing little gingham dress with a white pinafore and a red hooded cloak. She carried a basket of goodies and had the sexiest little red boots I'd ever seen. Jitty had found the perfect costume for Halloween.

"That's right," she said. "Only three days until Halloween. And you don't even have an idea for a costume. You can't be out on the streets of N'awlins in your civvies. I won't have it. You'd better get busy. Chop-chop."

"The locals hate it when people pronounce New Orleans like that. So you stop it. Chop-chop." Normally I let Jitty's shenanigans roll off my back, but this time I was truly, truly angry. She'd scared me badly. "I'm not having this, Jitty. I'm not. I realize you enjoy having fun at my expense, but this time you truly frightened me."

The look of contrition on her face was balm to my fluttering heart. "I'm sorry, Sarah Booth. I didn't mean to really scare you. It's just that . . ." She petered out, but a wicked grin lit her face. "You're so damn easy!"

"Easy? What the heck? The *Nain Rouge* portends doom and destruction. Death. Is Christa dead? Is Britta dead? Is this pointless? Is Coleman risking his safety for no reason? Am I going to die? Just spit it out. I'm sick of these games."

Jitty pushed back the hood of her cloak, and I could see she was truly worried. "I'm sorry, Sarah Booth. I didn't mean to upset you this much."

I sat down on the top step, the release of my anger weakening my legs. "I'm already worried about Christa and Britta and now Coleman. This harbinger-of-doom crap is wearing on me."

"Best to be prepared."

That was like a lighted match to a cannon. I jumped to my feet. "There it is again. You're all but telling me tragedy is about to arrive on my doorstep and yet you won't confirm it or deny it and you won't tell me how to fight it off. Either spill your guts or shut up and leave me alone. I can't handle this anymore."

"You loved these stories when your uncle Alton told them."

"My mama was alive then to hold me tight against her and make me feel safe." I realized the minute the words were out of my mouth that I wasn't so much mad at Jitty as I was feeling unprotected, insecure, a victim of fate yet again.

"Okay." Jitty transformed her Halloween getup to sweatpants and a long-sleeved thermal Henley. "Boy, did I hit your hot button. I'm sorry."

I couldn't stay mad at Jitty. "I'm sorry, too, but you really got to me. If there's something bad coming, just tell me, please."

"Folks either cry, run, or fight when they get scared. Glad to see you're a fighter. You were about to punch a mudhole in my butt and walk it dry."

I refused to laugh. She wasn't going to get by me with some insane praise. "Can it. Now tell me why you came here as the red dwarf. You must know something. Something awful. Just tell me." I was on the verge of begging.

"The only thing I really know, Sarah Booth, is that time is running out. You're like Dorothy in the witch's castle watching the sand drain from the hourglass. Find Christa and Britta, and be quick about it. That's all I can tell you."

"So they're still alive?" I would grasp any straw she threw out.

"Just hurry, Sarah Booth. Time really is your enemy."

There was the distant beat of drums and chanting. I thought for a minute it was coming from the blues club, but no, it was from a far distant vista where the Ottawa people performed a ceremony. Jitty did a slow spin and evaporated just as I heard footsteps on the balcony above me. I popped up into a standing position to see who was headed toward the stairs.

Addie Graham rendered an earth-shattering scream.

I screamed, too, because she scared me. We both just looked at each other and screamed again.

"What are you doing here?" she finally demanded. Apparently she was a fighter, too.

"Waiting for you to come out of hiding. I thought you were gone for a few days. I've been waiting to talk to you," I said. "I don't think you've been totally honest with me and we're going to fix that right now."

"My plans changed. I'm not in the mood to talk." Addie took in my vulnerable position on the top step and tried to push past me, but I blocked her.

"Not so fast, Addie."

"I don't have time for this, Sarah Booth. I'm supposed to be somewhere else."

"Where might that be?" I asked.

At last she sighed. "What is it you want me to tell you?"

"Let's start with the truth. You know more about Britta's and Christa's disappearances than you're saying." It was kind of a wild guess, but why else would she be so determined to avoid me and Frankie? She had to know something, and I suspected she was trying to honor her word to one of the missing women. This wasn't the time for honorable silence.

"Okay, okay. Maybe I do know something." She all but scuffed her toe on the painted boards of the porch. "I gave my word, though."

"Spill it. Please. You might save a life."

She met my gaze, and I realized her eyes were a striking golden brown. "I saw Christa maybe an hour before she went missing. She said she had a hot lead into that cult, the People of Eternity. She'd made a connection, and she was going to meet up with this person who supposedly had real information for her. They gave her a location where to find the group's meeting place."

"And why wouldn't you tell us this sooner?" I asked. My temper was already primed after Jitty's crazy stunt. Now to find out Addie had been lying to us—again—I could feel the heat building in my temples.

She shrugged. "I thought if she just stayed missing a day or two she'd miss the deadline and I would have a chance at that scholarship. Yeah, I'm selfish. But that's how you turn out when you don't have anyone who gives a damn about you. Christa had her mother at her beck and call. And friends everywhere. I didn't believe this was serious. I figured it was more of a stunt. And even though I am ambitious, I did give her my word I wouldn't tell anyone."

"And Britta?"

"Britta can manipulate anyone she wants. She can look out for herself. Trust me, wherever she is, she is just fine."

I motioned her back onto the porch. "We're going to sit out here and you're going to tell me everything you know."

"I don't think so. I really have to be somewhere. We can talk later." She looked longingly down at the parking lot where her car waited.

"Talk fast and you can go. Right now, I don't want to hear excuses, I want to know everything. If we hope to find Christa and Britta unharmed, we have to take action now and you're going to help me." Jitty's appearance as the red dwarf of doom left me with little room for tact. I wanted answers and I intended to get them, by whatever means necessary.

I called out for Frankie to join us on the porch. Whatever Addie revealed, Frankie had a right to know. She brought out a round of cocktails and I motioned for her to take a seat. It was time for Addie to fish or cut bait. We couldn't wait. We had barely less than ninety hours to find the girls if midnight on Halloween was the deadline.

But deadline for what? That's what I had to get out of Addie.

"I don't have anything more to tell either of you," Addie said. "And I really don't want to be here."

"You can make this easy on yourself, or hard. I'm tired of the games and the lies. You're going to tell us the truth or I'll have no choice but to cuff you and take you up to the Mississippi Delta with me for a long ride. I'm not going to hurt you, but I can disrupt your life in the same way Christa's and Britta's lives have been torn apart." It was an empty threat, but I sold it with everything I had.

"You can't do that. You have no authority to do any-thing to me." But there was doubt in her eyes.

"Addie, I'm not a cop. I'm not restrained by the law like Coleman is." What great timing that he wasn't with me or he would put a stop to this. "I can—and will—do things that he would never consider."

"I want my daughter returned to me safe and sound," Frankie said. "Whatever Sarah Booth decides, I'll help her and face the consequences later. If my daughter has been taken by some crazy cult, I need to know. Just tell us what *you* know so we can find her."

Addie looked from Frankie to me. She saw pain and suffering on Frankie's face, and grim determination on mine. It was apparently enough to move her to talk.

"Okay, I promised Christa I wouldn't ever tell. But she may really be in trouble." She leaned forward. "After Britta disappeared, Christa became very concerned. She'd heard rumors. Nothing proven, of course, but talk about the People of Eternity and the big ceremony they had coming up on Halloween. The man who'd offered Britta the commission was somehow linked to POE, or so Christa believed."

"His name is Renaldo. We've heard some type of cere-mony would take place at midnight on Halloween. When the veil between the living and the dead is thinnest," I said.

"Exactly. And apparently the deity this group worships is supposed to appear at midnight, October thirty-first."

"Yes, we knew there was some kind of deadline," Frankie said.

Addie rolled her eyes. "It sounds like so much horse fertilizer to me, but Christa was really excited about the whole thing. And when Britta disappeared, it freaked her out. She was more determined than ever. The whole ritual thing was both thrilling and horrifying."

"What was the ritual?" Frankie asked.

For the first time, Addie looked unsure. She glanced at me, but I nodded. We had to know, though Jitty appearing as the *Nain Rouge* had already alerted me to doom. "Tell us," I said.

"Look, Christa was too smart to investigate this without someone to help her. After Britta disappeared, it was me. What we learned was that to bring the goddess here, to the mortal plane, requires a sacrifice. Something valuable had to be given up." She swallowed, maybe only realizing as she talked how ominous her words would sound. "Once she is summoned, this, uh, this goddess will then take those she finds worthy with her to paradise, where they'll live forever, eternally young and able to experience all of the pleasures of the flesh with no decay."

"What does this have to do with Christa?" Frankie asked.

Oh, how I dreaded this answer, because I knew enough about mythology and gods to know that pretty women never fared well.

Addie fidgeted. "I don't even want to say this."

That made it worse than ever. "Quit stalling and tell us." I glared at her.

"Okay, okay, but when Christa gets home she's going to be furious with me."

"Better her furious down the road than me pissed off now," I warned her.

"Okay. The rumors Christa was tracking down involved human sacrifice. What she'd learned was kind of sketchy, but Christa was positive that cult was snatching up girls and using them for rituals. She was terrified they'd gotten hold of Britta."

"And?" It was like pulling teeth to get Addie to just tell the facts. Blood sacrifice, rituals, transcending mortal planes. POE sounded like a bunch of kooks with more money than common sense. Unless Addie knew more than she was telling.

Addie dropped her gaze and didn't answer me.

"Addie, tell me. Why was Christa afraid this group had Britta? Tell the truth and be specific."

"POE needs a beautiful young woman to offer the goddess to draw her to them. The goddess gets her power from the flesh of the sacrifice. That's what Christa said, and Christa feared that Britta would be that sacrifice. She said something about this not being the first time a young woman had gone missing."

"Sacrifice? Like a blood sacrifice?" I'd read enough mythology from around the world to know that often beautiful young women were killed or maimed to appease so-called gods. I'd done a little internet search into cults like Jim Jones's Peoples Temple, where more than nine hundred people drank poison—gave their children poison—because Jones told them to. Could Rhianna truly convince a group of well-off people to kill a young woman so they could be raptured up to an eternal youth? "Are you saying POE offers human sacrifices, as in kills people?"

"This can't be real." Frankie gripped the arms of her chair until her knuckles whitened. "This is insane. No one with good sense would believe any of this."

Rich people who were desperate to retain their youth might be convinced to believe a lot of things. But murder? Ritual murder? A truly powerful cult leader could persuade people to do a lot of crazy things. Kill their children. Murder their families. Drink poison. I hadn't fully understood the real potential darkness of Rhianna.

"And Christa also said that Britta had been lured and trapped." Now that Addie was talking, she had plenty to say. "That was a huge commission for a garden painting from an artist no one had ever heard of. The man who approached Britta was Rhianna's assistant. Christa was sure of that. Christa thought POE was trying to lure Britta to that location so they could grab her."

"But why Britta?" I interrupted. "She was visiting New Orleans."

"That's what made her perfect. She had no family here. No one who would miss her other than Christa, her roommate, and some friends. That's the third reason Christa thought Britta had been targeted: Britta was a vagabond, essentially, moving on a whim. She made it a point to let everyone know she didn't keep ties. Rolling stone, tumbleweed, she was really into that persona. She wore it like a beauty queen banner."

"In other words, the perfect abduction victim if a body was needed to disappear." This information chilled me to the bone.

Addie shrugged. "And Britta had a criminal past. Christa figured once the cops twigged onto that, they'd never put in any real effort to search for her." Her eyes filled, but she blinked back the tears. "I tried to stop Christa from pursuing this. I did. Even in the beginning when she first heard about POE, I tried to get her to drop it, but she wouldn't. She said the story had award-winning potential and Christa wanted that scholarship more than anything. Then, after Britta went missing, she was more determined than ever. Determined enough to confide in me."

She cleared her throat. "From the things Christa told me about POE, I feared they were tricky and dangerous, and if they realized she was working to expose them, they might hurt her. I warned her. She just wouldn't listen at all."

"Why didn't you tell us this two days ago?" Frankie was angry. Her face was a pale gray and her eyes blazed. "We've lost two days. Halloween is almost here. If what she told you is correct, she is in imminent danger. Possibly Britta, too."

"I swear to you, I didn't believe all of this. It's just too . . . preposterous. But the longer Christa and Britta are gone, the more I start to believe. I'm so sorry."

"Did Christa ever tie the man who offered to pay Britta that big commission to the People of Eternity?" Frankie asked.

"Christa didn't, but Carlos did. And Sarah Booth has, too."

That info caught me off guard. I'd spent a morning with Carlos and he'd had plenty of opportunity to help me out. He'd chosen not to. And then there was the issue of the earring I'd seen in the back of his car. Gooseflesh danced up my arms. "Carlos? When? How did he make that connection?"

"It had to be something Christa told him. They were, you know, involved. I'm sure she shared her secrets with him. She was over at his place a lot. You might want to check there for her computers. See if you can get into them. She might have made some notes."

"This assistant to Rhianna. What do you know about him?" I pressed. Addie had impeded my investigation in ways she'd never appreciate.

"His name is Renaldo. Christa found some literature

on the People of Eternity. He's high up in the church. He's like that Rhianna chick's concubine or male consort or whatever."

Anger shot up my spine, but I held it in check. "You should have told us this, Addie."

"Why didn't you?" Frankie asked, less angry now and more afraid.

"I was trying to be a good friend, a good partner to Christa. I did what she made me swear to do. I'm sorry." This time the tears spilled down her cheeks. She brushed them away. "I swore I'd keep the secret. Now I realize it was a very stupid decision."

"Very stupid, but we all want to honor our word." I didn't want to blame her, because I might do the same for Tinkie. Nonetheless, Christa was in far more danger than I'd known. "Did Christa ever say where she thought these people might be located?"

"She said they had to have a way to be found. Or how else would they attract new converts? Getting people with money to join was really important, Christa said. That's what she was working on. How do they spread their message to others? She was deeply into that when she went missing. Carlos was helping her. They had some kind of undercover thing going on, and they were trying to get invited to some of the sessions. That's what she said the last time I saw her."

And that was exactly what I would have to find out for myself.

# 20

I left Frankie to pull more details from Addie, and I went downstairs to stand under the oaks and a golden moon headed toward full for Halloween night. Hunter's moon? Harvest moon? Neither sounded good to me when I thought about Christa with a bunch of people who might spill her blood to attain eternal youth. I shuddered and looked up at the sky. Perfect conditions for unsavory acts, if folklore was to be believed. I dialed my partner.

"Tinkie, call Pouty and make sure she meets with you tomorrow. This has to happen." If Pouty was indeed a member of POE, she was going to have to come clean with me and Tinkie.

"What's wrong with you?" Tinkie could read me despite poor cell phone reception.

"I just found out that Christa may have been taken for some kind of ritual sacrifice. Like seriously, a human sacrifice. It's worse than we thought." Even saying the words made my skin crawl. Tinkie's silence spoke volumes.

"Are you saying that group of weirdos who think they can exercise their way to eternity are going to try to kill Christa?" she asked after a pause. "I mean, it's one thing to abduct someone and force them to participate in craziness, but ritual murder?"

"It's possible."

"Tell me everything you've found out." Tinkie's voice was firm with conviction. "Don't leave anything out. When I meet with Pouty I want to be sure I have all the ammunition I need."

I told her all of it while I watched the oak branches, pillaged by a breeze, shift back and forth across the moon. When she was caught up with everything I knew and feared, I felt as if a big burden had been lifted from my shoulders. Stuck in Zinnia, Tinkie couldn't fix anything, but she was plenty smart enough to help me think of solutions.

"We'll sort this out tomorrow when we have Pouty hemmed up. Tonight, you stay out of trouble and call me the minute Coleman returns," she said. "I know he's capable and all of that, but these people sound . . . nuts. People suffering from a deluded belief system can be very dangerous. Jim Jones, David Koresh, Kim Kardashian, Son of Sam, Vlad the Impaler. History is full of them."

"Kim Kardashian?"

"Cult leader if I ever saw one. She's just not mean or dangerous, but do you know how many booty implants have been done because of her?"

She was right. I just didn't want to think about it.

"You don't mess with people and their belief systems," Tinkie said. "If they truly believed that I or you or Christa or anyone else intended to come between them and their 'rapture up to eternal youth,' they might be extremely aggressive."

"You're right." Tinkie grew up as a princess, but she had a pretty good grip on the dangers of what fairy-tale witches desired.

"What I don't understand is how this group has worked for so long under the radar of the police," Tinkie said. "The NOPD should have at least had them under surveillance. Surely there have been complaints."

And once again, she was right about that. I felt a sudden tug of dread. We only knew of Leo LeMuse's financial complaints. What if there had been others that were covered up? New Orleans had many fine law officers, but it also had a history of corruption by the boys in blue. And Coleman might not see it in time. "Tinkie, I'll see you tomorrow. Promise Pouty whatever you have to. Just get that meeting set up. I can't wait to see you and Maylin." I had to stop long enough to ask. "How is the baby?"

"She has Oscar gobsmacked. He changes her diapers without complaint. She spits up on his expensive suits and he laughs. I never thought eight pounds of adorable flesh could render a man like Oscar helpless. And Harold is just as bad. He and Roscoe have been over here every day to make sure Maylin and I have everything we need."

I loved every syllable she said. "I don't doubt that Maylin has them both in her power. Now you and Cece drive carefully. I gotta go." I had to make sure Coleman was alert to all dangers.

Coleman would trust the police officers he'd met because they were law enforcement. There was an unspoken bond between the men and women who wore a badge and protected communities—a loyalty to each other. Was it possible some of the very lawmen Coleman was out with might be protecting POE instead of having his back? My fingers gripped my phone, but this was a call I didn't want to make.

I glanced back up at the porch to see Frankie leaning forward, talking intensely with Addie. I hoped they could give each other a little comfort. As for me, I knew what I had to do. Despite my promises to Coleman, I got my gun out of the trunk and jumped into the Roadster. The night chill heightened my sense of detail—and danger. The trip to Third Street seemed like a mistake, but I had to do it. An empty lot with possible leg traps, dark rituals, and a cult that might intend to sacrifice a human being was my destination.

As I drove past blues joints and jazz clubs, the lonely wail of a harmonica followed me down the road. I tried not to think about what Coleman's reaction would be when he saw me. He'd be mad, and I didn't blame him. Once I explained, though, he'd understand. I held firm to that belief even as I realized it was total rationalization.

Once I entered the Garden District, I slowed my roll and stayed on high alert. I cruised down First Street for several blocks, then doubled back on Second, calculating where the back of the property might be. If my estimates were correct, the lot owned by the now-deceased Rebus Mitchem extended all the way from Third to Second. It was an enormous lot; my best guess was ten acres. If it wasn't filled with death traps and devil worshipers, it was probably worth a mega million dollars. But those things were part of the locale, and maybe more. Anything—or anyone—could be hidden on that property. It was so overgrown that it would take someone with a machete to truly penetrate some of the areas.

On Second Street I stumbled across a weed-choked oyster shell driveway barricaded by a padlocked cast-iron gate that matched the Cerberus ironwork on the front. I pulled over, parked, and got out to inspect the drive. We hadn't had any rain since I'd been in New Orleans, so the tread marks in the sandy soil were barely visible, but they were there. Someone had been in that gate in recent days. The sandy soil likely wouldn't hold an impression much longer than that.

Had the person been there to set more traps, to sacrifice young women, to call on the devil to bring about their wishes and desires? I didn't know but I was going to find all of that out once I crossed the threshold.

First, though, I listened. Coleman and several police officers were on the property. It was a big piece of land filled with trees, shrubs, and thick underbrush, but if someone were close I should be able to hear them.

When I couldn't detect any activity at the empty lot, I got back in the car and drove around the block so that I was cruising down Third Street, the street the house had once faced. As I drew closer to the lot in question, I noticed two people walking along the sidewalk. They were moving slow, gawking while trying not to let on that they were gawking.

I pulled deep into a driveway three houses down, killed the headlights, and parked, hoping the pedestrians would think that I was someone who'd simply gone home. I just hoped the real homeowners weren't aware of me. If they came out to confront me or called the cops, my goose would be cooked. I needed the element of surprise.

I climbed out of the car, careful not to make any noise, and moved among the heritage camellias and azaleas in the yard. The moon was bright enough to cast shadows and illuminate portions of the yard, and I darted from bush to bush, trying not to attract any attention. I was opposite the empty lot when I realized the couple I'd seen walking down the street was opening the gate into the Mitchem property and going in. They wore coats and hoodies, and each carried a backpack. Were they cult members, tourists, cooking meth, or there for some other nefarious activity?

I considered running after them and warning them of the leg traps, but then I realized it was more likely they were the people who'd put the traps out. They weren't furtive in the least, and as I drew closer, darting from tree to shrub, I could hear them talking. It took a minute for me to realize they were speaking German. And who did I know who was German and missing? Britta! It had to be Britta's parents. Or at least some of her friends. It was too big of a coincidence to be anyone else.

They'd failed to latch the gate so I slipped past it without any noise and followed them, letting their voices and my memory of my last visit guide me. With each footstep, though, I anticipated the snap of a trap's jaws. If I could've used a flashlight, I would have found a stick to probe the ground before I took a step, but there wasn't time for that. And I had to remember that Coleman and several law officers were also on the grounds with loaded weapons. If those officers were against Coleman instead of helping him, they might shoot first and ask questions later. He wouldn't be the first person framed for a killing he didn't commit.

I squelched the desire to call out to him, to warn him. To do something to make sure he was on red alert. Instead, I did nothing except move slowly into the property.

The two German speakers jabbered away, though they were whispery in their conversation. I didn't understand a thing they said, no matter how I strained to hear. Were they here because they—and Britta—were part of this weird cult? Or were they potential victims, lured here for another purpose? I had no way to tell. I couldn't risk calling Frankie to ask some of the young people living nearby if they'd ever heard Britta talk about her parents, perhaps revealing what kind of people they might be. I'd failed to fully explore an avenue that could have given me helpful insight.

The Wagners, or the couple I believed to be them, moved past the foundation of the burned house, and I followed as quietly as I could. This was an area I'd never traversed, and I was moving blindly in the darkness, following their whispered conversation. The nearly full moon was a help, but too often the big oaks blocked out the moonlight or the path in front of me was clogged by tall foliage and weeds. I had no choice but to push forward, praying that each black clump of weeds I stepped in didn't hide a steel-jawed trap that could mangle my ankle beyond repair.

I heard the presumed Wagners arguing, and I was finally close enough to see they had a flashlight and were looking at a piece of paper. The man pointed left, but the woman started down a center trail that had likely been made by rabbits and other wildlife moving through the overgrown gardens. As I trailed them, I caught the scent of something sweet and delicious, some autumnal flower perfuming the brisk air.

I snugged my coat closer and continued on into the

inky blackness. I lost the drift of the trespassers' conversation and the little bit of moonlight that had aided
me. I'd stopped for a moment to get my bearings when a
work-roughened hand clamped over my mouth.

I tried to struggle, but an arm as strong as a steel band
went around my chest, crushing the air out of my lungs. I
tried to bite the palm, but I couldn't get my jaw open wide
enough to dig in. As I fought for oxygen, I began to feel
light-headed. My attacker was shutting off my air supply.
The only thing I could do was go limp and pretend not
to resist. Then, if I still could, I'd do some damage when
they finally released me.

"I caught her sneaking around," I heard a male voice
say.

"Let her loose," another man said.

"Really?"

I felt the arm around my chest relax to free my lungs.
I could breathe again. I drew in a lungful of air and was
just about to scream bloody murder when Coleman whispered in my ear. "Don't make a sound. I'll deal with you
later."

"You know her?" the first male, the one who'd grabbed
me, asked.

"Unfortunately, I'm very well acquainted with this
woman," Coleman said. "Give her a minute to catch her
breath. She's with us now."

# 21

The man released me instantly—so fast I almost fell to the ground. A strong hand grabbed my wrist and held me steady so I didn't kiss the dirt.

"You have an awful lot of 'splaining to do, Lucy," Coleman said in a pretty fair imitation of Desi Arnaz in his heyday on the *I Love Lucy* show.

"The Wagners are here," I whispered with great urgency. "At least I think it's the Wagners. A couple that speaks German. I—"

"I know."

That took the wind out of my sails. "I need to tell you something, Coleman."

"Not right now. Be quiet!"

"No, now." I tugged at his hand. "Private."

Coleman had a flashlight *and* a gun, which he holstered as he led me into some thick shrubs. When I stepped gingerly, he assured me there were no leg traps.

"You'd better have an excellent reason for being here. You could have been shot. Or mangled. Or worse."

"I was following the Wagners." I looked around, trying to ascertain how many men Coleman had with him. I could only see the man who'd caught me and he was bent down on one knee, watching what I presumed to be the Germans through expensive binoculars. "I had to tell you that I think someone in NOPD is working with the People of Eternity."

He was silent for a moment and I couldn't read his expression in the darkness. "That's a serious accusation," he finally said.

"Coleman, we know Dr. LeMuse reported them for . . . fraud or financial crimes. Nothing was ever done. The least of their crimes might be bilking people out of money, and you heard what Dr. LeMuse said. Over time it can cost hundreds of thousands of dollars to participate in this cult. And it could be kidnapping and murder. Two young women are missing and I haven't heard a single thing about it on the television news or radio. That isn't normal. Why isn't the NOPD being more proactive?"

"I have some leads on the People of Eternity," Coleman said. He pulled me closer to him because I was shivering from the chill night.

"Are you certain you can trust these police officers?" I still had my doubts.

"No." The word, uttered so softly it could have been a sigh, echoed in my ear, drowned out finally by the sudden loud beating of my heart. Coleman had come here knowing it could be an ambush.

"What are you going to do?"

"Watch them closely. And try to keep you from getting us both shot."

He had a right to be mad. He'd asked me to do something and I'd done absolutely the opposite. I wanted to try to justify my actions, but I stopped myself. The best thing I could do right now was be quiet and follow his instructions. If one of the cops he was with had gone rogue, I sure didn't need to agitate the guy by talking.

Coleman snugged me against him to maneuver me through the weeds. I knew he'd cleared the area of traps—he'd never put me in danger. He had some communication equipment on his chest and he touched a mic and spoke.

"We're hanging back. I have the woman, and I've got a bead on the couple with the backpacks. They seem to be alone. Do you have eyes on them?"

A male voice spoke. "Yeah, they're headed south."

"They seem to know where they're going," Coleman said. "Let's follow them."

I wanted to tell him I thought they had a map, but it wasn't necessary. I just needed to shut up and watch as we followed them. No arguments from me. I was as eager to see what they were up to as anyone else.

I stuck to Coleman like glue as we moved through the dense foliage of the lot. The sweet scent of a flower came to me again, and Coleman slowed us to a stop. The low murmur of people talking grew louder when Coleman parted some thick branches. I could see the Wagners. They'd cleared some debris into a pile, revealing an old wooden door in the ground. They were tugging like stevedores. My impulse was to rush them and stop them. Nothing good ever came out of a hole in the ground.

"Oh, great, secret tunnels. So what's in there? Tigers?

Bears? Aliens?" Coleman voiced my exact thought, but we didn't interfere. "Let's cross our fingers and hope it's the missing women."

The doors opened and the German-speaking couple descended into the earth—on stairs of some kind, I hoped, even though it looked as if they were floating down into the earth. It was possible they were really bad people with a date at the fiery lake.

"Will you stay here?" Coleman asked with just a hint of threat and annoyance.

"Yes." Because he would just tie me up and gag me if I resisted. "Go."

He moved with such grace and silence that I considered for a moment that he must be part panther or part ghost. Before I could react, he was at the doorway that opened into the earth. He started down and disappeared. I was left alone, praying that Coleman knew what he was doing. The police officer I'd seen with the binoculars was now gone. He'd left without a word.

A breeze kicked up, and the delicious smell of the flowers came to me again. I resisted the urge to go to the open door and see what was down in the hole. Instead I edged toward a mass of dark foliage where the scent of the blooms became stronger.

I couldn't see, but I felt the petaled head of a flower, and when a breeze shifted a few tree limbs, the moon illuminated a bed of angel coneheads. I thought they looked like big daisies, a flower I associated with sunshine and good times. The scent was a promise of paradise, and I closed my eyes and inhaled. For just a moment, I allowed worry to slip away and I drowned in the delightful perfume. The flowers were obviously protected from harsh weather to still be blooming in late October. Once established, the flowers would bloom each year, but this patch looked as if someone kept them up. In fact, around the bunker in the ground, there were a lot of plants that looked as if a gardener tended them.

In a bright moment of moonlight, I glanced ahead and stopped cold. In the silvery light, an incredible garden spread in front of me. It was in black-and-white instead of color, but I saw the different hues of mums, the black-eyed Susans, and the tall, stalky purple flowers that filled the woods at this time of year. This part of the property was tended with love, the flowers expertly banked with the smaller in front of the tall ones. Angel coneflowers bloomed in profusion, releasing their perfume. Had we found the gardens where POE met? I didn't know, but someone had labored long and hard in this place that appeared to be abandoned. It didn't make a lot of sense.

Coleman suddenly rose out of the underground area, and right behind him were the German-speaking couple. I stood where he'd left me, and they slowly made their way to me, the couple talking loudly to each other.

"Sarah Booth, meet the Wagners. They're Britta's parents."

I nodded to each but held my questions. Coleman was in charge, and he had far more experience at grilling people than I did.

"Tell Sarah Booth why you're here," Coleman prompted them.

"Our daughter," the man said. "We have come to pay the ransom. They left us a map and instructions. We must leave the money or Britta will disappear forever."

"You got a ransom request?" I was suddenly sick with creeping dread. Frankie hadn't received any ransom requests for Christa. The Wagners, though, had been given the chance to save their daughter. They'd flown all the way from Germany to attempt to buy her freedom.

"Yes, we were to find the underground place and leave the money." Mr. Wagner glared at Coleman. "But he has prevented us from doing as we were told. This man has killed our daughter."

# 22

It took all of my patience and skill to calm the Wagners down to the point where I could get information from them. Coleman threatened to handcuff them together, but when they agreed to cooperate, he slipped into the darkness with the other officer. I was left in charge of the prisoners. At last I was able to make them understand we would help them if they would only tell us who had demanded the ransom and where it was supposed to be left.

As we sat on smooth patches of grass in the moonlight, surrounded by the beautiful flowers, the Wagners explained that they'd received a call about Britta three days before. Coleman appeared out of the darkness and joined us, but signaled for me to continue asking questions.

According to Mr. Wagner, the ransom caller was female

and she said she'd taken Britta hostage and would release her when a fifty-thousand-dollar ransom was paid. They had not been allowed to speak with their daughter and they had no proof of life.

Mrs. Wagner slipped from her backpack and held it out to Coleman. "We booked a flight to New Orleans as soon as we arranged a bank draft to be picked up here in the city. We will pay." She motioned for her husband to do the same. "Here is the money for my daughter. Take it and give her back to me."

"We don't have Britta," I tried to explain to her, but she wouldn't listen. She was too distraught.

"Bring Britta to me. No questions. No police. Just take the money and bring Britta." She shoved the backpacks at Coleman. When he didn't take them, one dropped to the ground and the flap fell open, revealing stacks of hundred-dollar bills. They had truly brought the ransom.

"Where were you supposed to leave the money?" I asked.

"In the underground place," Mrs. Wagner said. She turned to Coleman. "Please, put it there and let us leave. You must leave, too. They said if anyone came with us they would kill Britta. If you insist on interfering, you will get our daughter killed."

Coleman had to call the next step. I couldn't do it. I had no right to try. I looked toward the underground shelter, aware that the police officer who'd been there earlier was gone. That made me nervous.

Coleman pulled me aside, where we had privacy. "Sarah Booth, will you take the Wagners to your car?"

I didn't want to leave him alone with people I didn't trust, and heaven knew what else might be lurking on the property. "It would be better if we waited here. To help you."

His hand touched my shoulder. "No, please. You need to leave. I'll put the money in the underground bomb shelter—"

"Bomb shelter?" Who had a bomb shelter these days? It must have been a relic from the 1950s or 1960s and therefore potentially dangerous.

"Yes, it's an old bomb shelter. There are gardening supplies in there now. We need to explore it more, but in the daylight. Now get out of here so I can find a place to watch. Maybe we can catch the kidnappers, and that, in turn, will lead us to Christa."

"Where are the other police officers?"

"I sent them back to the police station. Now that I know what's happening here, I can do more on my own," he said. "I'm fine. You need to get the Wagners out of here. Find out any details you can. Now go."

Coleman was tolerant of my stubborn streak, but now wasn't the time to test his patience. "Mr. and Mrs. Wagner, please come with me. We need to leave. Coleman will handle this."

"He will put the money in the underground place?" Mrs. Wagner asked.

"He will." Or at least I hoped he would. And I hoped he would catch the people trying to extract ransom from the Wagners. I just wished I could stay with him.

I took Mrs. Wagner's arm and we started back toward Third Street, with her husband behind us. This trip, they were silent. I knew they were scared and worried, but the best thing to do was to get them off the property and then talk to them.

When we made it to the Cerberus fence, I angled them across the street to where I'd left the Roadster. Luckily it was still there. "I'll take you back to . . . talk to Mrs. Moore, Christa's mother."

"She is paying a ransom, too?" Mrs. Wagner asked.

"No. She hasn't gotten a request for ransom." This was going to really upset Frankie, but it was best she knew the total score. And she could also help me keep an eye on the Wagners.

"Why isn't she paying to get her daughter back?" Mrs. Wagner persisted. "I would pay anything for Britta."

That was the big question of the night. Why hadn't Frankie gotten a ransom request? "I can promise you Christa's mother would pay if she could. She wasn't asked to pay a ransom. The same people might not be holding Britta and Christa."

"That is very odd. The woman who called me insisted on that amount. Exactly. I hope Sheriff Peters leaves the money." Mr. Wagner put his arm around his wife. "We only want Britta back. She is our daughter, and we love her."

"Did the woman asking for the ransom say why she had taken Britta?" I asked.

"Oh, she was angry about the *erpressung*." She waved her hands in frustration. "I know you know about it. The blackmail. They said Britta had been making up lies, blackmailing people. The woman, the kidnapper, said she was acting for one of the men." She leaned in closer. "Britta didn't tell us she would be in danger. Now we only want to pay these people and get her back. But it is all messed up because we were interrupted."

I felt as if the air had been knocked from my lungs. "It was about blackmail? Not about some kind of cult?"

"Yes, blackmail," Mrs. Wagner said. "If the money

isn't left there, my Britta may be hurt. This is wrong. It was not to happen this way."

I didn't have the heart to tell her what else Britta's kidnapping might be about—because it was possible Britta's disappearance had nothing whatsoever to do with Christa's disappearance or the People of Eternity cult. I needed to talk to Coleman about this. But it made no sense that the Wagners had been directed to a piece of property that was linked to the People of Eternity for a completely different reason. Something was fishy here.

I cast a critical eye at the Wagners. "Coleman will leave the money and he'll find this person who took Britta. I promise. He's very good at his job."

"He'd better be," Mrs. Wagner said darkly. "Now we must go to the hotel and wait. There's nothing else we're allowed to do."

The Wagners had left their rental car several blocks away. This was a nice area of New Orleans, but in a big city, anything could happen. "Hop in the car. I'll give you a ride to your rental and you should follow me back to the place where I'm staying to meet Christa's mother. We need to get some information from you. It might help us find both the missing women."

Mr. Wagner got in the back seat and his wife rode shotgun. I was so distressed by the news of the blackmail that I didn't feel up to making conversation. I just drove, following the directions Mr. Wagner gave me. They'd parked a heck of a long way from Third Street.

It took a little while to register that we were moving into a completely different part of town. Gone were the big houses set back off the street with elegant lighting. These streets were dark and the residences seemed sad and in a state of disrepair. The neighborhood was changing, too. Some houses were being renovated, and a few were abandoned. Gentrification at work. This neighborhood of spacious bungalows and Creole cottages would soon be upscale and out of reach of the average person.

"Where did you park?" They'd walked to the Rebus Mitchem property. This was a very long way in a city they didn't know.

"There's the car!" Mr. Wagner pointed past my shoulder to a sedan parked in front of an empty house. "We didn't know the area very well, and I misread the GPS."

I pulled in behind the sedan and put the car in park while they got out. Mrs. Wagner opened the passenger door, then turned back to me. "I'm so sorry."

The blow came to the side of my head and then everything went black.

# 23

When I came to, I didn't have a clue where I was. I'd slumped over in the front seat of the Roadster, creating a crick in my neck that screamed when I sat upright. Lolling my head around loosened the crick, but it did nothing for the headache that pounded. Or the confusion. I didn't recognize a single element of the landscape around me.

I had left the top down on the car, and a chill night had settled over me. I heard some voices, and I looked around. A trio of teenage boys was on the sidewalk staring at me.

"She's okay, see?" one boy said. "Let's get out of here before the cops come." He pushed a cell phone into his pocket. "We were going to call an ambulance," he said to me with way too much cheer. The other two boys laughed, and I realized robbing me was probably more in line with what the teens had planned.

"Where am I?" I asked them. I didn't recognize anything about the street or remember why I was there.

Instead of answering, the boys scampered away as if I were Typhoid Mary. A block down the street they turned around and called out an insult. I was left alone in the dark night in a place that meant nothing to me. The only familiar thing was the car, and I turned the key in the ignition. The car started. I flicked on the lights and sat for a moment, thinking about how I'd come to be in the place where I was.

When reality started to return, I felt the flutter of panic in my chest. The sedan the Wagners had said was their rental was gone. Where were they? What had happened? Had someone knocked me out so they could take the Wagners? Had we been followed from Third Street? That possibility upped my anxiety level considerably.

The real spike of dread hit, though, when I realized I'd last seen Coleman on the Third Street property where a cult might meet—and I'd left him there, alone. I checked my watch. I'd been unconscious at least twenty minutes. I put a hand on the side of my head and was rewarded with a jab of pain. Someone had cracked me good.

Had it been Mr. Wagner? Had I been sandbagged by the German couple?

I inhaled sharply at the thought.

Before I could do anything rash, my phone rang. Coleman! I answered it as quickly as my fumbling fingers would allow.

"Where are you?" He sounded tense with worry. "Frankie called and said she hadn't seen you and I know you've had plenty of time to get back to the apartment."

"I took the Wagners to their car—or at least I meant to. Someone knocked me out. The Wagners are gone."

"What do you mean 'gone'?"

"They were in my car, I was knocked unconscious, and when I woke up, they were just gone." I hesitated, remembering. "Before someone hit me, Mrs. Wagner said she was sorry."

"She's going to be a lot sorrier when I find her."

"What happened with you?" I asked. Coleman seldom made verbal threats. He was really annoyed with the Wagners.

"That sack full of money the Wagners were so eager to give to the blackmailer is counterfeit. They were passing off fake bills. I'm not sure what's going on here, Sarah Booth, but if the Wagners truly meant to ransom their daughter, passing fake bills could have gotten her killed."

"Oh, no." Instead of being angry at the couple, I was distressed. Was Britta in serious trouble because her parents were criminals? Had the Wagners' illegal endeavors pulled Christa into danger, too? It seemed every lead on this case turned into something completely different from how it started out.

"Where are you, Sarah Booth? Check your GPS app. Are you hurt?"

"I'm not sure where I am, but I know how to get out of here. And I'm okay to drive. I was just stunned, but things are coming back to me." Things I didn't necessarily want to know. "I'll call Frankie and let her know I'm on the way home. What happened at the Mitchem property?"

"Nothing. Absolutely nothing. Either they knew we were there or the property is a dead end. No kidnappers arrived to pick up the ransom and no cult members appeared casting spells or performing rituals."

That wasn't what I wanted to hear, either. "What's our next move?" I didn't have another ace up my sleeve or any fallback plan. Britta and Christa were just as gone as they'd been when we first took the case. And another whole day had ticked away from me.

"We'll talk when I get back to the apartment. Just put the car in gear and move. Right now. If you feel funny at all, I'll send a police officer to drive you."

"I'm perfectly okay. I swear." And I did exactly as he told me without a single complaint.

I sat on the porch of Christa's apartment sipping the Jack Daniel's Frankie had made for me, waiting for Coleman to return. I'd told Frankie everything that happened. She looked as defeated as I felt. She kept glancing at her watch and I knew she felt the pressure even more than I did.

"I'm sorry." I'd said it a dozen times and meant it more with each repetition. "She should be home."

"Sarah Booth, I don't know what else you could have done. I should have investigated Britta when she moved in with Christa. I know better than to take people on face value. She just seemed like a nice young woman—very European in her attitude and with a quest for adventure. I thought she would be good for Christa. I wanted Christa to live, to travel and experience life before she got trapped in a career or marriage."

"So many parents work hard to protect their children from new or different experiences. Don't blame yourself."

"Libby and I talked about rearing our children. Well, we mostly talked about you and how much your mom wanted you to be safe, but not to be afraid. I so admired her, the way she risked her heart to allow you to make choices. She said it was the greatest gift a parent could give a child—the self-confidence to really live life completely."

"My mom talked about that?"

"She did. We both agreed. Now, I only wish I'd been more diligent in protecting Christa. Freedom is fine, but caution is not a bad thing."

"Christa would have done exactly as she wanted anyway." I'd learned at least that much about her.

"You're probably right about that." Frankie sighed. "I called the hotel where the Wagners said they were staying and they've checked out. They're gone. I didn't suspect them of anything either."

"It seems that everyone we've met has different motives than we assumed. I can only hope that Christa saw more than I did." I finished my drink. "If we could determine whether Britta's disappearance is linked to Christa's, then we'd at least have a direction. Now it seems we chase down one path only to hit a dead end that indicates the two disappearances have no connection at all. But that just seems impossible. How did the Wagners, paying a ransom for Britta's blackmailing, end up at the same property where Coleman was looking for a cult?"

"I know," Frankie said. "How improbable that two missing female roommates, who both know the same piece of abandoned property and also have a connection to POE, would be taken by two separate forces."

I simply couldn't accept that they weren't connected. Perhaps it was that hardheaded determination to make a link that didn't exist that was keeping me from finding Christa.

There was a gentle rap at the bottom of the stairwell

at the side of the balcony. Frankie called out, "Come on up."

I stood, wishing I had my gun, but it was still in my car. When Addie appeared at the top of the stairs, I relaxed. Frankie waved her over to a chair. "Would you like a bourbon?" she asked her.

Addie grinned. "You ladies have brought out the hard stuff. Just a light one with water."

Frankie made the drink and handed it to her. She took it with a frown. "I have something to confess," she said.

"What's that?" I felt my scalp prickle. I'd had about enough unpleasant surprises for one evening.

"I didn't mention this earlier because I really thought Christa would be home by now. She and Britta were so close. They were more like sisters than friends, and I didn't want to step on their toes or get in the middle of their business."

"Spill it, Addie." I'd noticed her use of the past tense. "If you know something. Anything. Tell us now."

Addie realized I was well and truly pissed at her and she turned red in the face and floundered. "You don't understand. Christa and Britta had a deep friendship. They could finish each other's sentences. Britta wasn't interested in journalism, but she was always helping Christa with this project. She wanted Christa to have that scholarship."

Did Addie know the real relationship between Christa and Britta? It seemed to change every time Addie opened her mouth. "Just tell us," I said.

She swallowed a gulp of her drink. "You don't know the real truth about Britta, either. She came here looking for someone. A schoolmate of hers from Düsseldorf who disappeared in New Orleans last year at Halloween. She is a terrific painter, but that isn't what brought her here."

My hands clenched at my sides and I swallowed the bitter, angry response I wanted to hurl at Addie. "Why didn't you tell us this sooner?"

"Christa and Britta are my friends. If I say things that make Britta look bad it's going to come back on me. I wasn't going to say anything until I found this." She reached into her purse and brought out a photograph.

I leaned back to allow the porch light to illuminate the photo of a beautiful fountain in a garden. The garden was awash in color, and even in a photograph it held a special light—a Monet wash infused the colors of the flowers and the sky. There was statuary, sculptures of what looked to be Greek goddesses. I recognized what appeared to be Pan and Venus. Sunlight reflected off the spouts of water from a fountain centered with a beautiful maiden kneeling in the water as she filled a cup that overflowed.

I handed it to Frankie, who studied it and gave it back to me. "I don't know that place," she said. "Do you, Addie?"

"No. But I think it's connected to both Britta and Christa."

The lighting on the porch was dim at best and I went inside to Christa's desk. There was something about the figure in the fountain. I couldn't see her face, but her body was graceful and perfect. It was only when I snapped on the desk light and studied it under an intense bulb that I saw the reflection in the water. It made me catch my breath. One half of the young woman's face was breathtakingly beautiful, but the other was old, ugly, malicious, a twisted rictus of negative emotions. It was the contrast of the maiden and the crone. Youth and age. Promise and consequence.

I'd walked over a lot of the Third Street property and found some beautiful plantings and flowers, but nothing like this fountain.

I went back to the porch where Frankie and Addie sat in silence. "Check out the statue in the fountain."

I passed the photo to Frankie, and I heard her sharp intake of breath. "What the hell is this?" she asked.

Tinkie was the partner with the fine arts sensibilities, but I could take a wild guess. "It's symbolic of age warring with eternal youth. This has to do with POE."

"It's a bastardized version of Hebe, cupbearer of the gods in Greek mythology. She granted eternal life to the gods with her drink of ambrosia." Addie's voice was quiet but firm. "The beautiful half of her face and the pose comes from a famous Italian sculpture. But the aged version, that's something I've never seen. It's pretty creepy."

"How do you know all of this?" Frankie asked.

"I looked it up. After I found this photo."

I glanced at Addie, wondering if we should shut this conversation down until Coleman got there. Was Addie trustworthy? Had she really just found the photo or was this another excuse for her lack of forthrightness?

"Where did you find this?" I asked her.

"I don't want to say."

"It doesn't matter what you want," Frankie said gently. "My daughter's life hangs in the balance. You have to tell us the truth, Addie. This may be the garden Britta was to paint. It may help us find a location. Please."

"I found it on the floorboard of Carlos's car. I know how bad this makes him look. I don't really believe he would do anything to jeopardize either of them, but especially not Christa."

"Is this the photo the man left for Britta, to show her the commission work?" I asked.

"I think so," Addie said.

"Did Christa or Britta tell you anything?" I asked Addie. "Now's the time to let us know. It may not be too late to save them."

"Christa suspected that this garden was some creation of Rhianna's. A blending of Greek mythology with whatever else Rhianna is selling in a beautiful setting. Christa felt Rhianna had developed her own belief system around this deity she created. She can make all the rules, determine all the policies. She has total control. At least that was Christa's thinking."

"The woman that Britta came here to look for. Did you get her name?"

"Gerritje Krieger. Britta called her Gerri. They were schoolmates or something like that."

I'd heard so many stories about Britta and why she was in New Orleans and what she'd done or not done that I wasn't certain I could believe any of this. But I knew someone who could check it out.

"I need to go home," Addie said. She didn't give us a chance to dissuade her. She got up and disappeared down the stairs to head over to the other apartment.

"Why didn't she tell us this sooner?" Frankie asked.

I shook my head as I dialed Coleman on the phone. "Maybe she was trying to keep her word to Christa. Maybe she didn't realize how important what she knew would be."

"Do you think this has cost Christa her life?" Frankie asked the tough question.

I shook my head again. "Don't give up hope now. If Halloween is some kind of deadline, we still have time to find her."

Coleman answered his phone at last, and I could tell by the commotion around him that he was at the NOPD. "Can you look for a report of a missing girl? Gerritje Krieger. She used the nickname Gerri. She supposedly went missing last Halloween. Britta was allegedly here looking for her."

"Where'd you get all this info?" Coleman asked, his skepticism easy to hear.

"Addie Graham, the neighbor and friend. And she had the photo of the garden Britta was to paint. It's not on the Third Street property where we've been looking."

"Damn. I'll check about the other missing girl," he said. "I'll call you back."

"Are you coming here soon?" I had a sudden longing to see my man.

"As quick as I can. You just stay put."

"Any sign of the Wagners?" I asked.

"They're in the New Orleans international airport, where they were trying to get a flight back to Germany. They must have gone straight to the airport after they knocked you out. The NOPD is bringing them back to the Quarter for questioning. No one is certain exactly what's going on with them and the counterfeit money."

The Wagners' capture counted as good news. Whatever they knew about what was going on with their daughter, they hadn't been truthful. I wanted a chance to really grill them—or at least watch Coleman do it.

"Sarah Booth, they're running that info now. Hold on."

Before I could object, he put me on hold. "Coleman is

checking now," I told Frankie. I knew she was impatient, and so was I, but there was nothing to do but wait.

After a few moments, Coleman was back on the phone. "I got a hit on Gerri and a detective is here waiting to talk to me."

"Give me the basics if you can."

"Okay, hold on a minute." Coleman lowered the phone but I could still hear him talking with the other officer. When he came back on, he talked fast. "Gerri was reported missing last year, around Halloween. Same age as Britta and Christa, also beautiful, same situation, as far as the law officers know. She was in the French Quarter going to meet a friend for lunch and she never showed up. She was never found. From what the missing persons report indicates, she was another young woman living in New Orleans without close family and friends to look for her. And it was Britta Wagner who reported her missing. This doesn't look good for any of the young women."

"When y'all have the Wagners in custody, I have some questions for them. A lot of questions."

"That makes two of us," Coleman said.

# 24

On that happy note, Coleman hung up. I walked to the edge of the balcony and looked out on Esplanade, a thoroughfare that was scattered with posh residential areas and businesses, blues clubs, fortune-tellers, high-dollar restaurants, quick stops, medical buildings, and lawyers' offices. If you drove the length of Esplanade, eventually you could find just about anything you wanted.

A couple of blocks down the street, neon sizzled and signaled a blues joint. Folks went inside, and others came out. Laughter echoed back to me. Smokin' Hot Blues was the name of the club, and the music drifting out of it was old Parchman prison songs that I'd grown up listening to with my parents. The band was hot, hot, hot.

Frankie slipped up beside me, putting an arm around

my shoulders. "Your mama loved that music and she sure had the moves. She and James Franklin could have been in that *Dirty Dancing* movie. Lord, they had fun."

"She did love to dance." When I thought of my parents, one of the first images was their dancing to old romantic tunes in the parlor. They could dance anything from jitterbug to rhumba, but my favorite thing to watch was just the good, old-fashioned close dancing when they would look into each other's eyes. They'd been so in love.

"Your father was a remarkable man," Frankie said. "He was often serious, a man with a lot on his mind." She hesitated. "You were just a child, Sarah Booth, and I doubt either of them talked to you about some of the things they suspected. Some of the trains they stepped in front of in the name of justice." She held me closer. "They wanted only to protect you. But you have to know, they were perfectly matched. They loved together and they fought together. I know they'd be happy with the man you settled on, with the things you've done with your life."

"They would appreciate Coleman." They'd known him as a boy, a good kid who worked hard and did his best to stay out of trouble. But he'd grown into so much more. He was someone who shared their values. Coleman's path hadn't always been straight and narrow, but he'd developed integrity and a keen sense of justice that served him well as a lawman. Sunflower County hadn't always been a place where officers and elected officials upheld the law. To the surprise of many, Coleman had won the office and set about cleaning up the corruption that had infested the sheriff's office, the board of supervisors, and the other public offices. Once the light of honesty burned bright, the cockroaches scurried back into the dark. For the most part.

"Thanks, Frankie. I think they would, too."

"Your mama had such big dreams for you, Sarah Booth. How you loved the stage! For a shy kid, you came alive in those little school plays they did each year."

I remembered performing little skits of history reenactments and productions of classic children's stories, some of which I even "helped" to write. I had loved to be front and center, which was odd because I had been shy. "I ate that up, and Mama always made sure I had a great costume."

"Lord, I remember when she got that glue gun and Bedazzled everything!"

That was a bad clothes period. Everything I owned had glittery jewels or brads at the seams. We both laughed at the memory. "She did go a little wild. She was going to Bedazzle Daddy's boots, but he wouldn't have it."

"Thank goodness that period didn't last long. I remember one of your little jackets went from about a pound to at least seven pounds due to all the things she glued to it."

"The whole Bedazzling period peaked with the butterfly costume I had in third grade."

"I remember that," Frankie said. "She had so many glittery things on your wings they fell off in the middle of the play. Shortly after that the glue gun disappeared, along with the big box of fake jewels and stuff she'd bought."

"Aunt Loulane said Daddy threw it away one morning after he left for work. The story was that he gave it to a costume jeweler from Mobile who went on to create all of the best Mardi Gras trains for the court queen coronations during the ball season." I had to laugh. "Mama never said a word. She wouldn't give him the satisfaction of admitting she missed it."

"That was Libby through and through. Now you know

if she'd really wanted to Bedazzle more things, she would just have gone out and bought a new glue gun and more costume jewels."

Frankie was right about that. My parents didn't really fight. And I knew if Bedazzling meant that much to Mama, then Daddy would never have objected to it. He would have worn Bedazzled eyebrows to make her happy.

Frankie's voice changed. "Isn't that the same black SUV that was scouting out these apartments the first day we were here?" Frankie pointed across the common ground to a black vehicle cruising slowly. I couldn't tell who was in the SUV or what they were looking at, and surely New Orleans had a million such automobiles. Still, I longed for a pair of binoculars to get a closer look. There was just something sinister about that vehicle, and I thought of Rhianna and her henchman Renaldo. Were they watching us?

The SUV disappeared down Esplanade and Frankie motioned me inside. I lingered on the porch a minute, waving as Burt and Leitha came from the parking lot to their apartment complex. I went to the railing to call down to them. "Come up!"

"Sure." They clattered up the outside stairway and joined me on the porch.

"Any word about Christa?" Burt said.

"Or Britta?" Leitha threw in.

"Nothing definitive," I said. I still had the photo of the garden Addie had provided. I picked it up and showed it to them. "Recognize this place?"

"I don't think so," Leitha said. "That's a weird fountain, though. I'd remember it if I'd seen it. I'm sure."

Burt took the picture. He studied it in silence for a long moment.

"Do you know the place?" I asked.

"I don't, but I know someone who does."

"Who?"

He hesitated, but when I caught his gaze he nodded. "Carlos. He's photographed that place before. He has to know exactly where it is."

"Why wouldn't he say something?" I was at a loss. These young people knew I was desperately trying to help Christa and Britta, yet they'd all kept things from me. And Carlos, with the earring in his car and now the photograph of a garden I felt had to be where POE had a connection—why wouldn't he act to save the woman he claimed to love?

"Carlos may think he's protecting Christa," Leitha said softly. "We've talked about it a little between us. Christa was so . . . determined. She wanted this story, and she was clear that we weren't to interfere in any way. Carlos cares for her."

"Carlos is back?" I asked.

Leitha frowned. "As far as I know, he's in town."

"Please don't say anything about this to Carlos." The last thing I needed was for him to take off before I could talk to him.

"I won't," Burt said, and Leitha agreed.

"And don't say anything to Frankie, either. She's worried enough."

They nodded. "We should go." They both looked down.

"If you think of anything else, please, please tell me. I need your help, and so do Christa and Britta. Once they're safely back here, you can sort it all out amongst yourselves. But if they end up hurt or dead, you'll never have that chance."

Tears slipped down Leitha's cheeks and Burt looked hangdog. "We'll tell you anything we come up with," Burt promised.

They clattered down the stairs and I heard them whispering as they walked to the next-door apartment duplex. I was tempted to go inside and call Carlos, but he was already scheduled to photograph the luncheon with Pouty, Tinkie, and Cece. I'd catch him there and wring the truth out of him.

It was midnight when I left Frankie's apartment to head to my own bed. The blues club across the common ground was wide open, and the wail of an alto saxophone made me pause and listen. So much talent in New Orleans. I had a yen to talk to Coleman, so I called him.

He was still wading through the red tape of bureaucracy at the NOPD. The Wagners were safely in custody, but not even Coleman could get through to talk to them. My chances were infinitesimal.

"Catch some sleep," Coleman counseled me. "Tomorrow, you've got a busy day with the meeting with Pouty."

"You haven't heard anything?" Police departments were like hospitals or other institutions—filled with gossip.

"The Wagners are denying that they knew about the counterfeit."

My concern wasn't on fake money, but on missing girls. "Are the feds buying that?"

Coleman shook his head. "Nope, and that's why they've blockaded access to the Germans."

Terrific.

"Go back to the apartment. I'll be there as soon as I can. And get some sleep."

"Okay."

"Be careful, Sarah Booth. There's more to this case than meets the eye."

"What did you find out?" Coleman had learned something.

"Rebus Mitchem. The cops ran his fingerprints and he had a criminal record."

"Don't tell me, counterfeiting."

Coleman chuckled. "Nothing that fits so neatly. More like trafficking of young women."

"Are you serious?"

"Don't jump to any conclusions, but I'm deadly serious," he said. "Keep in mind, he was charged, but never convicted of any crime."

That was interesting. "What are you thinking?" I asked.

"Nothing. I'm absolutely not thinking anything," Coleman said, "except that maybe Mitchem knew some things he could tell us and that's why he's dead."

"That's a distinct possibility. Do the cops have any idea who killed him?"

"If they do, they aren't sharing with me yet. If I learn anything else, I'll tell you when I get back to the apartment."

"I'll be waiting."

"I know how hard that is for you, Sarah Booth, but that's the exact right thing to do."

"See you soon." I hung up without argument or pointing out that doing "the exact right thing" seldom paid out for me in the coin I was anticipating.

A clattering sound in the parking lot drew my attention and I eased out the front door to check it out. Something across the street had caught my eye. There was a woman hiding behind one of the oak trees, every so often peeking around the trunk. Her behavior creeped me out, aside from the fact that she looked familiar. I felt that I knew her.

I stepped into the shadows cast by a nearly full moon and the oak trees that framed the apartment property. Standing in deep shadow, I felt somewhat protected, and I moved closer to the dense tree trunk for good measure.

The woman was dark haired, tall, wearing jeans and boots and a sweater. I waited in the shadows, wondering if she'd do anything but stare at me. And what about me could possibly be so interesting?

I edged around the tree, playing her game, to see what she was up to. Maybe we were just two foolish adults caught in a game of peekaboo, but I didn't think so. There was something off about this woman. People who came in and out of the bar give her a wide berth. Folks walked past her without even a nod or acknowledgment. It made me wonder if she might smell bad or if she simply gave off an unfriendly vibe.

While I was looking, she stepped out from behind the tree. She was very thin. I ducked back behind my tree and waited a few minutes, trying to muster a plan. Should I confront her? See if I could help her? Turn away, go inside, and lock the door? Something about her really got under my skin, and I felt the beginning churn of panic in my gut. There was something . . . supernatural about this woman.

A terrible thought occurred to me. Was this something Rhianna had conjured up to watch me, to report on my movements? Were the bar patrons ignoring her because *they didn't see her*? That thought scared me even more.

Taking a deep breath, I shifted my head out from behind the tree.

"Crap!" The cry escaped me before I could stop it. The woman was standing in the common ground. She'd closed half the distance between us and stood under a streetlight. I could see the pitiful, thin body, but her features were still unclear. I knew her, though. I didn't know how, but I knew who she was—and she scared me. Traffic streamed in either direction as she stood in the middle, staring at me.

I considered calling out for Frankie or some of the young people, but I didn't. First, I had to determine what I was dealing with. Who was this woman and what did she want? She didn't look strong enough to be of real danger, but it wasn't the physical threat she represented that scared me. It was what else she might be. Ghost, demon, golem, some creature animated by voodoo or magic to harm me. That was one explanation for how both Christa and Britta could so easily disappear—and perhaps the missing Gerri before them. Magic. That would certainly explain it. I was normally a rational, skeptical person, but standing in the shadows of a New Orleans street with voodoo, covens, fortune-tellers, and a cult that believed in eternal youth and immortality all around me, I wasn't nearly as skeptical as I wanted to be.

I had to take some kind of action. I could confront her or run. My feet were itching to fly off in the other direction, but I held steady and forced myself to look around the tree.

"Oh, god no!" The woman was standing not ten feet from me. She'd moved across the busy lane of traffic in record time. An impossibly short time. And worse! Worse than anything else, I was staring at my own reflection. A poorer, sicker version of myself, but there was no doubt it was my own image. It was me!

# 25

Doppelgänger!

The word ran through my brain. It took me a moment to find my feet and back slowly away from the creature who looked back at me with features ravaged by illness or starvation or something seriously badass in the way of flesh desiccation. Wherever this doppelgänger had come from, I knew it was not a good thing. Either I was being visited by a creature that in folklore was a harbinger of my own death, or I had completely lost my mind and was hallucinating.

"Sarah Booth." The creature spoke in a voice I recognized as my own, although hollower. I had the sense the creature was an empty shell. It looked and spoke like me, but there was nothing there. Papier-mâché. I could punch my way through it/her/me if I had to. Except I wasn't about to touch that thing.

"Get away from me."

She was suddenly three feet closer and she hadn't moved her feet. She coasted just above the ground, like a ghost or spirit. I'd seen that move before in a number of demon-possessed movies.

"Who sent you here?" If this was something meant to harm me, someone had conjured it and set it about this task. I certainly hadn't invited it.

"You. You summoned me." Her grin was terrifying. "I came for you."

That was a damn lie. I believed in ghosts—hell, I had one that tormented me day and night. I knew there was more to this world than the three dimensions we could all agree on. But I had not summoned or invited this apparition.

"I did not call you, and I want you to go."

The creature's smile turned melancholy. "You love to argue so much you'd bicker with yourself, wouldn't you?"

Now that was a smart-ass thing to say. "You stay away from me. Go right back to the person who sent you. But first tell me the name." I was ready to put my bets on Pouty. She was a cult member, delving into eternity spells and rituals. I wouldn't put it past her to learn black magic if she thought it would help her keep her youth. Or it could be that Rhianna had finally gotten word that I was on her tail and she'd sent something she'd conjured up to frighten me away.

"I am here for you," the apparition said.

That was one thing I didn't want to hear. I knew a doppelgänger was the ghost of a living person, a spirit double. It was said that if a person caught sight of their own doppelgänger, they were about to meet their maker. This visitation was nothing more than an attempt to scare me off this case.

"You can't hurt me." I picked up a stick and threw it at the creature. The stick passed straight through. "You look like you've got consumption anyway. Get out of here. You can't scare me into quitting."

"I have a message for you." It tried to come closer but I backed away. I'd read enough horror novels to know that doppelgängers were known to whisper malicious lies and bad advice if they could get close enough. All designed to drive the person to a faster death.

"You can't hurt me." I tried to sound firm, but then I had to go and add, "unless I let you."

"Care to take any bets?"

There was something in that last question. Something familiar that had nothing to do with me. "I know what you're up to."

There was the cackle of laughter and the creature began to fill out and assume my plumper proportions. When it looked exactly like me, a healthy me, I knew what was going on. My anger was in direct proportion to the fear I'd felt.

"Jitty, I am going to kick you out of Dahlia House!" I was so mad my hair was about to catch fire. "You have already been around here trying to scare me. Go back to Zinnia."

"I had you going!" The creature morphed quickly into my familiar haint. To add insult to injury, she was wearing my favorite jeans and sweater.

"Think on this. You just scared my ovaries into an early grave. Now I'm never going to have a child." I threw the biggest bomb I had at her. "You'll have no one to haunt once I'm dead, and you just took ten years off my life span with this stupid trick."

She frowned, patting her beautiful hair that she'd combed into a high bun wrapped in a brightly colored cloth. "That's pretty extreme payback for a practical joke, don't you think?"

"You scared the snot out of me. I almost ran into the road to get away from you. What if I'd been hit by a car? What would you do then, Miss Smarty Pants?" The more I talked, the hotter I got.

"Look, it was a joke. I figured you'd snap on it and have a good laugh."

"Am I laughing? Do I look like I had fun?"

"Calm down, Sarah Booth, I made a miscalculation."

"Don't you ever do that again. I'm serious. You really scared me."

"That's a reaction you should have kept to yourself," she said, and I knew she was right. Now that Jitty realized I could be spooked with some of her foolishness, she was bound to try it again.

"Doppelgängers are not funny. They're awful. I read that Abraham Lincoln saw his own doppelgänger in the mirror just before he left to attend the theater. He was dead within hours. Now you show up and hide behind a tree, watching me like a ghoul. I . . . I . . ." I couldn't think of anything bad enough to say.

"I'm sorry, Sarah Booth."

Jitty hardly ever apologized. I was as stunned by that as by her awful prank. "Really? You're truly sorry?" I wasn't being a wiseacre, I was genuinely taken aback.

"Yes, really, but if you're going to be a jerk, I'll rescind my apology."

"You can't do that."

"I can."

"Cannot."

"Can. And will!"

I burst into laughter and so did Jitty. Covering my mouth, I looked up to the balconies of the nearby apartments. If Frankie or Burt or Leitha heard me out here arguing with myself and laughing like a loon, they'd think I was nuts. And maybe I was.

"All jokes aside, why are you here as my doppelgänger?" I asked. "Tell me the truth."

"You were knocked in the head tonight. You were left in an open convertible on a bad street near a property where strange rituals were possibly performed. You could easily have been killed by a cult member or just a street felon. You're taking too many risks, Sarah Booth. Too many. You fuss at me about scaring you into danger, heck, you jump right into it every fifteen minutes."

She was right about that. "I didn't suspect the Wagners. They caught me flat-footed. I should have been more suspicious, you're right. They weren't the grieving parents I'd assumed they were."

"I came as your doppelgänger because I wanted to make a point. Be careful. You aren't immortal, and if you got hurt or killed, a lot of people would suffer. I think you sometimes forget how many people care about you."

She'd been gracious enough to apologize, so I would return the favor and heed her warning in the spirit it was given. At least until I could think of a way to pay her back. "I'll be more careful. More alert. It's hard to take some of this ritual hocus-pocus and the ceremonies for eternal youth seriously."

"You better get yourself an attitude adjustment then. Folks willin' to pay thousands and thousands for the promise of eternal paradise, they ain't messin' around, Sarah Booth. You get between them and that rainbow to eternity and they'll slit your throat."

Jitty had a good point that I'd failed to weigh seriously. In all of the lurking about in the dark I'd forgotten the money aspect of the case. Expectations of eternal youth and immortality—not in my wheelhouse. Cash on the barrelhead, now that I could understand as a motive. "Thanks, Jitty. You're right about that."

"Go to the apartment," Jitty said. She slipped behind the big oak I'd been using as a shield. "Hurry. There's a bad moon on the rise."

"Stop it with the spooky crap, and you can't defile Creedence Clearwater Revival!" Now that was absolutely against all rules.

"Black SUV." She pointed down the road where a black car was slowly cruising toward me. "Run!" she said as she completely disappeared. "Run fast!" Her voice echoed through the empty night and I turned toward the apartment and put everything I had into getting away.

# 26

The lights were out in Christa's apartment so I assumed Frankie had gone to bed. I walked past that duplex to the next one where Coleman and I were staying. The parking area was empty except for the Roadster; apparently Coleman remained at the NOPD working. A sudden longing to join him swept over me in a wave. For that split second, I felt really alone. The emotion was so strong, it caught me by surprise.

Laughter from the blues joint floated on a breeze, and the loneliness eased away. This was the city that care forgot. Life marched on with good times to be had. I could never reclaim the past, but my present was pretty darn good. I had to focus on that.

The apartment was an up and down. A den, half bath,

and spacious kitchen comprised the first floor. A luxurious bedroom and huge bath covered the second floor. I opened the front door and slipped inside, aware of a chill in the house. A window must have been left open.

I trudged into the dark apartment, locked the front door behind me, and went to check the windows. This was a relatively good neighborhood, but New Orleans wasn't Zinnia. Folks didn't run off leaving windows open and doors unlocked. I checked the windows upstairs, all were closed and locked. There was a definite chill in the place. I found the thermostat and kicked the heat on higher.

My stomach growled. I couldn't remember the last thing I'd eaten, but there wasn't any food in the apartment and I wasn't going out to buy anything, though some barbecue from the blues joint across the street did tempt me for a brief moment. I checked the refrigerator on the off chance Frankie or Coleman had leftovers there. Nada. Bottled water and one cola. Otherwise empty. A strong chill caught me and made my teeth chatter.

The cold draft had to come from an open window. I checked the kitchen and dining nook, but all the windows were closed and locked. I could feel the warm air blasting from the vents. It didn't make sense.

As I turned to go into the den, I caught the acrid scent of cigarette smoke. Like the cold draft, it didn't make any sense. I was imagining strange things, but I had a plan to quell the willies. I'd read for a while, waiting for Coleman. I hadn't completely shaken my sense of aloneness and I needed some snuggle time with Coleman to set me right.

All thoughts of snuggling and cravings fled my brain when I saw the orange glow of a cigarette in the darkened den.

Someone was in my apartment. Someone bold and un-afraid of being caught. Which meant it was someone who felt they had the upper hand. I didn't even have a flash-light, much less a weapon. I froze so I could consider my options. My gun was outside.

My first assumption was Jitty. "Don't do this to me, Jitty. I don't like to be scared."

"Who's Jitty?" The voice was male and self-assured.

My assumption was inaccurate. And the cold grew more intense. "Who are you?"

"I'm not here to scare you, I'm here to save you." The last held a bit of humor.

"Tell me who you are or get out." I hid my fear. He had the upper hand, but I didn't have to telegraph it to him.

"You've been looking for us. That has to stop."

"The only person I've been looking for is Christa Moore, and you certainly are not her."

"I make it a point to know who's asking questions about Rhianna and her business."

"And what business might that be?" I had regained my composure, and now I was eager to talk with him. This was likely the man who'd tried to commission Britta for a painting. I could see his outline in the chair, tall and lean, but I couldn't distinguish any features and I had no idea how he'd gotten into the apartment.

"The business of eternal life, of death without pain, of preserving youth until the end of time. I know it's hard to accept, but Rhianna has gifts to offer those who are willing to take them."

"Like every televangelist, the redemption you offer comes at a steep price."

"You're quick with words, Sarah Booth Delaney, but there's so much more to life, and death, than you understand. But I have a warning for you. Stay away from Third Street, the People of Eternity, and Rhianna. This is your only warning. Go home. While you still can."

"Or what?" I asked softly.

"Or you might not be able to. Rhianna is powerful. New Orleans is her home and she doesn't want to leave. Don't make her feel threatened. I tell you that to help you."

I saw headlights turn into the parking lot and I prayed it was Coleman. If I could simply keep this man in the apartment until Coleman arrived, we could make him talk. I felt certain he had plenty to tell us.

The figure in the chair stood also, and I knew he'd seen the headlights. He stepped past me to the door.

"Leave New Orleans," he said. "Tomorrow. Stop poking around or you'll regret it."

I moved to step in front of him but he shoved me hard enough to send me sprawling. The door opened and he was gone. By the time I got to my feet, Coleman was walking in. "What's wrong?" he asked.

"The man who just left. Did you see him?"

He turned to rush out the door, but he stopped. "There's no one out here."

"He was just in here. He warned me to leave town and stop poking around Rhianna and the People of Eternity." I was over being scared or worried. Now I was angry.

Coleman shut the door and locked it. "We'll find this group and put an end to these threats," he said in a tone that held total determination. "This isn't going to end pretty for the People of Eternity."

# 27

I faced the morning after a restless night. Coleman and I had discussed every possibility for my "encounter" with the stranger and he'd agreed that Rhianna had sent a henchman and that she was the person we needed to find first and foremost. Coleman had high hopes of interviewing the Wagners, and whatever he could glean from them would be a boon to us. We had a plan.

Coleman took the Roadster to the police department. Frankie would drive us to our appointment to meet Tinkie, Cece, and Pouty. I had some serious questions for Pouty. But first more research. I had at least an hour to kill before we needed to set out for the early lunch Tinkie had set up.

I'd done due diligence on Rhianna and found nothing

of interest. Her name as a spiritual leader was mentioned in several small stories, but there were no details and no pictures of her. None. In this day and age of cell phones, social media, TikTok fame, memes, and video clips, that was really hard to believe. How had she escaped the limelight? Instead of staying on Rhianna, I changed my tactic. This time, I went in backward, googling eternal-youth cults and some other keywords. Ninety minutes later, I was better prepared to attend the luncheon meeting.

One helpful piece of information I'd uncovered involved Hebe, the goddess of eternal youth and cupbearer of the Olympic gods. There were several images of her, all similar in that she was young and lovely and had cascading curls. Most often she stood in the center of a fountain, pouring water to quench the thirst of the gods. A goddess in training.

I picked up the photo of the gardens that I assumed Britta was supposed to be commissioned to paint. The maiden in the fountain was certainly supposed to be Hebe, goddess of eternal youth. But this was a darker, twisted Hebe. Rhianna had taken bits of Greek mythology, youth cults, the notion of a fountain of youth, and blood sacrifice and combined them into a potent brew for her followers to believe. But there were so many questions. And Pouty was my first line of attack.

I checked my watch and grabbed my purse to walk over to Frankie's. It was time for the early luncheon meeting—and I honestly couldn't wait to see Tinkie and little Maylin. We needed to arrive a little early so Frankie could set up at a table beside our table to record the conversation. Just in case Pouty revealed something.

Frankie looked at me and shook her head. "We both look like we've been up for a week."

"I know. But this is coming to a head today. We're going to find Rhianna and then find those missing women. Don't give up yet."

The Little Easy, the restaurant Tinkie had selected, was dark and private. Frankie set up at a nearby table while I watched the parking lot. There would be no reason for Pouty to be suspicious of Frankie, sitting at a table working on her tablet, since she'd never met her.

Tinkie was the first to arrive, and when she got out of her car with little Maylin, I was almost beside myself. The baby had grown. It had only been a few days, but she looked at least two inches longer, and her hair had filled in. I waved at the baby through the window and she waved back. Folks would say it was my imagination, but I knew better.

I hurried outside and Tinkie put the baby in my arms and then wrapped us both in a bear hug. "I've missed you," she whispered. "Don't tell anyone I'm such a sap."

It felt as if a sheet of ice around my heart melted. I could have sworn Maylin smiled at me even though she was too young for such charms. Her little toothless gums chomped on her own fist. I'd never seen anything more beautiful. Maylin was perfection in a diaper.

Cece nudged my arm. "You look like you've been struck dumb. I never thought a baby could make a fool of you, Sarah Booth."

"Me and everyone else who sees her." I kissed the top of her little head.

"Let's get busy, Sarah Booth, because Oscar, Maylin, and I want you back in Zinnia where we know you're safe. Chop-chop! Let's find those missing women."

I couldn't agree more.

Fifteen minutes later, when Cece, Tinkie, and I were sipping iced teas, Pouty arrived. She drove a sporty BMW and got out of the car with grace and a dazzling wardrobe. I checked my watch. Carlos was late and I had a terrible feeling he wasn't going to show up. According to Addie, he knew a lot more about POE than he'd told me. And possibly a lot more about Christa's disappearance. The earring I'd seen and the photo Addie had discovered in his car hovered in my mind all the time. While Tinkie and Cece were busy waving Pouty to the table, I took the opportunity to text Coleman and ask him to check on Carlos if he had time.

"I'm here, everyone!" Pouty swept past the hostess and came right to the table.

Pouty sure knew how to take over a room. Her big hat coquettishly covered half her face, but not because she didn't want to be seen. She was beautiful, no doubt about it, and she looked not a day over twenty-five. Whatever she was doing for a skin regimen, she looked dewy fresh. She hugged Tinkie, oohed briefly over the baby—but did not touch Maylin—and gave Cece a beaming smile and an air kiss. She ignored me completely.

Once the drink orders were in, I sipped an iced tea and held Maylin while Cece talked about the Thanksgiving fashion spread and how she wanted to feature Pouty again. Pouty warmed to the subject quickly, getting excited about the possible wardrobe shots.

"We've had a minor snafu with our photographer," Cece said, giving me the eye as if I could produce Carlos on demand. "But we'll have that straightened out when it's time for the actual shoot," Cece said, smoothing over the missing photographer. "And you, Pouty, are going to become the face of fashion. I've got a lead on selling the article to one of the big fashion magazines. They're talking an eight-page spread."

Once the flattery was done, Pouty turned her attention to Tinkie. "Could we speak privately?" Pouty asked.

I hadn't anticipated that, though I should have. But Tinkie apparently had. She was unflappable in her response. "I think that's the perfect plan," she said. "Cece, Sarah Booth, can you manage Maylin while Pouty and I have a chat? Looking at Pouty, I want to know everything about how she stays so youthful. This is such an opportunity, once I lose the baby weight."

"Oh, dear Tinkie, that will fall away under the guidelines of Rhianna's program. Trust me. Good nutrition and exercise are all part of the plan."

Tinkie looked at me and winked so that no one else saw her. "You good with Maylin?"

"Unless I have to change her." I told the truth. Babies frightened me a little. They were so fragile. So easy to break. So filled with baby poop!

"I've got it covered," Cece said, pulling out an assortment of baby necessities from a large purse that was color coordinated to match the baby's adorable outfit. Tinkie wasn't slacking on wardrobe for her offspring. Maylin wore a little corduroy onesie with a matching band of cloth chrysanthemums on her head. Tinkie also had a matching hair band and minidress, complete with tall boots. Tinkie had dressed for her role.

I had only a few misgivings as Tinkie and Pouty left the table and moved to the empty bar to talk. I glanced at Frankie, who looked completely done in. We couldn't really talk to her, but I texted her a thumbs-up. Tinkie would find out everything we needed to know. And more.

She was a gifted interrogator and far smarter about finances than I'd ever be.

Tinkie and Pouty fell deep into conversation as Cece and I took turns playing with Maylin and watched them. I took pity on Frankie and texted her to go home and sleep. Since Pouty had made it a point to move out of hearing, there was no reason for her to be at the meeting. Tinkie and Cece would give me a ride and also give me a chance to find out what information Tinkie had pulled out of Pouty. I watched Frankie go, shoulders slumped and defeat in her posture. Worry and anxiety were draining the life from her.

"We've got to fix this," Cece said. "She looks awful."

"I know, and we will."

While we ordered and ate, Cece caught me up on the latest developments with the celebrity/paranormal column, *The Truth Is Out There,* that she and Millie had begun. It was such a relief to spend time with Cece, my practical friend who weighed everything I told her and urged me to trust my own instincts.

"Trust hasn't gotten me very far," I told her after I'd filled her in on my and Coleman's time in New Orleans.

I sighed and glanced back in the bar. Tinkie and Pouty were deep at it. I wanted desperately to hear what was being said, but I knew if I tried to listen in, they'd stop talking. My cell phone rang and I answered Coleman's call.

"I'm coming by the restaurant to pick you up," he said.

"What's wrong?"

"I ran over to Carlos Rodriguez's place, as you requested. His place has been ransacked, Sarah Booth. I don't know what happened, but Carlos may very well be dead."

I hadn't expected this. I was surprisingly fond of Carlos, and I recognized his talent. It was going to be a blow to Frankie, because of his close connection to Christa. And because we'd so hoped to get more information from him. "This is awful news. No one has located the body?"

"Not yet. It looks like a rug is missing from the living room. The NOPD's best guess is that he was attacked, wrapped in the rug, and his body removed. At least that's what the cops are saying."

"Any suspects?" These were routine questions, but it gave me a focus and a chance to get over the shock of Carlos's strange disappearance. And why? Had Carlos photographed something useful to finding Christa and Britta? Or something detrimental to POE?

"Yeah," Coleman said. "Christa. A bloody knife was found in his kitchen sink and it had Christa's fingerprints on it. I think someone stole the knife from Christa's apartment to frame her."

"Why would they have Christa's fingerprints on file?" I asked.

"She worked as a bartender for a little while."

"Christa loved Carlos. She wouldn't harm him or anyone else." I was exasperated. "People have been in and out of that apartment the whole time we've been there." I didn't believe the young woman had killed anyone.

"I know. The police know it, too."

"And that Renaldo guy was just in our place. He got in somehow. He could have gotten the knife from Christa's place while he was in the area. He's a lot more likely to be the kidnapper than Frankie's daughter!"

"I know." Coleman exhibited patience in the face of my excitability. "But the NOPD is going to have to act on the evidence, Sarah Booth. There's no way around it."

"Think about it, Coleman. You know these people tried to frame you for Rebus Mitchem's death. Now they've framed a young woman who's been missing for days for the disappearance of her boyfriend."

"I know. And you'll likely be the next fall guy. Whoever is behind this is smart and has thought things out. If they eliminate us by making us suspects, they'll be able to do whatever it is they want."

"Which is?"

Coleman hesitated. "I don't know. Kill two young women in a ritual sacrifice? Sell those women into the sex trade? That's a big part of our problem. We can't solidly connect both disappearances together, and we have more motives than we can shake a stick at."

"And I'm tired of not knowing. The women are missing, Carlos is missing. Rebus is dead. Who's going to be next?"

"I don't have the answers, but I know we have to prove the facts if we want to help Frankie."

Coleman was right. Arguing wouldn't change the facts. "Where are you?"

"Outside the restaurant. Tell the girls hi and give the baby a kiss. Let's hit it."

I explained to Cece, who promised to call me before they left New Orleans. We had to catch up with everything to plan our next move. I gave Maylin a kiss on her chubby cheek and was surprised by the physical pang that shot through my heart. I had an intense urge to simply hold her—for the rest of the day, at least. I forced myself to hand the baby over to Cece and hurried outside.

Coleman had no lights or siren, but he drove like he did. We got to Carlos's house and parked behind three cruisers. "Just follow behind me," Coleman said.

I did as he said, and I was surprised they allowed me into the crime scene. I should have stayed outside. Carlos had struggled. His place was trashed, and the altercation had been brutal. Coleman pulled me aside.

"I'm going to divert the cops. See if you can find anything to help our case. You'll have a better chance of not drawing attention than I will." He nodded toward the back. "Check it out."

"You bet." It was one time I was happy to be told what to do.

# 28

Easing away from the watchful eye of the law, I scoped out Carlos's kitchen. He'd been attacked in the front room or den, and the area rug I remembered from my previous visit was certainly gone. Police officers and crime scene specialists worked the area. The kitchen looked like a hurricane had hit. Dishes were crashed and broken on the floor, drawers upended, and contents spilled on top of the broken dishes. Was the culprit looters looking for valuables or someone intent on destroying every reflection of Carlos's life?

As I poked in cabinets and even the refrigerator, I could hear the coroner talking with the police. The front door was undamaged and the back still locked from the inside. It appeared Carlos gave access to the person who attacked him. Someone he knew? Was it someone from his past or his present, was the more pointed question.

I moved back to the bedroom where at least three computers had been smashed to bits. I couldn't help but notice that one of the computers had a Kappa Tau Alpha emblem on the outside of an Apple laptop.

The journalism society sticker stopped me. That was Christa's computer. It had to be. Carlos had lied about having it, but when I'd visited his place, I hadn't seen that computer. It was possible someone had deliberately left it there. And someone had made absolutely sure that anything on it was destroyed. They'd sledgehammered it. Intuitively I knew they'd done this so that Frankie and I would stop looking for it, otherwise they could have taken it with much more ease. Now I had to wonder if Carlos was a target because of what he knew.

Several of his cameras had also been smashed, and the senseless destruction made me ill. I borrowed a pair of evidence gloves and checked for memory cards, but they were too badly damaged to even extract.

Carlos's cell phone was also smashed to bits on the floor, and I left that, too. The CSIs for the police department might be able to retrieve the information there. I had no way to do that. I searched through the rest of the apartment, trying very hard not to remember Carlos as the charming young man I'd shared breakfast and a photo shoot with. When I was finished I went outside to sit on the stoop and wait for Coleman.

"Can you catch an Uber?" he asked when he came out the door, his forehead creased with worry. "I want to talk with the investigators to see what they're thinking. Did you find anything that might give us a motive?"

"Someone went to a lot of trouble to trash Carlos's

cameras and computers. Christa's laptop was there, too. Carlos had it all along. Looked like someone ran over it with a truck." I mentioned the memory cards in the cameras in case the NOPD had experts. "Maybe you can load them in another camera and see what you get."

Coleman took my hand and stepped around the side of the house into a little alley. He pulled me into his arms. "I'm sorry about Carlos. You said he was very talented."

I realized then that my distress must be apparent to anyone who looked. "He was talented. He *is* talented. And he's a liar, too."

"Certainly nothing that warranted this brutal attack."

I sighed. "You're right about that. I'm just frustrated by Addie withholding facts, and now Carlos. No telling what Burt and Leitha know and haven't told us."

He held me tighter.

"I'm afraid we're going to be too late to save them," I confessed.

"I'm worried, too. But I need to get back inside the house to see what the police are saying. You're good to get back to the apartment? You could take your car and I could catch a ride with the guys."

"You keep the Roadster in case you hit a hot lead. Just text me and let me know what's going on."

"You bet." He kissed me soundly. "I'll wait with you until your car arrives."

"I'm going to wander down a couple of blocks of the French Quarter. Maybe pick up some beignets at the Café Du Monde. Delicious for dessert tonight." I wasn't telling him the complete truth, but he had enough on his plate.

"The simple pleasures. Like . . . dessert."

I pushed him back. "Get to work." I hustled down the

street and got to the corner. When I turned around he was still watching me. I gave him a wave and speed-walked toward Jackson Square. I wanted to talk to some of the artists there. They might have a line on Britta.

Walking briskly in the lovely October day, I took in the bustle of my favorite city. New Orleans was a place where many contrasts collided. Rich and poor, tragedy and comedy, beauty and squalor, history and the most contemporary pop scene.

While I was walking, I dialed Tinkie. If they'd finished with Pouty, maybe we could meet at the Café Du Monde. Tinkie, who'd once been so rigid in her weight, now ate whatever she wanted. Nursing a baby gave even a Daddy's Girl a healthy appetite.

"Sarah Booth, where are you?" Tinkie asked without even a hello.

I looked around. I had cut through an alley and I wasn't certain exactly where I was. "Headed to fresh, hot beignets. Can you meet me?"

"Wild horses couldn't keep me away." Tinkie laughed at her use of such a corny line. "I am so glad to see you. I've missed you. And Maylin has, too. I'm going to teach her to say your name as her first word."

That was Tinkie. She'd give me that generous gift, because she could. "'Mama' or 'Daddy' might be easier for her."

"She's a genius. You'll see."

"I don't doubt it for a minute." At the head of the alley a black SUV moved slowly along the street.

"Tinkie, I think someone is following me."

"Who?" She was on it instantly.

"Someone from the People of Eternity. A man. He's been casing the apartment and last night he slipped in. He didn't harm me or do anything but he threatened me and told me to leave town." But someone had surely harmed Carlos. I turned around to retrace my steps and get back out onto the busy street.

The black SUV blocked my exit. A tall man in a suit got out. When I looked in the other direction, two men in suits were walking toward me. I could clearly detect guns on their hips.

"Tinkie, I'm being abducted or killed. I'm in an alley near the back of the cathedral. I'm—"

One of the men grabbed me and knocked the phone from my hand. The other placed a chloroform-soaked cloth over my nose and mouth. I felt myself slowly falling.

# 29

I had no idea how much time passed. I was in a room, but whenever I opened my eyes, the room spun. I closed my eyes and darkness swallowed me again. At times, I was aware of people coming in and out. They injected something into my vein whenever I started to regain awareness.

At those brief moments when the end of the drug began to release me, I heard a calliope, the happy music lifting and falling as if carried on the wind. Laughter swelled but slowly drifted away. The sounds of people talking waxed and waned.

"Where am I?" I asked once, when I became aware of a man standing over me, holding my arm as the needle slid in once again. "Where are my friends?" Coleman, Tinkie, and Cece would be frantic. Did they know what had happened to me, where I was? How could they know what I didn't even know? And at the edges of all those questions was the darker one. The one that skittered into my brain and then oozed away. What was going to happen to me? I knew I was in danger, but I didn't know why.

At last, I slowly came to awareness. My lips were cracked and I was thirsty in a way I'd never been before. My throat was raw. "Water." I tried to speak aloud, but it was more of a croak than a request.

A hand slipped beneath my head and held me up as a cup of cold water was pressed to my lips. I drank greedily, and the water seemed to sharpen my mental abilities. I began to take note of the room I was in. The curtains were pulled tight and the room was dark, with a lamp lit in one corner.

"Drink more." The hand slipped behind my head and lifted it. The cup returned to my lips and I drank the cold water, draining the cup.

"Where am I?"

"Asking questions is what got you into this in the first place." The man stepped back and I could see him better. Still he was more of an outline—no facial details were visible. He was tall, broad-shouldered, lean, and his profile showed a high brow and an aquiline nose. He moved with catlike grace, and the thought that he'd been in my apartment came to me. This was the man in the black SUV. If my assumptions were correct, this was the man connected to POE and Rhianna. Renaldo.

"Finally, you're awake."

I closed my eyes instantly. I was regaining my senses, but he didn't need to know that. This man had kidnapped and drugged me.

His hands grabbed my arms and pulled me into a sitting position, and I realized I was on a bed. He leaned me against the bed frame. "Open your eyes. You're awake and you have to eat something."

I shook my head but didn't open my eyes.

"Eat or I'll force-feed you."

He put a warm plate in my lap and the smell of jambalaya was tantalizing. I was starving and felt like I hadn't eaten in days.

"Eat. You have to be able to walk."

I wanted to question him, but he left the room and I heard the door lock behind him. When I looked around the room, I realized I was in a small bedroom in an old building. I could be anywhere in the French Quarter. The food was impossible to resist, and I ate the jambalaya with gusto. It helped bring my mind to clarity.

First things first. I wasn't restrained. I wasn't tied or cuffed to the bed frame, and there was a reason for that. No obvious means of escape. There was a window high up on the old brick wall, which led me to believe I was in a basement room. But New Orleans didn't have basements. The city was below sea level. And the bars set into the old brick told me I wasn't escaping out of the window even if I could climb the wall to get to it.

I listened for sounds outside, but nothing. There was none of the laughter or chatter or music that I'd heard when I was drugged. Had that all been hallucinations brought on by whatever they'd injected into my arm? Had I been moved? Anything was possible, and that frightened me. I felt like I'd lost time.

I searched my pockets, but they'd taken my cell phone. I'd been talking to Tinkie when I'd been grabbed, so at least I could count on the fact my friends were looking for me. Coleman and Tinkie would tear New Orleans apart to get me. If I was still even in New Orleans.

Though I was still unsteady, I got up and tried the door. I jerked and tugged as hard as I could but it remained locked from the outside, and I was very weak. Aggravatingly weak. I couldn't give up, though. This might be my only chance to try to escape.

I climbed on the bed and pulled back the heavy curtain from the window. The only thing I could see was a blue sky filled with golden light. October. But it looked like a morning sky, the pinks and mauves brightening just behind the outlines of the tops of the buildings that I could see. It jolted my heart.

The room contained a bed, a desk and chair, a lamp, and three books on the desk—tales of Marie Laveau, a history of magic in New Orleans, and a copy of voodoo terms and spells. Ominous reading at best.

I tried to remember the number of injections I'd been given and I checked my arms to see at least three distinct needle marks, maybe more. The bends of my elbows were badly bruised.

If I'd lost an entire day, then the date was October 30. We had twenty-four hours to find Christa, if the thing I dreaded was true. But I calmed myself with the fact that we'd never found any proof Christa had been taken by the cult for nefarious purposes. Neither Coleman nor I had found any real evidence of blood sacrifice. Yes, there were young women missing in New Orleans. Three who were connected—Gerri, Britta, and Christa. And now Carlos, possibly gravely injured, was also missing. But that did not mean they were slated to die. The women could have been sold into the sex trade—not exactly a happy alternative. But Christa's research had greatly influenced the way my thoughts had run. Christa had assumed the kidnappings were part of a ritual sacrifice. I could no longer allow myself the luxury of unsupported suppositions.

With the food and water in my system, my clarity and determination returned. I tried the window and door again. No possibility of escape that I could find. Inside my head was a ticking metronome of time slipping away—for Christa and Britta and maybe for me.

The door of the small brick room opened. I'd pulled back the curtains from the window and the light fell on a man who was matinee-idol handsome. I hadn't seen his features in my apartment but I knew it was the same man by the way he moved. He was stealthy and graceful.

"Hello, Renaldo," I said, leaning back against the bed's headboard. "I'm ready to leave now."

He smiled, completely in control of the situation. "I have to insist that you remain my guest for a bit longer, Ms. Delaney. Your life is in danger, and I don't intend to be blamed for any accidents that might befall you."

"An accident like getting kidnapped?" All of the drugs in my system must have made me feel invincible. Renaldo only smiled. "Or maybe stabbed, like Carlos?"

"Whatever you think, you don't know the truth. And, further, I have no idea what happened to the young man."

I swung my feet off the side of the bed and sat up. "So, tell me. What the hell is going on here and why are you holding me against my will?"

Renaldo took a seat in the chair by the desk. "Do you remember when you were taken?"

I thought back to the alley. The black SUV that stopped in front of me. The other one that blocked the end where

I'd entered. Two men had jumped out of the first SUV, put a chloroformed cloth over my nose and mouth, and that was all I remembered. "Some of it."

"My men were in the SUV closest to you. We took you, to prevent the other men from getting their hands on you. We saved you from serious harm." He leaned closer to me. "You have stirred a hornet's nest with your nosy questions." He leaned in so close I could smell his expensive aftershave. "You should be thanking me."

I laughed. "I'm to take my captor's word for this? By the way, why did you kill Carlos?" It was a ploy meant to elicit a response.

He watched me for a minute, and I realized that his light brown eyes were unreadable. He was a handsome man, with an olive complexion and longish dark hair. He wore a suit with elegance. Nothing in his eyes gave away what he was thinking or feeling.

"I haven't killed anyone, and I think we're done here." He stood up.

"Tell me about the People of Eternity," I said. "Please." This might be my only chance to talk to him because, as soon as I could, I planned on escaping. "This leader, Rhianna, can she deliver on her promises?"

"Rhianna is a powerful woman. I tried to warn you away. You just don't listen, Ms. Delaney. You have almost been caught more than once. And, trust me, had I not been able to get you away, you would not be alive now."

That gave me pause. Did I believe him? Not completely. "Who wants to harm me?"

He shook his head. "The more you know, the more trouble you'll get into. You need to go home."

"I'm looking for two missing women. I've been paid

to find them and I intend to. If the People of Eternity aren't involved in their disappearances, why am I in danger?"

"You've been paid to find one of them, at least," he said, demonstrating that he knew a lot more about my business than I knew about his. "The other, the German girl, have you been paid to find her, too?"

"No, but the two disappearances are connected." There seemed no point in lying. "Christa needs to be returned to her mother. Is she okay?"

"I have no idea."

"I think you do. And the other woman, Britta Wagner. Her parents are in town looking for her."

"So I've heard." He gave me a direct look that revealed nothing. "I don't know anything about these women. My work with Rhianna is strictly financial. I take care of the books, her money, her investments. Nothing more."

"And yet you say you abducted me to keep me safe. That doesn't sound like a financial concern."

His smile moved from slight to amused. "I suppose you have me there."

He was losing interest in this conversation but I had to keep him talking. I had to find his weakness, if I could. "You were going to hire Britta to paint some gardens for you. Or was that a ruse to lure her into danger?"

"She's very talented."

It wasn't a real answer. I didn't want to press so hard that he left, but I had to try. "You offered a lot of money for a young painter without a name."

"Finding talent is my talent," he said. "In time, Ms. Wagner's paintings will be very valuable. I would consider my offer to be a bargain."

"Artists are often more collectible after their death."

He laughed out loud. "The bitter irony of the art world. But since Ms. Wagner never consented to paint for me, I don't own her work. I have no motive."

He made a certain kind of sense. In a crazy way. Time to change directions with my questions. "What is Rhianna actually selling? She's as bad as the televangelists marketing salvation with prayer cloths and magic holy water."

"She's selling the one thing that people with money want more than anything else on Earth. Time. Eternal youth. Immortality. The rich have everything, except time. She sells them fresh, hard bodies and more years to enjoy them."

I chuckled. "And you expect me to believe that? That she can push back the hands of the clock that ticks for all of us."

His brown-eyed glare intensified and a chill passed over me. I'd relaxed, forgetting how dangerous Renaldo might be.

"There's real magic in the world, Ms. Delaney. There's power you have no comprehension of. You don't see it because you don't believe it exists. Some people are open to the wonders Rhianna offers. Others are not. Rhianna has been touched by the goddess, but she can only do so much. She can't make anyone believe."

"Yes, like miracles offered up by the hucksters on television, Rhianna's eternal youth and ticket to paradise won't come to me because *I* lack the proper faith to access the wondrous healings." My words were edged with anger. It was always the way with charlatans and liars to try to put the blame back on the person seeking help. "Or maybe if I had more money, I could buy back a few years of youth from the Rhianna eternal time bank."

"Conjuring the magic required to roll back time takes

tremendous effort and energy. Rhianna earns every penny, and she doesn't waste herself on those who cling to skepticism. Amazing how people limit their potential, even the potential to receive the goddess's grace and miracles."

"Goddesses or demons?" I asked. "Does the name 'Abaddon' mean anything to you?"

He shook his head. "Rhianna isn't responsible for those who walk the dark path."

"What about Rebus Mitchem? I know POE has used his property on Third Street for some ceremonies. And Carlos Rodriguez? Is she responsible for that?"

He flinched, but only for a split second. "She is responsible only for what she does herself, and she brings youth and eternity to those who are strong enough to accept the gift."

"I don't believe in this foolishness. You can bilk people like Pouty out of hundreds of thousands, but I know better. I believe in science and facts. There is no fountain of youth or goddess who can make people stay young. I don't know how she's pulling this off, but I suspect it involves moving often."

His laughter was full and rich. "You really are a . . . hardheaded woman."

"And you're a charlatan trying to sell a fantasy to someone who knows better."

"How old do you think I am?" he asked.

"Oh, at least four hundred years." I'd heard the same foolishness about Rhianna—that she dated back centuries.

"I lived during the time of Anne Boleyn. Her brief marriage to Henry VIII was traumatic for most of the country."

"Most especially for her when her head went rolling down the stairs of the gallows."

He looked at me with pity. "Unless you understand the space-time continuum, you'll never understand. We are all destined to have brief lives, but there are ways to change that. To retain a youthful body to enjoy the time we live. Anne could have taken a different path, but her father chose to use her as a pawn in a power grab. She had great powers, but failed to learn to use them. The end result? She lost her head."

He was loonier than I'd thought, and I knew I shouldn't poke the bear, but I couldn't help myself. "But she died eternally young," I pointed out.

He actually laughed. "You're a clever woman. That's good. Now if you'll just broaden your mind, you could experience many wonders. There are things in this universe that most people can't dream of. Rhianna dreams, and she dreams across the star-spangled sky. Over the many years, she's made bargains with . . . entities. She always delivers on her end. It's not always pleasant, but once a bargain is struck, the price must be paid."

"And who does she bargain with?" I asked.

"Above my pay grade. I am merely her financial agent, the person who delivers the tedious portion of the agenda. Investing, paying off the people who must be paid." He frowned. "It's easier in some countries than here. If I have my way, our time in New Orleans is drawing to a close."

"And do you supply the women to be sacrificed? I see you're very good at staging abductions."

He shrugged. "To make an omelet you have to crack a lot of eggs."

His remark, and the offhanded way he spoke, infuriated me, but I couldn't let him see that. "It's not too late to save yourself. Tell me where Christa and Britta are. Let me save those women and I'll make sure the prosecutors know how much you helped. You can come out of this in a better position than you think."

He looked genuinely perplexed, but I knew better. Renaldo was a lot of things, and among them was terrific actor. I couldn't believe he actually thought Rhianna could grant eternal youth. "Oh, I doubt that." He turned away but not before I saw the smile that pulled up the corners of his mouth.

"What are you planning to do with them?"

"I have no plans."

"I'll bet you don't. I want to meet Rhianna."

"You're not the kind of person she associates with. In fact, I daresay you're the kind of trouble she works hard to avoid."

"Renaldo, you have to tell me. Is she going to kill Christa and Britta at midnight on Halloween?"

He checked his watch, the sly grin visible yet again. "Well, you have about sixteen hours until you find that out, don't you?"

My stomach jolted. "Sixteen hours? What day is this?"

"It's Halloween. The city is ready to party, too."

"How long have I been held here?"

He stood up. "Tomorrow you'll be released, unharmed. All you have to do is behave until then."

"You can't keep me here." Real panic was welling up. He was crazy as a squirrel in a roomful of cats. He hadn't admitted to taking the two young women or Carlos, and I had lost many valuable hours.

"You haven't been harmed, and you won't be. Just a little longer now. I didn't want to drug you any more but, remember, I can. If you create trouble or make noise."

I started to snap back, but I stopped. I could not be drugged again. If I had any prayer of escaping, I couldn't be knocked loopy with a sedative. "Will you at least let Coleman Peters know that I'm okay?"

He shook his head. "Nice try. I'm not stupid. Your friends have torn up the French Quarter looking for you, which was half of my goal. They've been so busy trying to follow the leads I left scattered about you that they've allowed Rhianna time to prepare for the final ritual."

"You cannot kill those women." I didn't want to make him angry so that he'd drug me, but I had to say something. I had to try.

"You're not in a position to tell me what I can and can't do. But as I've told you, I have nothing to do with the rituals. Rhianna works the magic. Rhianna decides the sacrifices. Then she bestows youth on those she deems worthy."

"How does Rhianna bestow youth?" I kept my voice calm, just a curious question, like "is it going to rain today?" Renaldo's face had taken on a glow. His eyes were fevered. He wasn't acting. Either he was a true believer or completely mad.

"It's transference. She takes the years from the true believers and gives them to the . . . nonbelievers. She doesn't kill anyone. The years, though, they take a heavy toll. Sometimes people die. Sometimes they don't believe enough, or trust Rhianna enough."

"Can't you see that killing people is wrong?" Again, I tried to be reasonable. I had to get out of that room and I'd use whatever tool I could come up with.

"No killing!" He pulled the chair closer to me. "Rhianna wouldn't harm anyone. That you have to believe. She can't grant everyone youth or make the goddess take everyone to paradise without suffering the pain of death. But that isn't her fault."

I wondered if he was taking drugs, or if the power of Rhianna was that of an intoxicant itself. Whatever Rhianna sold, Renaldo had bought into it.

Cynicism and greed were a dangerous combination. But true belief—that was how suicide bombers and racists with a desire to kill and maim were born. Those who believed in their own superiority and special powers often harmed others.

He stood and walked quickly to the door. "Behave and tomorrow you'll be released." Then he was gone, the lock clicking into place behind him.

# 30

Not only was I imprisoned in a small room with no way to escape, I didn't have a clue if I was still in New Orleans or had been moved to another location. The jambalaya made me think I was still somewhere in the New Orleans region, but that might be wrong. Jambalaya was popular wherever Creole cooks roamed.

I searched the walls and floor of my prison, and examined the door hinges and the lock, which were old but seemed sturdy enough. At least they didn't give after my repeated kicks and bashes with one of the books from the desk. Not the one about Marie Laveau. I'd already determined to take that with me if I could escape.

I didn't have a car key or credit card because I didn't have my purse. When I'd been snatched, the things I'd had with me had disappeared. They were probably kicked to the gutter in the alley. I wondered if Coleman might have found them—and that rocked me with a wave of dread.

When I stopped long enough to imagine the dark thoughts and worries he and my friends were enduring, it made me queasy. They'd assume the worst, of course. And while I was a prisoner, I didn't seem to be in imminent danger. I was apparently too old to be of interest to Rhianna. If Renaldo could be trusted, the intent was to keep me here, locked away, so that I couldn't interfere in their plans.

That simply would not do!

I searched the room for any type of tool, trying to knock a piece off the bed frame with no results. I pushed the bed under the window and put the chair from the desk on top of it. Then I had a better idea and pushed the desk over beneath the window and put the chair on top of the desk. A much more stable arrangement. I climbed up and had a good view out the window at an empty street. Cobblestones. In the distance I could hear traffic and humans interacting and moving about.

It still looked like New Orleans, and that was a relief.

I managed to get the window up and realized if the bars weren't in the way, I could slither through. Could I land safely on the other side? I didn't know. And the iron bars, sunk into the cement and brick, were not going to disappear.

I grabbed the rails like a prisoner from some noir film and shook as hard as I could. At the base of the bars, cement crumbled and clattered down to the street. I shook again. More crumbling cement.

The buildings in the French Quarter carried a lot of age. If the owners hadn't maintained and repaired this one . . . it was possible I could dislodge the bars. I almost couldn't believe my luck. For a woman who made antiaging her crusade, Rhianna was going to be pissed. It would be the age of cement and mortar that could allow me to escape.

I relentlessly assaulted the bars, shaking and heaving, satisfied with the continued clatter of pieces of cement. When the bars became loose, I wanted to stop and rest, but I didn't. I worked harder, until I'd freed the bottom of the bars. Once I could push those out of the windowsill, the top also came loose. I held the bars in my hand as I pushed up into the window. The only thing that could stop me now was a long drop.

When I gained the window ledge and was sitting there, I realized it wasn't that much of a drop, but it would be a hard landing on cobblestones. The alley was narrow and deserted. At the moment. I had no time to think, worry, or plan. I could make a break for freedom, or risk getting caught and moved to a more secure cell.

Still holding the heavy iron bar grate—I feared dropping it because of making noise—I slid to the edge of the window ledge and prepared to drop. It was only about eight feet, but a wrong landing could result in my recapture.

"Jitty, I'm calling on you and Marie Laveau to help me through this." I patted the back of my jeans to be sure the book was still securely tucked there. Taking a breath, I eased out of the window and hit the ground.

Pain shot up my ankles and legs, but I landed on my feet, and after taking just a split second to make sure I wasn't injured, I started jogging to the end of the alley, where I could see occasional traffic. I had to find a place with people. A restaurant, or dry cleaners, or whatever, where I could hide and call my friends.

When I turned the corner onto a street, I was still lost. I loved the French Quarter, but I wasn't an expert on where things were located. I relied on the GPS in my phone, which I no longer had. Disco music drifted down the street to me and I paused. Disco? I'd heard a lot of music in New Orleans, but disco had come and gone. Still, it was New Orleans.

I hustled forward and came to a corner. To my right, the street was empty except for a few passing cars. To my left—I inhaled. Someone in a Darth Vader costume stood on the corner showing his disco moves while five or six people stood around throwing money into the hat he'd put down. Watching the caped figure of darkness swivel his hips like a comic book Patrick Swayze, I gawked, open-mouthed. Darth had some lethal dance moves. He was pure John Travolta and he performed with a flare that pleased his audience.

Glancing behind me, I happened to see a black SUV turn the corner about six blocks down. I hustled into the shadow of a building and raced toward the performing Darth Vader. I could mingle in with the crowd that had grown to more than three dozen.

Darth ended his dance with one finger pointing in the air and a hip swivel. The music changed, and he slowly looked around the crowd. Without any warning, he came forward, grabbed me, and pulled me onto his "stage." With the flip of his wrist, he threw off the Darth mask and cape, revealing a black suit, skinny black tie, and a handsome man with a slicked-back ponytail.

When "You Never Can Tell" sung by Chuck Berry

blared, I knew I was in deep trouble. It was *Pulp Fiction*. The famous dance scene.

"Twist it, baby," someone in the group of gathered tourists called out. To my surprise, the dancer was a big draw. The crowd had grown to nearly a hundred people and they were hooting, cheering, and dancing with one another.

My parents danced and I loved dancing with them, but I was way out of practice with the twist. Nonetheless, I put on my best Uma Thurman face and posture and went to town. I danced toward him and he chased me back. We rolled through variations of the classic twist and swim until we came to the end of the song. I was smiling and bowing when I saw the five men in black suits on the fringes of the crowd, watching me with evil intent.

They'd realized I'd escaped and they'd come to take me back. Nope. Not going to happen.

I grabbed my dance partner by the hand and moved into a tight frame for slow dancing. "Those men are trying to hurt me. I need a diversion. And I don't know where I am. They were holding me captive."

In the world of Darth Vader and John Travolta street-corner dancing, I was just another ten-minute interlude in his day. "I can handle that." He spun me out and brought me back tight against him. "Next spin, let go of my hand and run. You'll be headed toward the river. You're about ten blocks off Rampart, but there are a lot of shops along that route. Your best bet is to lose them."

"Thanks." I didn't have time to linger. He wound me up into a close boogie step and spun me out while at the same time grabbing a couple of the men and tangling his legs with theirs until they were a writhing mass of falling bodies. I saw them go down and then ran with everything

I had in me. When I'd gone three blocks I took a left, looking back to see that the street was a mess of bodies struggling to get up and then falling again. I wondered if Darth, my hero, might be a stuntman for the movies.

Twenty minutes later, heaving and sweating, I entered a small shop that advertised estate sale jewelry, dishes, and furniture. The place smelled deliciously of wood polish and the comfort of well-loved antiques. I sighed and went to the older man behind the counter in the back. He willingly gave me his cell phone and I punched in Coleman's number.

"Hello?" Coleman sounded suspicious. And tired.

"It's me. I'm okay. I've escaped and I'm at Graceland Antiques. On the corner of—"

"I'll find it. Are you hurt?"

"No. Renaldo abducted me, but I got away. He kept me drugged for . . ."

"You've been gone two days. We've been crazy with worry."

"I know. I was out of it until this morning. Is Tinkie okay?"

"She and Cece and Maylin are still here in New Orleans. She wouldn't leave with you missing. I think she may have threatened Pouty into cooperating, because I've finally got a location on the place where POE meets. I'm on my way to get you."

I looked out the window and saw one of the SUVs cruising the street. I quickly ducked behind a stand of beautiful old hats. The car didn't stop, and I looked at the shop owner, who was watching me closely. "Hurry, Coleman. They're looking for me."

I handed the phone back to the shopkeeper. "Thank you."

"If you're in trouble, young lady, you should go see Father Joseph at St. Lucy's Catholic church. He'll help you, as long as you aren't a felon."

Father Joseph. It couldn't be coincidence that his name had come up again. "Thank you. I'll do that."

"Until then." He handed me a wonderful old lettered jacket from one of the parish high schools, circa about 1960. "Wear this." He grabbed a baseball cap off another hat rack. "And this. You'll blend in with the tourists and it gives you a little protection."

"I don't have any money." I didn't have money, identification, or a phone. It was possible I wasn't a citizen of the twenty-first century.

He laughed. "Pay it forward, dear. Now just be alert."

I waited in the shop for fifteen minutes before I risked stepping out onto the street. In the jacket and hat, even Coleman would have trouble recognizing me. But I could absolutely identify the car he would be driving since it was mine. I pulled the cap low and window-shopped, using reflections in the glass to identify Coleman.

I'd been on the street less than ten minutes when the Mercedes pulled over. The relief on Coleman's face was the best thing I'd ever seen. I hopped into the passenger seat and leaned over to kiss him on the cheek as he pulled into traffic. "Boy, am I glad to see you."

"Ditto." His hand curled around mine and held it tight. "I was worried."

There was no point apologizing. "I was drugged." I took off the jacket and showed him the bends of my arms. "Renaldo said he was going to let me go after tonight. It's the ritual. I'm so sorry I worried all of you, but that's not important right now." I checked his wristwatch and saw it was two in the afternoon. Ten hours left before the midnight deadline when the veil between the living and the dead was supposed to be near. The time when a sacrifice would be made, if that was the fate waiting for Britta and Christa. "Did you find out anything that might help us find the missing women?"

"Yes. Let's get with Frankie and your posse and I'll lay it all out and we can plan."

"I think Renaldo took me to shift your focus away from the search. We must have been getting very close. What about the Wagners? Are they still in town?"

"Yes. They admitted to the counterfeit bills, but said they didn't think it was a crime to pay a ransom with fake money." He chuckled. "They kind of have a point."

"They won't be charged?"

"I don't think so, but that's really up to the NOPD. Passing fake bills . . . I'm pretty sure they'll get a pass because of the abduction." He squeezed my hand. "I'm not so sure I'm willing to let them off the hook for hitting you in the head. They confessed. They knew the bills would get them in trouble and they were desperate to flee back to Germany."

"They were just going to abandon Britta?" That appalled me.

"They didn't have any money to pay the ransom. They thought if they were gone, the kidnapper might just let Britta go. There was nothing to gain by keeping her or harming her."

It made a wonky kind of sense. And the Wagners were strangers in a place that even natives had trouble understanding at times. "Where are the Wagners?"

"At the police department, being held on a bunch of

charges. It's a way of keeping them pinned to one place in case we need more information."

"Thank you." I knew Coleman had leaned heavily on the NOPD for this amount of cooperation.

"They'll be held as long as the law can do it without creating problems."

"We only need another ten hours."

"That's the good news and the bad news."

When we were out of the thick of the traffic, Coleman pressed on the gas pedal and sent the Roadster hurtling. I closed my eyes and trusted his driving skills. We had to develop a plan and take action quickly. There wasn't time to fool around.

# 31

Tinkie paced the apartment, which suited Maylin just fine. She liked motion, action, movement. She was a mini-Tinkie, with eyes that I knew would be cornflower blue and a smile that could melt hearts in under ten seconds.

She watched me, cooing and chewing on her little fist. I didn't know much about babies, but that seemed to be a highly sophisticated move for a newborn. I didn't understand it, but whenever Tinkie passed by, I wanted to reach out and grab the baby, who was quite happy riding in some kind of sling that Tinkie had fitted to her chest. Of course, the baby holder matched the bow on her little head and the high-top-sneaker-looking socks she wore. Maylin, showing a jogger's chic, was Fashion with a capital F.

We'd holed up in Christa's apartment, and I found I was victim to a range of emotions that passed over me like summer storms. Carlos was missing still, and the NOPD wasn't forthcoming on details of what had happened. Not even with Coleman. I had no idea if he was another victim of a crazy cult or if the whole scenario in his apartment was meant to hide his complicity with POE or something unrelated. He'd certainly lied to me and had known more than he'd let on. Had he betrayed Christa? I honestly didn't know.

It was clear that Frankie took his disappearance to heart. If his name was mentioned, tears welled up in her eyes. She'd decided that Carlos was a link to Christa. Whatever else he might have been, he was forever associated with her daughter in her emotions. And he was a helluva photographer. I had no doubt that a brilliant career could have been his. There was no time to rue his fate, though. Lives were still on the line, and it was up to us to find Christa and Britta.

Pouty was hiding out in her fancy home. Tinkie and Cece had pretty much terrorized her until she'd spilled her guts about Rhianna and the cult. Now she was afraid for her life. Rhianna had let everyone know that things didn't go well for blabbermouths. I'd feel sorry for Pouty later, too. There was no time to feel remorse for what we had to do. As Aunt Loulane would say, it was time to grease the wagon wheel and move.

"Tell me everything," I said. "I didn't learn anything except that Renaldo wants to appear to be the good guy in all of this. He drugged me, but he didn't hurt me. And he could have. He claimed that he abducted me to keep someone else from taking me. Another team in another black SUV."

"Do you think he was telling the truth?" Coleman asked.

I shook my head slowly. "I have no idea. He's an accomplished barker. He can put a spin on anything."

"So he's selling pig shit as appetizers?" Cece said.

"Pretty much, and filling his own pockets. But I have no way of determining what is true and what is the story *du jour.*"

"I wish you'd gotten some photos of him," Cece said. "He'd make a fascinating subject for a column of *The Truth Is Out There.*"

"If I'd had my phone, I would have called home," I said with some amusement. Cece was ever the newshound.

"Oh, your phone!" Coleman went to the table in the study and picked up my phone. "I found it in the alley where you disappeared. Along with this." He fetched my purse from the back of a chair.

I was glad to see them both. "Thank you. So now you know everything I discovered, which wasn't much. But you all were very busy. Spill!"

Tinkie wasn't shy. "Oscar is going to divorce me because I've taken Maylin and he is having withdrawal." She wasn't totally kidding, but she was smiling.

"You should go home." Reality jolted through me. Oscar probably was missing his daughter and his wife. They'd been gone days and the plan had only been for a New Orleans lunch. I was surprised she was still in the Crescent City, and it was definitely time for her to get home to Zinnia.

"I'm good until tomorrow," Tinkie insisted. "Oscar is fine. He knows I'll keep Maylin safe." Tinkie handed me the baby as she adjusted her skirt.

I looked at Tinkie's outfit, which was gorgeous and

matched Maylin's. Obviously she'd found a moment to shop for clothes. "Really, Tinkie. Let Cece take you home. Coleman is here. We'll handle things."

"I'm not leaving until this is done," Tinkie said. "We're here. Oscar can come if he wants. But I'm working the phones and staying safe. Cece is calling the newspapers to see if she can pick up on any leads. Coleman is working every angle, though we were all deflected from our purposes by your abduction."

I felt tears threaten. My friends. They never, ever let me down. They showed up when I needed them.

Tinkie took Maylin out of my arms and paced the living room again. "Pouty couldn't tell us where the grand mansion that Rhianna lives and holds her gatherings in is located. She said she was blindfolded every time she went. She said it was a good distance, but that they could also have driven in circles to confuse her." Tinkie bit her bottom lip. "She isn't the most observant person I've ever met." She narrowed her eyes. "And she is probably lying. I think she's afraid of Rhianna."

"Afraid for her life or afraid that Rhianna won't give her the magic youth juice?"

"Probably both," Tinkie said. "But she's supposed to call me tonight about the gathering."

I took a swat at her backside when she walked by me. "You could have told me that. You've got a mean streak, Tinkie."

"I just wanted you to know that I'm indispensable. Even with a baby in tow, I'm your partner. I'm waiting on Pouty's call, and if she offers, I'm going with her to the meeting of those wing nuts tonight. If they intend to sacrifice anyone, I'm going to be there to break it up."

Tinkie's statement really scared me. The one thing I

couldn't allow was for her to put herself in danger. She had a baby now. A child that counted on her. But Tinkie was every bit as hardheaded as I was, so I knew a direct challenge wasn't going to work. "Coleman mentioned he had a hot lead, too."

I reached out and he came to sit beside me on the sofa, pulling me close against him. It was a moment I relished. "What's the clue?" I asked.

"I actually owe this to Cece, who put me on this path. When she mentioned that Rebus Mitchem owned properties with connections to criminal activity, I got my friends at the NOPD to check for more. Rebus Mitchem owns a big old house outside of New Orleans. There's a large tract of land south of New Orleans, where the house is located, and there's also an awful lot of gossip from the locals that things aren't what they should be on the property."

"Meaning what?" Frankie asked. She looked like she'd aged a decade since I'd been held prisoner. I knew she'd been worried about me—as all of my friends had been. But Frankie had felt responsible, and helpless. Both emotions took a heavy toll.

Coleman reached over to her and put a hand on her knee. He, too, realized the stress she was under. "I think we may have pinpointed where Rhianna lives."

"Really?" This was great news. "Let's hit it." I was ready to boogie. Being held prisoner and drugged had left me with a need to take aggressive action. I wanted to rip the place apart until we found Christa. "Address?" I had my phone out, ready to activate the GPS.

"It's not that simple," Coleman said. "And there's more news. There's a moving van at Pouty's home. Lots of frantic action. One of my detective friends has been keeping an eye there. I figured she might make a move."

"Pouty didn't say anything about this at lunch," Tinkie said. "And she hasn't answered a single call since then. She just texted and said she'd pick me up to go to the meeting tonight."

That didn't sound good at all. But at least we had locations to check out, and somehow I was going to have to convince Tinkie she couldn't go anywhere with Pouty or any member of POE.

"Let's plan this out," Coleman said, giving me a meaningful look. "No one is going to put themselves at risk."

It was a fine thing to say, but I didn't know if Frankie, Tinkie, or I would be able to give him our words about that.

# 32

We had less than ten hours to find Christa and Britta. I had no doubt Rhianna or her henchmen would kill both women if they truly felt it was necessary to attain the crazy promises Rhianna had made to her followers.

With maps and GPS, we discovered that the property Rebus Mitchem owned was not far from Avondale near the Jean Lafitte National Historical Park and Preserve. From the quick research Frankie did, it looked as if the area was as much water as land. Alligator heaven.

Coleman was on the phone trying to rent an airboat while I plotted out directions and Tinkie kept trying to call Pouty. Cece and Frankie were looking up the history of the old house known as Shadowvale, a name that didn't really inspire excitement and optimism. It seemed

Rebus Mitchem had a fascination with property with a dark history. Abandoned and destroyed properties.

"Shadowvale was once the home of John Randall Waldrop," Cece read aloud. "A big game hunter who was injured by a hippopotamus." She looked up, eyes wide. "It says he was involved in the ritual slaughter of animals, and that the Africans on safari with him said the wild beasts had come to extract revenge. Waldrop was gravely injured, his face was horribly maimed, and he left polite society behind and moved into his family's mansion on the highest ground in the area. According to the article, Waldrop found solace in the isolation of the swamps. He continued hunting, often leaving the carcasses of alligators along the main road. The locals thought he was mad and dangerous."

"He sounds like a jolly fellow," I said. "He's dead, I presume?"

"Doesn't say," Cece said. "Only that he was last seen in the area in 1969. He was still a young man, but it says his injuries were severe."

"That was over fifty years ago," Coleman said, thinking aloud. "And the house has been empty all this time?"

"Unclear," Cece answered. "It only says that Shadowvale is reputed to be haunted. Locals avoid it at all costs. No one will go there after dark."

"Hey, I found something else," Frankie said, looking over her laptop. "It says that area residents saw lights in the area of the house up until the mid-1970s, but now the place is totally overgrown. The assumption is that the house has been taken back by the swamp. The article says that the road to the house has disappeared and no one can locate the property. Some believe it's been veiled by a spell."

Now my interest perked up. "A spell?"

"I guess a concealment spell. It's in all magical literature," Frankie said. She took a deep breath. "The last time I talked to Christa, she mentioned a charm or glamour, where you cloak or hide things from sight. It's there but no one can see it."

"So Christa was definitely thinking magic," Tinkie said. "As much as I don't want to, we have to look into this."

"In this heat and humidity, if a place isn't maintained, the swamp will quickly reclaim it. There might be nothing left there. And it's deep in the swamp," Coleman noted.

"I want to believe it's a dead end," Tinkie said. "I don't think Pouty would go to a place in the swamp. She's not an outdoors kind of person. And she said that the place where Rhianna held her services was off the old River Road. More of a plantation. Very elegant. But . . ." She put a hand on Frankie's arm. "We have to check this. The swamp would be a perfect place to get rid of . . ." She pressed her lips together, aware of what she'd almost said.

"Of a body," Frankie finished for her. "Yes, I know. I was thinking the same thing."

We couldn't be at both places, and time was running out. We had no choice. We had to split up. After some deliberation, it was agreed that Cece would come with me, and Coleman would take Frankie with him to the swamp. Tinkie would stay safe with Maylin.

"Do you think we can get some backup from your law enforcement friends?" I asked.

"I'll check." But the look he gave me told me much more. He didn't want to take any of the officers. They had no jurisdiction, and Coleman didn't say it, but I knew he was distrustful after what had happened at the old abandoned house on Third Street. On top of that, my abduction—even though I'd safely escaped—had left him with a bad taste in his mouth when it came to trusting anyone but the people in the room.

"What about the Wagners?" I asked.

"They'll keep until we get back."

"Do you think they were truly trying to buy Britta's freedom with counterfeit money?" I just didn't see that.

"It's possible. They don't have the kind of money for the fifty-thousand-dollar ransom demand they received. They were desperate enough to go to an abandoned site with fake money in the hopes of getting Britta. As I said, they'll be held until we resolve this. If we find Britta, we'll have good news for them."

"Why would they get a ransom demand and I wouldn't?" Frankie asked. That ate at her. She would have sold her soul to get Christa back, but she never got the opportunity to pay a ransom for her own daughter. "Do you think if I tried to talk to the Wagners, they might tell me more? If there's a way to contact the kidnappers, I'll pay them whatever they want."

"It's worth a shot," Coleman said. "But right now, I think we have to focus on the two locations for the possible ritual tonight. The Wagners aren't going anywhere anytime soon. I'll arrange for you to talk with them after tonight."

Frankie's dejection was easy to see, and my partner stepped up to try to help. "Did Renaldo say *why* they'd taken Britta?" Tinkie asked. "This seems . . . too coincidental. Last year they took another girl Britta knew. Britta comes to look for her missing friend, Gerri, and receives an offer of a commission, then she's mysteriously taken. Why? What was it about those two girls?"

I'd given that some thought, actually, and so had Coleman.

Coleman spoke first. "I believe that Gerri's disappearance brought Britta here, to New Orleans, at the same time of year that her friend went missing. Britta was hoping to reproduce whatever happened to her missing German friend. I've checked with the artists along Jackson Square and several of the more established ones remembered Britta. Lele is a jeweler and he remembered that Britta requested the same stall that Gerri had used, and that Britta asked a lot of questions about Gerri and what had happened to her. She was definitely on the trail of her missing friend."

"I'm so glad you had a chance to talk to the artists around the square," I told Coleman. "I was going to meet Tinkie at the Café Du Monde and then head there when I was abducted."

"Did you find anything we can use?" Tinkie asked Coleman.

"The artists change out often, but I found a few who remember both women. They remembered who Gerri and Britta were talking to. What they were saying."

"Any leads?" Frankie asked hopefully.

"Britta was telling everyone that she was alone in New Orleans. That her family wouldn't look for her because she'd made mistakes in the past. That she was on her own in a country that didn't care if she made it back to Germany or not."

I understood. "In other words, she was baiting the trap to be taken. No one would miss Britta if she disappeared. Just like no one would miss Gerri." My opinion of Britta just rose several notches.

"Yes!" Tinkie and Cece high-fived each other and little Maylin threw a drooly, chubby fist in the air.

"That baby is way smarter than anyone thinks," I pointed out.

"But how is Christa mixed up in this?" The dismay on Frankie's face was so clear, I got up and put a hand on her shoulder.

"Christa is the fly in the ointment here, Frankie. Don't give up hope. I don't think they wanted to abduct Christa. Britta was the one they wanted, the one no one would really track or care about. I think Carlos and Christa got too close to the truth."

"And now my daughter is going to be a blood sacrifice at midnight." Frankie looked stricken.

"We don't know that." Tinkie lifted Maylin from her papoose and handed her to Frankie. The baby was like some kind of magic totem. The minute Frankie touched her, she calmed a little. "We don't know what's really going on, Frankie, and so you can't turn this into a tragedy. Not yet anyway."

"Give us a chance," Cece said, her voice soft. She picked up Frankie's hand. "We won't leave here until we have some answers. I swear it."

I nodded. "Frankie, are you good to go with Coleman?" I was worried that in her emotional state she'd put herself and Coleman in danger.

"I am." She sat up tall and squared her shoulders. "We'll find Christa and bring her home. I'll be an asset to Coleman, not a liability. I swear."

"Good deal," Cece said. "Now let's go, Sarah Booth."

"Where?" I looked at all of them. "Do you have a location?"

Coleman grinned with pride. "I do. The house on River Road is off the beaten path, but it is supposed to be a mansion with great wealth and access to the Mississippi River. It's very isolated and it's about the distance that Pouty said she thought she'd traveled in going to the meetings." He came to me and pulled me to my feet so he could hold me. "I want to go with you, but I have to go to Avondale to check there. Our time has run out."

"You really believe one of these two locations is where we'll find Rhianna?"

"Rhianna, Christa, and hopefully Britta and Carlos," Coleman said. "You just have to get close enough to see if that's the right place. Then call me and I'll shift directions and head your way. If I find evidence our quarry is being held in the swamp, I'll let you know to come help and bring the cavalry. Now we need to get after it while we still have daylight. Once it's dark . . ."

He didn't have to finish his thought. Once it was dark, we'd be at the mercy of terrain we didn't know and surprises that could prove deadly. Also, we'd be that much closer to the witching hour of midnight, when the sacrifice would be made. I looked at my watch again, even though I'd just checked the time. Midnight was fast approaching.

Coleman tossed me the keys to the Roadster, grabbed his backpack, and handed me the one he'd prepared for me. Flashlights, flares, my gun—the essentials of life. I sidled over to Tinkie. "Thank you for staying here with Maylin. You can do more good here."

"That's not true, but my baby has to be first right now. She needs me. But I am with you in spirit, and I'm waiting on Harold to give me a call about both properties. I can find out a lot about a place via the financials."

"You can." I kissed her cheek. "You're a financial genius, and Harold is just the man to help us."

"I want to whine and complain, but who can moan about their lot when holding Maylin," she said. "Sarah

Booth, this is so much better than I ever imagined. Every smile, every noise she makes is a miracle that stirs my heart."

"I can't wait to finish this case and get back to Zinnia where I am going to teach that baby all the bad things I know."

Tinkie rolled her eyes. "Now that's a threat, Sarah Booth."

I pulled her close and kissed her cheek. "You bet it is!"

"Let's go," Coleman said. He was worried and he wanted to get this over with, plus our time was running out. Cece took the gun he offered her. "Both of you. Don't hesitate if you're in danger. I think about Jim Jones, who urged his followers to kill themselves and others. A narcissist, with power over an audience, is a dangerous thing."

# 33

I watched Frankie pull out of the parking lot with trepidation. Coleman was in the passenger seat, a solid bulwark against danger and fear. I was glad he was with Frankie, but I sure wished he could be with us, too. Cece was a stalwart friend when trouble hit, but Coleman was dead-eye Pete. He was the best shot in the entire Southeast.

As I maneuvered the Roadster onto Esplanade, I looked back at the apartments. Addie stood on the balcony, gripping the railing with both hands, as if she was preventing herself from jumping to the ground and coming with us. I didn't feel a need to share our plans with her, and I knew Tinkie wouldn't either. Addie should have told us the truth when we first asked. We might not be in such a predicament had she done so.

She waved goodbye and I waved back. She started down the exterior stairs and I wondered if she was going to visit Christa's. Tinkie and the baby were there alone, so that might be a good thing. Addie could keep Tinkie occupied so she wouldn't worry so much.

Coleman and I had agreed to check in with each other every half hour, but the truth was, the places where we were going might not have cell reception. Both locations were isolated and in areas where hurricanes often destroyed the grid, cell towers, and phone lines. As fast as the utility companies worked to put things back to rights, the weather churned to tear them down.

Cece was checking her phone in the passenger seat, and I felt a rush of love for my friend who was here with me, putting herself in possible danger. Not because she didn't have plenty to do but because in Zinnia, I'd found my family of choice. We knew we'd be there for each other. I felt bad that Cece would also confront whatever danger I found along River Road, and I feared it would be awful to witness. Isolated cult gatherings weren't known for good outcomes.

"Don't feel like you dragged me into this," she said, as if she could read my mind. "I want to be here, and if Millie had a chance, she'd be in the back seat. So would Madame Tomeeka."

She was right about both of our friends.

Cece's eyes widened. "Hey, that's an idea. I'm going to call Tammy and see what she has to allow. We haven't heard from her all day. I hope Coleman let her know that we recovered you safe and sound. She was very worried."

Madame Tomeeka, known to us childhood chums as Tammy Odom, was a formidable psychic who could sometimes see things in the future. She worked off symbolism that we often didn't understand, but she was eerily accurate. So accurate I didn't really want to talk to her. I had enough anxiety. "Wait! Just text her I'm okay. I don't think I can take—"

Cece's cell phone rang. She took a look at the screen and lightly punched my arm. "It's Madame Tomeeka."

Tammy did eerie stuff like that all the time. I loved her but she sometimes creeped me out.

"Hi," Cece answered. "I'm putting you on speaker. Sarah Booth and I are driving out to an old plantation on River Road looking for a cult getting ready to perform a blood ritual. Sarah Booth is fine. She escaped on her own, just like you said she would. And we're going for the cult people right now. If Christa is their prisoner, they may try to kill her tonight at midnight."

"Have you two lost your minds?" Tammy asked. "Cults, blood rituals, old River Road near New Orleans. Don't you dare go poking around that place. That's the land of Marie Laveau, and you know tonight is Halloween."

"We don't have a choice," I said. "It may be our last chance to find Christa Moore alive. Maybe another missing woman and man, too. Her friend Britta Wagner disappeared and her boyfriend, Carlos Rodriguez, was taken a few days ago. I'm certain all of the abductions are connected. We have to find them."

"I understand the need to help your mother's friend, Sarah Booth, but keep in mind, you poke the wrong alligator, you may end up dead."

Tammy wasn't kidding. She was always up front about what she saw in her dreams and the strange messages that came to her.

"Where's Tinkie?" Tammy asked suddenly. "Tell me she isn't with you. And Maylin, is she safe?"

"They're back in New Orleans. Tinkie's working the internet and the financials to see what she can dig up on this crazy cult. Her buddy Pouty is supposed to come by and pick her up to take her to a spiritual meeting tonight, but word is Pouty is clearing out of town, so I think Tinkie is fine."

"She can't go." Tammy sounded scared. "You can't let her go."

"She's not going," I assured her. "Tinkie and that baby are going to stay safe in the heart of New Orleans. Pouty wouldn't dare show up, and Tinkie is smart enough not to go anywhere with her." But it did make me wonder what had spooked Pouty to the point that she was packing a van. It could be that it was merely a domestic issue. Whatever was going on, some of Coleman's law enforcement friends were watching Pouty and would tail her wherever she went.

"Thank heavens," Tammy said. "Now you girls turn right around and go back there, too."

"We can't," Cece said. "We just can't. Two young women may die if we don't find them."

"Where's that lawman Sarah Booth uses as a bounce toy?"

I snorted at her description, but Cece answered. "He and Frankie have gone down toward the Lafitte Historical Preserve. There's another possible location there. A report of an abandoned mansion where strange things happen. Because time is so short until midnight, we had to split up."

"Not good," Tammy said. "I had a vision."

This I dreaded. Still, I had to hear it. "Tell us."

"Sarah Booth, you were on a little spit of land. There was water all around you filled with that green algae found in bayous around the big cypress trees. Two logs floated close to you, only they weren't logs, they were alligators. They watched you, eager for a chance to snap you up. You were looking for someone. Desperate to find them."

"Who was I looking for?" Tammy made me sick with anxiety. "Was it Coleman?" He was the one headed into the swamp. He and Frankie. What if something happened to both of them?

"I don't know who you were looking for," Tammy said. "But there was a woman there. She wore a white turban around her hair. She was exotic, beautiful, and she wore a white dress that rippled around her when she walked. She moved among the cypress trees like she was walking on the water, and she spoke out loud. I didn't understand her words, but the alligators heard her and began to follow her in the water as she moved away. She was charming those alligators."

This didn't sound so bad. "Who was she? One of your friends?"

"Not a friend, exactly," Tammy said. "Sarah Booth, I know you believe in me, but you don't always believe in magic or the power of spirits."

No point arguing with her. I believed in Tammy and in Jitty. I believed that sometimes my parents visited me from the Great Beyond to bring me comfort or to give me hope. And sometimes to let me know I needed to straighten up. But I didn't believe in voodoo curses or youth cults or blood rituals or the darkness that some people thought could give them great power. The history and power of Marie Laveau was well-known lore, and I wouldn't dispute it. And I wouldn't turn down her help if she was showing up in Madame Tomeeka's dreams. But my touchstones were good people, loving people. A few of them just happened to be dead.

"Listen to me, Sarah Booth, New Orleans belongs to Marie Laveau, but she wasn't the dark sorceress some would have you believe. She was a healer. Sometimes she grants the wishes of those who ask. She is not to blame for those who ask for bad things. Many who work in the magic world simply hold up a mirror. Those who look into it see themselves, good or bad."

"Is Marie Laveau connected with Rhianna or that cult of youth?"

I heard Tammy sigh. "No. Or I should say I don't know, but it doesn't seem likely. What I am saying is that you should think of her as a friend. If you're afraid of the situation you find yourself in, you'll receive some guidance from her. She is not what people have painted her to be."

If I were ever going to believe anyone about the reputation of a woman attributed to have the power of voodoo, I would believe Tammy.

"What else did you see in your dream?" I asked.

"The place you're going, the past lingers there in layers. One lifetime is overlaid on top of another, making it seem impenetrable. You must pierce the distance of time and find the answer you seek. You must find the thing that is missing. You are the seeker, Sarah Booth."

"Christa Moore is the person missing and I do have to find her," I said. "Her mother is worried sick about her. Can you tell me where she is?"

"I can't see her location, but she appears in many guises, a young woman with many lifetimes. Marie walks with her in the swamp, and neither are afraid. The snakes and reptiles follow them like members of their court."

"Is she dead?"

"I don't know," Tammy said. "She is comfortable in the world of spirit, but I don't know if she lives there or is merely a visitor."

"How do we invoke Marie Laveau?" Cece asked. She was making notes.

"You merely ask. Understand she is a holy woman of great power, and ask only for something you truly want. Then you must leave an offering for her in the cemetery where she is buried."

"Got it," Cece said.

"Tammy, do you have any specific information about either Christa or the other missing woman, Britta Wagner? Or maybe Carlos?"

"I see nothing about the man. The women are surrounded by jungle, by the lush growth of the subtropics, the smell of water not far away."

Coleman was headed to an area near the Gulf and I was driving toward the Mississippi River, both aquatic locales. Both in areas where vines like kudzu grew twelve inches a night. The Lafitte Historical Preserve would feel the ebb and flow of the tides, little affected by the passage of time. Many of the fabulous old mansions built in that area had been lost to hurricanes, but it was possible some still existed, abandoned in an area unreachable most of the year when the rains were plentiful.

River Road, where I was going, had once been a seventy-mile stretch between New Orleans and Baton Rouge featuring the mansions of the super-wealthy sugarcane plantation owners. Those plantation homes lined both sides of the river, a display of great wealth and Greek Revival architecture. The pre–Civil War era had celebrated the beauty, graciousness, and elegance of that time period. But, oh, the cost in terms of human misery.

In the last fifty years, though, many of the homes had fallen into ruin and been abandoned. There were plenty of places where a secretive cult might blossom. Thank goodness we'd been able to get an address or else we might have wandered the area for months.

As we drove along the road that followed the Mississippi River, I found the turnoff that quickly went from poorly maintained to awful. Was this another false rabbit trail where I might get Cece and me stuck on a rutted dirt road with no way to get home and no cell phone service?

"We wasted a lot of time because of me," I told Cece. "I was certain POE was in the Garden District. I've had Coleman and his officer friends running around in circles at the Third Street address."

"And you had plenty of reason to believe it was the right place. That fence with Cerberus, the sigils and ritual markings, the fire, the overgrown gardens. Heck, if you leave a garden for twenty minutes down here it's overgrown. That place could have been in recent use. And eventually that place led us to these properties owned by Rebus Mitchem, right?"

That was true.

"So, it wasn't really a waste, was it?"

"We'll find out soon enough," I said as I pulled to a stop on the faint dirt trail surrounded by weeds taller than my car. "I think this is it."

# 34

I took the opportunity to call Coleman while I still had one bar of telephone service. Time was oozing away from me. It was almost five o'clock, and we had only seven hours left. We had to find POE while we still had some daylight. Once the sun set, dark would come quickly.

"By the way, Pouty is definitely loading up to move," Coleman said. "You were right. After that lunch with Tinkie, she decided to cut and run. She must think she's in trouble, that maybe she revealed too much."

"Do you think she's in danger?"

"I have someone watching out for her. The good doctor isn't going with Pouty."

"How do you know that?" I asked.

"Because he's at the house and he's been moving things

out of the van. She has her movers load something up and then he has his crew remove it and put it back in the house. They're threatening to kill each other."

"I didn't mean to wreck her life." As much as I hated to admit it, I felt a little guilt at using Pouty.

"You may have saved her life, Sarah Booth. Now Frankie and I are down in the preserve and the cell reception is spotty at best. Text me if you can and I'll do the same."

"I love you." I couldn't say it often enough. Coleman had become part of my family. Coleman, Jitty, and the critters. "Have you heard from DeWayne?"

"All is well at Dahlia House. I just wish he and Budgie were here to help me but someone has to mind the store in Sunflower County."

"We'll be home soon, and I'm sorry this is your vacation."

"No one is hurt, and we're on two solid leads. It could be worse. I know you'll make it up to me when we get home."

"You can count on it." But I didn't know if he heard me or not. The connection was lost.

When I looked around me I felt swallowed by a sea of green. This was the alluvial soil that could grow anything. Like the Mississippi Delta, the land once fostered a way of life that was long gone. Good riddance. The sugarcane fields were the most brutal of all agricultural work. The region still suffered under the legacy of that time—a sharp divide between the wealthy few and the many poor in states like Louisiana and Mississippi.

"You okay?" Cece asked, and I realized I'd been sitting at the turn for too long.

"Just thinking. About the past. About what life was

like here for the rich landowners and then people like Jitty."

"Jitty?" Cece frowned.

"Oh, an old family friend." I'd slipped up. Cece didn't know about my relationship with the Dahlia House ghost. I put my foot on the gas to forestall any further comment.

As I drove down the pig trail, the car was engulfed in green. It could have been any lush tropical area, with many plants I didn't recognize. The only thing that made me go forward was the tire tracks I followed. Someone had been down this road recently. Several someones.

The drive seemed endless, and the sense of claustrophobia grew as the foliage around me changed to taller plants and some densely leafed trees I didn't recognize. I couldn't name any of the plants, which only deepened the feeling that I'd driven out of the South I knew and had entered some strange land of eternal green. Fitting for a youth cult.

"You're mighty quiet," Cece said.

"Sorry. I'm disoriented. This green is like being under-water. It's . . ."

"Disturbing?" she finished.

"Yeah." Out of the corner of my eye, I thought I saw a flash of white moving through some trees. I stopped the car and focused, but whatever I'd seen was gone. Though not without leaving chill bumps behind. I thought of what Tammy had said about Marie Laveau. Her white dress.

Or, it could have been an egret or a white paper bag skittering along the ground. The wind had kicked up a little, and the tall green fronds around me swayed in the breeze like lazy dancers, a hypnotizing rhythm.

"Did you see anything over there?" I pointed.

"No. What did you see?"

"Probably nothing." I pressed the gas lightly and we moved down the road. Our only saving grace was that it hadn't rained in the last few weeks. We were experiencing a dry and golden October. Tonight, the moon would be full, a spectacular hunter's moon. And it was Halloween. My favorite holiday, and one I'd be celebrating in a dark swamp.

Tinkie had created wonderful costumes for herself, Maylin, Oscar, and Sunflower County Deputy DeWayne Dattilo, who was probably thanking his lucky stars Tinkie was out of town. Now, though, Tinkie and Maylin were stuck in New Orleans and Tinkie couldn't show off Maylin to all the local residents who'd awaited the baby's birth for what seemed like an eternity. I had a lot to make up to my partner.

"What was your favorite Halloween costume, Sarah Booth?" Cece asked.

I almost said a fairy, because I loved the costume so much and it was during my mother's Bedazzling phase so I had loads of glitter and jewels. "An evil doll," I decided. "I practiced walking like a doll for weeks beforehand. I had a blue-checked pinafore dress, like Dorothy, only there was blood all down the front of it. Mama had painted black eyes on my eyelids so if I closed them, it looked really awful. Other children were terrified of me. I made Randy Fulton cry."

Cece snorted. "And you loved it."

"You bet."

"Hey!" Cece pointed down the road where the trees thinned and the pale coral walls of a large house emerged from the green jungle. "Would you look at that. Rising out of the weeds—it's like a mirage."

The house made me think of *Arabian Nights*. The pale

coral stucco exterior contrasted with an umber tile roof with parapets and archways and a glorious fountain with nymphs frolicking in the water. Beneath the windows mosaic tiles brought in the blues and greens of the sky and plants. If the house had ever fallen into disrepair, I couldn't tell. Unlike the majority of other homes that had characterized River Road, this had a Moorish influence, not the Greek Revival that was traditional, leading me to believe it might be a newer structure. The house was enormous, a mansion, and the grounds fell away behind it to what looked to be a gentle slope to a bayou or inlet from the Mississippi River. A huge boat was tied off to an elaborate dock.

The soft breeze ruffled the lush lawn grass and swayed the Spanish moss that decorated the tree branches. Nature was alive with motion—and not a single human being. No people. No cars. No curtains gently being pulled back for a curious person to investigate who was arriving. There was an air of emptiness about the house that I knew was deceptive.

We'd arrived at our destination.

I let Cece out of the car while we still had the cover of all the plants. In front of me was the neat, cleared circular drive of the house. "Be careful." I had no intention of giving away the fact we were there.

"Roger, wilco." She grinned impudently. "I always wanted to say that. A vestigial desire from my Cecil days."

I wanted to hug her tight, but I only shook my head at her comedy. Coleman had gotten three handguns from his NOPD friends, so we were both armed, as was Frankie. I felt real apprehension as I watched Cece slip into the folds of leaves and plants. One minute she was there, the next she was gone. Cece, too, had some stealth moves, possibly from the many duck-and-dove hunts she had been forced to endure with her privileged family when she was Cecil. How she'd hated those hunts. Cece didn't have a pet because her heart was so tender toward animals that she couldn't bear to lose one. Killing held no attraction for her. Her teen years among the Buddy Clubbers had been harsh and needlessly cruel.

I tried my phone but there was zero cell service. Cece and I were on our own with the mission of spying. Coleman had made me promise I wouldn't attempt to extract Christa if I found her. I was to spy, photograph, and memorize the layout of the grounds, then drive to a place with phone service and call the parish sheriff's department.

While Cece made her way through the overgrowth, I had the problem of parking the car somewhere it couldn't be seen but from where we could make a quick escape if necessary.

I'd seen another pig trail a hundred yards back, so I reversed and backed in. I was pointed in the right direction for a speedy escape, if necessary. Even better, the car, which was low profile to begin with, disappeared in the tall greenery. Even someone looking from the third floor of the mansion couldn't see it.

Cece had taken the east and north areas. I would go west and south. Unlike most of the houses on River Road that fronted the Mississippi, this house was set at least a half mile back from the river. The inlet allowed access to the Mississippi, though. Something I needed to keep in mind if I did discover something amiss. Should Rhianna and her crew attempt to flee, they could easily go by boat.

I busied myself snapping photos. I could only thank

my lucky stars for a dry, cool October because otherwise we would have been eaten alive by mosquitos and yellow flies. Insects buzzed around me constantly, but they weren't biting. That might change as the sun sank on the horizon and the blue hour of the gloaming arrived. Some people loved this time of day, but it always made me melancholy. I was a woman who liked beginnings, not endings.

Watching the light fade from the sky alarmed me on another level. Where was everyone? The lights in the mansion were coming on, and I heard a mechanized noise I identified as a big generator. To the west of the house, a wide space had been cleared for large solar panels. This place was self-sufficient for energy. It was a high-end setup. But who would want to live so far out in the boonies?

A cult leader, that's who.

I felt it in my bones that I'd found Rhianna's lair. As I eased around the southern side of the mansion, I came upon something that stopped me in my tracks—bones. Human bones. They were neatly stacked, with the larger bones on the bottom, the femurs and tibias. The ribs and other bones went on top of that, and finally the skull. It looked to be one complete human skeleton.

Stones with various markings surrounded the bones, and kindling had been stacked close to it. A bone-burning ritual? But whose bones?

I was so caught up in the gruesome discovery of the bones, I didn't hear anyone approaching from behind me, from the river side of the property.

"You've sought me out in my home. So here I am."

I turned around to face a woman of dark, savage beauty. Her black curls contrasted with skin so white it reminded me of cold marble. The red lipstick cut her face like a slash of blood.

"Rhianna." I knew who she was.

"Yes, and you are Sarah Booth Delaney. A woman who has suddenly become a problem for me. But I have a remedy for that." A gun came out from the folds of the black dress she wore and soon I was looking down the bore of a .357. Rhianna didn't play. My job became survival and protection of Cece. It was going to be a harrowing Halloween.

# 35

The barrel of the gun pointed squarely in the middle of my chest left me no choice. When Rhianna told me to walk in front of her to the house, I did so. I desperately wanted to pluck my cell phone from my front jeans pocket, but I kept my hands hanging at my sides. I needed to warn Cece, to call Coleman, to alert the authorities. I could do none of those things. My best bet was to hope that Rhianna wouldn't think to take my phone and that I'd have service if I ever had the chance to use the dang thing.

"Do you really have the power to grant eternal youth?" I asked Rhianna.

"Shut up and walk."

There was a trace of an accent in her words, but I couldn't place it. "Where are you from?"

The gun cocked and a bullet whizzed into the ground not twelve inches from my foot. I controlled the impulse to jump away, and I contented myself that the shot would alert Cece to danger. She'd get help. All wasn't lost yet, but Rhianna was serious about making me walk fast to the big house.

Movement at the edge of the lawn caught my attention. Something white slipped into the weeds. It could have been a plastic bag blowing in the breeze, but it looked like the same thing I'd seen earlier. A chill touched my neck.

"Where's Renaldo?" I asked.

The gun cocked behind me and I wondered if she'd shoot me in the back. I just kept walking.

At last we got to the front door and I marveled at the varnished wood, the details of the carvings on the door. Some of them I recognized from the sigils at Third Street. This was a house guarded by magic. Not the good kind of magic, either. I'd never believed in dark magic . . . until now. Foreboding oozed from the house as I opened the door and stepped into a foyer with a black-and-white-tiled floor.

My footsteps echoed in the large room that offered parlors to either side and a staircase curving up to the second and third floors. It was impressive.

"Have a seat to the left," Rhianna said. "Renaldo and I have some questions for you."

I started to pop off with a smart-aleck answer, but I didn't. This woman had a pile of bones in her yard. I suspected she wouldn't hesitate to add mine to the heap.

The parlor was furnished in traditional Southern style with loads of antiques, art, figurines, and plush materials. I took a seat in a wing chair while she sat opposite me.

"Who knows you're here?" she asked.

"I'll answer your questions if you answer mine."

She smiled. "You don't have a lot of room to negotiate, Sarah Booth. May I call you that?"

"Sure, Rhianna. So where are Christa Moore and Britta Wagner?"

"You might not like my answer."

Oh, I knew I wouldn't like her answer. But it was the first step in figuring out how to find them and get them out.

"So, who knows you're here?"

"Coleman Peters, the sheriff of Sunflower County, some law enforcement people in New Orleans, some friends." I shrugged. "I tend to leave a big trail of bread crumbs when I'm searching for a psychopath."

She laughed out loud, a real belly laugh. "I like you. You've got chutzpa."

"Give me my friends and I'll leave. You can do whatever it is you want to do with those bones out there."

The humor left her face. "You're not leaving."

"If you take off now, you can get away." I offered her escape, which was more than she was going to offer me. "You can lock me up so I don't interfere. Make a clean getaway, take up your life somewhere else."

"I don't think so. Tonight is the conclusion of months of work here. You've already scared away one of my investors. Such a pity. But Pouty wasn't the only person interested in eternal beauty and a painless passage to immortality."

"Can you really offer that?" I played naïve, hoping for more information.

"You don't have the kind of money necessary to ask that question."

So far, the vibes I was getting from Rhianna had nothing

to do with spiritual matters, magic, or eternal youth. She was pure financial cutthroat.

"How do you convince these people of your powers?"

She actually considered my question. "People desperately want to believe that what they want most in life is available. There's a time when each person is ripe for the picking. It's in that moment, when the thing they cherish the most seems to be slipping from their grasp, that a convert can be made. It doesn't take a lot of convincing. They are desperate to believe."

Rhianna's answer didn't surprise me, but her absolutely cold assessment of the people who believed in her did. Rhianna had a talent—she could assess weakness and desperation in people. And she acted on it. She was a cult leader cut from the same cloth as Jim Jones or any of the messianic figures. She seemingly felt nothing of compassion for those she fleeced.

"You're a real piece of work," I told her. She only smiled, revealing perfect white teeth. Rhianna was physical perfection. So interesting how such a beautiful body could house such a dark soul.

"You're a bit more of a challenge to me," she said. "People who want physical beauty, they're easy to pull in. Those who desire a deeper spiritual meaning are more difficult, but there's always a moment when I finally understand what each of them wants. Then I'm able to refine what I offer." She watched me with a cold, clinical look.

I could literally hear a clock ticking in another part of the house. Tick-tock, tick-tock, tick-tock. She kept staring and I refused to flinch.

At last she smiled wide again. "I know what you want, Sarah Booth."

I couldn't resist. "What would that be?"

"You want the past, not the future. How interesting." She got up and came over to me. When she put her hand on my head, I felt a vibration of energy. I wasn't imagining it. "Yes, I understand now." She backed away so I could see her eyes. "I can give it to you."

"You can't make the past real," I scoffed, but my head was still buzzing from her touch.

"Oh, but I can. The past is known. That's easy, but I can't give you back the things you lost, the years. Yet I can help you achieve your desires, just not in the way you imagine."

She spoke with such certainty. I realized how much I wanted to believe her. "How?"

"When someone offers you the thing you most desire, at no cost, are you going to question how?" She seemed amused.

"Do I have to believe in you?" I asked. This was always the great cheat by all who offered miracles, because when the miracle failed it would always be the supplicant's fault—they didn't believe enough.

Rhianna was amused by my question. "In this instance, no. You don't have to believe in me or my connection to the deities who grant my requests. I have discovered the power of worshiping numerous figures of abundance."

"In this instance?"

"You're a special case, Sarah Booth." The smile flashed again, but it didn't reassure me.

"Yes, my mother always told me I was special."

"She says she was right."

That stopped me. Sometimes Jitty had messages from my mother. Sometimes Madame Tomeeka would dream a message from her. This woman had no right to pretend to be communicating with my mom. "Don't mess with me about this."

Rhianna's grin was pure wolf. "She said you deserved all the Bedazzling in the world."

"Bedazzle." The word slipped from me. How did Rhianna know? I'd only been talking with Frankie about this hours ago, and one thing was for certain, Rhianna hadn't talked to Frankie. My mother's friend was with Coleman in another part of the greater New Orleans area.

"Don't look so shocked. I have powers. Special gifts. You don't have to believe it, but it's true."

"Why are you even wasting your time on me? I don't have the kind of money you can get from your other clients."

"You have property. I've been told about your home and the land. Sounds like good collateral."

That snapped me out of the spell she'd been weaving over me. She would never get her mitts on Dahlia House no matter how many games she played with me. "Forget it. What I want is to find Christa Moore, Britta Wagner, and Carlos Rodriguez. All I want is to retrieve them, and to leave. Then you can do whatever you wish with your followers. You can have a happy Halloween."

She shook her head and pasted a little frown on her face. It was interesting that her eyes never seemed to change. They were cold, like a cobra's. "No, that just won't do, Sarah Booth. You came here and interjected yourself into my business. I tried to offer you an easy out, but I guess we'll do this the hard way."

Two double doors opened beside a bookcase and four men stepped into the room. They were fit and had guns.

"Take her," Rhianna said. "Put her in the cleansing

hut." She reached over and removed my car keys, phone, and the gun tucked in my boot. I hadn't reached for it because I'd hoped not to draw attention to it. Poorly played, Sarah Booth.

Two of the men grasped my arms and yanked me to my feet. My toes barely touched the floor as they frog-marched me out of the parlor, then the house, and across the beautiful lawn to what looked like a solid cement structure. The cleansing hut. I didn't like the sound of that.

# 36

When we got to the door of the hut, they opened it and pushed me in. My hands were unrestrained so I was able to catch myself before I stumbled and fell on my face. The lighting was dim in the hut, coming from two windows high up the cement wall. There were no furnishings that I could see in the dim light. Not even a chair or mattress on the floor. The circular hut was cement, inside and out. I didn't see a source of water or electricity or a toilet. This was going to be very, very unpleasant.

That is if I had to stay there.

I didn't see a lot of exit options, but I wasn't a quitter. I'd noticed that the door dead-bolted on the outside—not the most sophisticated locking system, but effective at keeping me stowed away.

I focused on the fact that Cece was out there some-where. I could only hope she'd seen my captors toss me in here and that when darkness fell completely, she would come and set me free.

Another scenario: Coleman would come looking for me when he couldn't contact me by phone.

I sat on the hard cement floor thinking it was just a matter of time until the cavalry arrived. Just a matter of time. All I had to do was keep positive and not give in to panic.

I stood and began pacing. If I had to stay in that ce-ment cell a lot longer, I would need a good cleansing. My bodily needs were making themselves known. I was thirsty and I needed a toilet. I wondered if Rhianna had some way of watching me. Like a hidden camera. If she was getting pleasure from watching me stew.

I inhaled, sat down again, and leaned back against the chill wall. I'd never realized how hard and cold cement could be.

Noises came from the outside, and I moved closer to the door, putting an ear against the wood, hoping to figure out what was happening. It was useless. The wood was too thick or the people talking were too far away for me to hear anything useful. But at least I knew that multiple people were out there, and one of them was a woman other than Rhianna. I had no doubt that other people were on the premises, but I hadn't seen a single sign of them.

I'd tried to memorize the layout of the grounds in the brief time I'd had to explore them. If there was a gath-ering tonight, a ritual, where would it be? Luckily, they hadn't taken my watch and I could read the digital dial in the deepening dark. It was going on eight o'clock.

I had to figure a way out of this prison, and I had to do it quickly.

The light coming in the two windows had slowly faded to black. If the moon shifted or a cloud covered it, the room would be totally dark. I moved along the walls, searching for anything I could use to affect an escape. I found a few gouged-out places in the wall below one window, and I realized that someone had been in this room and had attempted to at least gain a view of the outside by climbing the wall. My fingers were skimming the surface when I found scratches. The light was already gone but my fingers traced over the letters. C H R I S T . . . I inhaled sharply when I found the A. Christa had been in this room. She had been here, on these premises. And likely she was still somewhere on the property.

Yes, I was in an ugly predicament, but I felt closer to finding Frankie's daughter than I had so far. I was on her trail. I could almost smell the goal within reach. If I lived long enough to save her.

I paced until I thought I might go mad, but only forty minutes passed. Midnight drew ever closer. My attempts at climbing the wall led to my falling to the cement twice. The heels of my hands were scraped up but I was otherwise uninjured. At last I scaled the wall and pulled myself up by the window ledge until I could see out over the lawn. I had a river view. What I saw made my breath catch.

Some fifty people were gathered on the lawn holding torches. They wore white robes, and I couldn't distinguish if they were male or female. Their features were obscured with white, gauzy cloth. Strange words echoed on the night as they chanted and began to move slowly, fanning out to make a semicircle toward the water.

"We call upon the handmaiden of the gods." Rhianna's voice was suddenly clarion. She had some electronic amplifiers—and she had climbed onto a dais where she stood above the worshipers. "Hebe, be with us tonight as we embark on the journey to paradise for several of our congregation, those you have chosen to bestow your favors on. We have studied your lessons and served you honorably. We understand that the power to hold on to youth and life lies within each of us, with your blessing and help.

"We call Papa Legba and the Ghede to bring your gifts of access to the spirit world and the passing from life to death. Gentleness is what you've promised us, an ascension to paradise without the death of our mortal vessels. We praise and honor you. Our debts will be paid."

I was far from an authority on the voodoo faith, but while I recognized Papa Legba, the spirit or guide or god—I was uncertain of his exact status. Legba allowed humans to communicate with the other loa, or powerful spirits. Fascination replaced fear as the striking figure of Baron Samedi came from the darkness of the trees and began to dance. In his top hat, skull makeup, frock coat, striped trousers, and with a cigarette in one hand, he commanded my attention. Even though I knew it was someone dressed to play the part, I was still powerfully affected. Baron Samedi controlled access to the land of the dead. Rhianna had combined a number of belief systems to come up with her sales pitch for eternal youth.

The white-robed congregation, or whatever they should be called, formed a circle around Rhianna. They began to slowly dance and whirl in a clockwise direction. Another, larger circle of humans formed outside that one. They danced with abandon, moving in a counterclockwise direction. Their white robes fluttered in the night, giving the ceremony a ghostly slant.

"As we move the hands of time backward, we achieve the moment of ascension," Rhianna said. "This is what we've worked so long and hard for."

Rhianna began to dance on the dais, and even though my arms were trembling from holding up my weight, I couldn't look away. She had the grace of a trained dancer. It was as if the gods had touched her with beauty and suppleness. Though she claimed to be hundreds of years old, she was ageless.

The full moon rose in the corner of my window, a beautiful golden globe with light so strong it cast shadows. Around the dancers, the white robes and black shadows created a kaleidoscope effect of dark and light, a chilling reminder that if good existed, so must evil.

The dance began to speed up and, behind Rhianna, there was the crackle of lightning that forked across the cloudless sky. A strong wind turned the marsh grasses surrounding the yard into a susurrating, chilling song.

Holy criminy, she seemed to have some influence on the natural elements. I no longer felt the strain on my arms. I was completely absorbed in the events happening on the lawn, and my toes had found a tiny purchase in the walls. I hung on for dear life, mesmerized by the motion of the bodies and the play of moonlight and shadow. I realized then that some of the participants were falling to the ground. I couldn't tell if they were permanently injured or just dizzy and resting.

Rhianna called out and lifted both arms high, then crisply brought her arms to her sides. All motion stopped. "I've told you all that not every worthy applicant will be chosen for the transcending journey to paradise. Not everyone here will be granted youth and eternal life. Hebe and the Ghede make the choice, not me. Not you. We willingly serve those who hold our fates, the handmaiden of the gods, who provides them with the nectar of eternal youth, and the loa, who brings sweet death. Arise, so that Hebe and the Ghede may choose from your midst."

The participants slowly got up from the ground. They were silent and seemed slightly disoriented, but I couldn't be certain. I wondered if they might be drugged.

Movement at the edge of the manicured lawn caught my attention. Cece! At last. But the moving shadow merged into the darkness and I couldn't tell if it was Cece or Bigfoot.

"Bring out the prisoner!" Rhianna cried.

My hopes of a rescue by Cece were dashed as my journalist friend was roughly led up to the dais by two muscled security men. She was frantically looking around, and I knew she was worried about me. I wanted to signal her, but I dared not call attention to myself, still clinging to the window. What was about to happen wasn't something I or anyone else was supposed to see.

# 37

They hadn't harmed Cece—only danced and chanted around her—by the time my arms finally gave out and I fell to the floor. I landed on my butt with enough force to make me fear I'd broken my coccyx. I was writhing in pain when I heard someone at the door, unbolting the lock. I jumped to my feet and pressed my back against the wall. The door opened to the outside, and a figure stood before me, appearing to survey the inky interior of the round hut. My only advantage was that my eyes had adjusted to the gloom. The open doorway actually gave me a little moonlight to work with.

When my prison guard tried to enter, I was going to ka-bong him as hard as I could with my bare hands. Or maybe I would trip him and push him headfirst into the opposite wall. In any case, I was going to take action.

The door slowly creaked wide open. Whoever it was, his features were swallowed by the darkness. I only had a sense of a tall person with broad shoulders. He hesitated to enter.

"Ms. Delaney. Sarah Booth." The slight accent told me it was my previous captor, Renaldo. Some nerve he had. I kept quiet.

When he started into the room, I stuck out my foot and tripped him, but instead of going headfirst, he lurched toward me, falling on top of me as we both hit the cement floor hard. The insult to my butt bone sent me into jerks and twitches that bucked him off me and onto the cement.

"Ms. Delaney!" He pinned my shoulders to the rough floor. "Are you having a seizure? Do you need medicine?"

"I'm in pain," I howled, glad the door had closed behind him when he came in. "Let me up!"

Slowly the pressure on my shoulders decreased and I was able to shift to my side to take the pressure off my butt.

"Help me up!" I was aggravated and showed it.

When he saw I wasn't going to swallow my tongue or aspirate my own vomit, he offered a hand to help me to my feet. "You have to get out of here. Now."

I couldn't believe what he was saying. "What?"

"You need to make an escape now, while they're occupied with your friend."

"You're helping me escape? Wait a minute, I can't leave Cece here to be . . . sacrificed."

"You can't stay here or you'll be the next one to be

killed. Rhianna doesn't play with those who interfere with her plans."

I couldn't believe what he was saying. Was he really going to release me? And why? "What's in this for you?"

"Rhianna is drunk on her power. This . . . human sacrifice is not what I agreed to do, but she's concocted a foolproof scheme that in the past has made her a very wealthy woman. Once you're out of danger here, I will follow. Wait for me at your car and we can go for help together. You can talk to the authorities and tell them I never agreed to be a part of this."

"You think we can just slip away from here? I don't even have the keys to my car. Rhianna's men took them off me when I was captured."

Renaldo held up a key ring with my distinctive fuzzy dice hanging from it. "I have your key."

I reached for it, but he drew it back. "I will keep it until we can leave together."

"You're really going to cut and run?"

"Indeed I am. Rhianna values loyalty, and I fear I have betrayed her. She'll kill me in the blink of an eye for doing what she always does—looking out for herself."

"I won't leave Cece here. Or the two young women. I can't."

He shrugged. "Then you will die. Your choice. I'll take my chances telling the police my story without your help. Here there is only certain death for me. With the law, at least I'll have a chance."

"Let's rescue the others and we'll leave. I will vouch for you. You were telling me the truth when you captured me and held me prisoner. You were trying to save me."

"Yes, and yet here you are, a prisoner and on the extermination list."

"Why is Rhianna doing this? She can't give people eternal youth or ascension to paradise. Why does she kill people?"

"She kills the young women because it's a necessary part of her plan. Me, she will kill because she'll derive pleasure from it. Possibly you, too. We've committed the unforgivable sin of complicating her life. She doesn't like that and punishes it harshly."

"She can hold all the ceremonies she wants and kill all the beautiful young women she can get her hands on, but she can never deliver what she promises," I said. "Eternal youth. Ascending to heaven without dying. All of that is impossible, and all the magic in the world can't give people immortality."

"You don't understand what's going on here at all." Now Renaldo was impatient. "Get out of here and head toward the car where you left it. It's still there."

"Not yet. First, you're going to fill me in on what's really happening here."

Renaldo waved me into the night. "Leave! There's no time for explanations. They'll be coming for you any minute." He started dragging me toward the exit, reaching out to open the door. He sounded sincerely afraid.

"Why are you helping me?" If he was acting in my best interest instead of Rhianna's, he would likely pay a steep price. If he was caught, Rhianna would hurt him. I could understand his growing panic and desire to flee.

"What is Rhianna up to?" I asked. "Tell me."

He peeked around the open doorway in both directions. His hand grasped my wrist and he pulled me out with him, then quietly closed and locked the door. "Shush!" he said when I tried to talk. "When the patrol comes by, they'll see the locked door and maybe think you're still in there."

Very carefully he led me around the cleansing hut and across the dark lawn toward the road and where I'd left the Roadster.

"Where are Christa and Britta?" I demanded.

"They're here, but they're being guarded. Forget about them and get out before you're caught and killed." Renaldo looked toward the area where the dais and the dancers still seemed to be going strong, if the chanting was any indication.

"I have to get them and Cece. I can't run away and just leave them. Rhianna will kill them. You said so. But why? What's the point of killing someone for no result?"

Renaldo at last looked deep into my eyes. "Rhianna won't kill them. Not herself. But she will have one of the people who follow her do it. That's how she assures a flow of income. She implicates all of her followers in the murders, and then she has all the dirt she needs to blackmail these people for the rest of their lives. They become willing accessories to murder and then there's no escaping Rhianna or her demands. She's really furious with you about Pouty. That was a rich plum Rhianna was aching to pick and you ran her off. Rhianna really has it in for you."

# 38

"Why Britta and Christa?" I asked. I wasn't leaving the spot I stood on until I had more answers. It was all beginning to make horrible, insane sense to me now. Somehow Pouty had gotten wind of what was going down tonight and she'd had the good gumption to try to flee, but I wondered if Rhianna would actually allow her to get away. At the moment, though, she wasn't my concern. Cece, Christa, and Britta needed immediate rescue.

"Britta was the chosen target for tonight. A foreigner, a young woman with a criminal past. No one would look for her. No one would care. No one would know when she simply disappeared. I found out that Rhianna has done this before in other countries. She's perfected her selection of victims. She's bragged that she's never even been under suspicion. Now you've changed all of that. She's on the police radar, and she's very angry. She'd hoped to stay in New Orleans for another few years, but you've driven her out."

"Where's she going?"

He laughed. "I'm not on her list of confidants any longer. If she catches me, I'll be one of the human sacrifices."

"So it doesn't have to be only beautiful young women."

He stepped close enough so that I could see the moonlight in his eyes. "It's whoever Rhianna says it will be. Never forget that. She makes the rules and she breaks them. Her word is the law to these people."

"How many people are here?"

"Fifty. Maybe sixty. When the police started searching the Third Street property, some of the newer people left. They didn't like the scrutiny or the implication that POE was illegal or underhanded. Rhianna was furious. That's when she ordered her hired hands to abduct you. She's got it out for you big-time."

Terrific. Nothing like being at the top of the enemy list. And I had no doubt the people I'd seen dancing would do Rhianna's bidding. I had a sudden flashback to Frankenstein's monster being pursued by a mob with torches. We did have to get out of there before she sent someone to drag me to the execution site.

But I wasn't leaving Cece to be killed.

"Take my car, drive someplace where there is phone reception, and call the sheriff to come right away."

"I need you to validate my story. Otherwise Rhianna will take me to the electric chair with her. I've watched you and I know that big lawman will believe you. He'll convince the New Orleans police that I wasn't part of these murders."

I needed to clear up a factual point. "Louisiana doesn't use the electric chair any longer."

"Are you dense?" He was agitato. "That doesn't matter! They still kill people."

I couldn't argue that. "You go. I'm staying. Tell Coleman I said pink opossum."

"Why?"

"That way he'll know you helped me. That's secret code between us. You don't need me if you have that phrase. He'll believe you and help you. Just go!" I pushed at him. Then had a thought. "Do you know where Rhianna put my gun? Or where I can get ahold of a weapon?"

"I wish I knew where there was an AR-15. I don't care if you kill them all. And remember, they've been drugged with hallucinogens and brainwashed. Don't think they're just a bunch of innocent rich people. They'll kill if Rhianna tells them to. They've done it before. She showed me pictures." He sighed. "She probably left your gun in the office in the house. Top right desk drawer. There may be another gun there. Maybe not."

"Where are Christa and Britta?" He had to tell me that or I'd kill him with my bare hands.

"Rhianna has taken them to the gardens. There's a stone hut there. They've been drugged and fasting, so they're likely weak."

"And Carlos?" I asked.

He stared at me. "There is no man detained here."

I felt he was telling me the truth. If Carlos was here, Renaldo didn't know about it. "Where are the gardens?"

"Beyond the dock, to the north. Upriver. They're to be brought down to the dock on a floating barge, dressed and ready for sacrifice. Rhianna fancies herself something of a Cleopatra type."

"Thanks. Now get out of here and get me some help."
I was putting a lot of trust in a man I didn't know, but I
didn't seem to have another choice.

He disappeared into the night like a whisper. I was on
my own.

The big house was unlocked, which didn't surprise me.
I was smart enough to realize there were cameras everywhere and that if I lingered, someone would be sure to
realize I was there. I breezed through the unlocked front
door and toward the back of the house where I assumed
an office would be. Rhianna's hubris would be her undo-
ing. She'd left everything wide open because she'd assumed she was invincible.

At any other time I would have loved exploring the
house. Both the architecture and the furnishings were incredible. Now, I only wanted the weight of a gun in my
hand. Or at least some type of weapon that could give me
an advantage against sixty or so adversaries. A Gatling
gun would be more helpful.

I found the office, the desk, and the drawer, but no
gun. There wasn't time to go on a hunt, but also there was
no way I could save Cece or the young women with my
bare hands. Nothing I saw seemed useful, until I opened
the closet door in the office and found a plastic container
of fireworks. It wasn't a real solution, but it would buy me
some time and maybe the element of surprise.

Actually, it didn't matter. The boom-booms were all I
could find and I heard someone coming in the front door.
I grabbed the tub of fireworks and a lighter from the
desktop and headed out the back.

The first place I stopped was the firepit filled with human bones. Grunting with disgust, I tossed the bones
out on the grass, found some dry sticks and grass, and

quickly built a fire. It wouldn't last long, but long enough. When it was going good, I tossed in a handful of Black Cat firecrackers and ran like hell for a big tree.

The fireworks sounded like multiple gunshots and I heard screams coming from the area where Rhianna was performing. If my plan worked, the people, who would still be addled from the drugs Rhianna had given them, would rush over here to check out what sounded like gunshots. Then I could sneak over and free Cece. I was assuming they'd tied her up there. I could only hope I was right.

I skirted the area where I knew they'd gathered and came up from the back side. Someone had lit a huge bonfire, and the glow revealed Cece, tied to a pole too close to the fire. It had to be hot and uncomfortable. I didn't have a knife or any other tool except the cigarette lighter, so I had to believe the bonds that held her could be untied. As I'd hoped, Rhianna and her enforcers had gone to investigate the gunshots.

"Cece!" I whispered in her ear when I was behind her. "Be still." I worked the knots, glad the rope responded to my fingers. New rope never tied as tightly as old. "Just hang on a minute."

"Hurry," she said. "I don't know if they were planning to kill me before they cooked me but my skin is scorched."

The heat from the fire singed my skin in a very unpleasant way. When I worked the last knot, she freed her hands and we rushed away from the bonfire and into the night. And not a second too soon.

"Where is she? She's escaped!" Rhianna's angry voice rang out from the direction of the mansion. "Find her. No excuses. Find her and bring her back. Get the other one out of the cleansing hut. We'll start with her. We must have a ritual now to call the goddess to us."

"But it's more than an hour until midnight," one of the men said.

"We'll have the eternal youth ritual at midnight. This ritual, this cleansing ritual, will give me the power to smite my enemies."

Cece grabbed my arm and pulled me hard toward the driveway and the road to freedom. She'd once been part of the track team in high school, and she'd never been a smoker. I knew I was in for a workout.

"We've got about five minutes before she realizes you're gone and I'm gone. And then it's going to be hounds and hares. If they catch us, you know what hounds do to rabbits?" she asked.

"Yes, I do." It wasn't a very pretty image to contemplate as I ran with everything I had in me. We were in luck that the lawn was well tended and level because in the darkness, we could barely see where we put our feet. A hole could have resulted in a broken leg or worse. We made it to the edge of the tall weeds and trees before we heard the uproar from the cleansing hut. My absence had been noted.

I hesitated at the tall grass. Stepping into that was like shifting to another planet. And one with snakes and alligators, marsh grass that cut like a blade, and unexpected pools and streams of water.

"Come on!" Cece snatched my arm.

"Alligators." It was all I could choke out.

"Take your pick. Alligators or crazed cult members. I'll take my chances with the gators," Cece said, tugging me behind her. "We just have to get deep enough into the swamp that they won't come after us."

"Wild boars." I knew what lived in the swamps.

"Rhianna," she countered.

"Moccasins."

"Burned at the stake."

"Dragged underwater and stuffed in a hole for a later gator snack."

"Executed for rich people to go to paradise."

I sighed. She had me there. I'd rather be eaten by a gator than be a ticket to paradise for someone who bought their way there. "Okay. Since there's no cell reception, let's use the light on your phone."

"And make ourselves the perfect target. No."

I held her hand as we stepped into the thick curtain of leaves and shrubs. We tested each step before we put our full weight on it. The one thing we didn't want to do was sink into waist-deep water that might contain more than we'd bargained for.

"I wish you could have gotten a weapon," Cece whispered.

"Me, too. I had a tub of fireworks but I left them by the pole where you were tied."

"By the pole?" Cece sounded suddenly excited.

"Yeah, why?"

"It was pretty hot there. If a spark . . ."

"That would be pretty damn excellent," I said.

"Keep walking," she said. "Is your car still here? We have to get out of here, get a signal for my phone, get some help, and then get back here to save Christa and Britta."

That was an awful lot of gettin' to get done. But first I had to tell her that Renaldo had taken the car.

"You think he'll actually find help?" she asked.

"I don't know. But it was better to send him on the chance he will do it than have him following me around." I tried not to think about our chances of escaping Rhianna and her goons. Without a car, they were nonexistent. There was only one road in and out, and even if we stayed off that road, we'd have to parallel it or risk the grim prospect of being lost in the swamp.

A terrible idea bloomed in my head. "Cece!" I grabbed her arm. "We're going in the wrong direction. The boat! Tied up at the dock. We can take the boat!"

"Do you have a key to the boat?" she asked.

"No. But we should turn the boats loose so they can't use them. That would be smarter than hiding in the swamp."

"Jesus, Sarah Booth, now you think of that."

"I was inspired by stomping through a swamp where alligators, snakes, and wild hogs live."

"Let's go."

We trudged back through the tall weeds and finally came to the edge of the lawn. The area around the bonfire looked quiet and deserted. The cult people had to be there, but I didn't see them. Not a single one. Where had sixty or so people disappeared to without a trace?

Cece and I darted from one hiding place to the next. I saw the tub of fireworks right beside the bonfire but there wasn't time to get it and I didn't know what to do with it anyway. At last we made it to the dock. Somewhere in the water I heard the hiss of a large animal. I knew it was a gator. Been there, done that.

"If we get on one of the boats and they come after us, the gator will eat them."

"I'd kind of like to see that," Cece said. "But let's turn the boats loose and look for Christa and Britta. We can't float off down the Mississippi and leave them. Let's complete the rescue mission. If you don't want to hide in the swamp, then we need to find them and get away. Or at least find a really good hiding place. Rhianna and her crew are at the same disadvantage in the dark that we are."

She was correct about that. Saving my own butt had almost made me forget about saving the young women. Now that I knew where they were, we had to get them and get out of Dodge. One thing I suspected about Rhianna was that she truly enjoyed her revenge served hot. She would kill Christa and Britta just to prove she could do it. And if she went down, she meant to take everyone she could with her.

# 39

Cece and I settled on the plan of finding the kidnapped women, *then* setting the big boat free, and *then* trying to float out to the river in a smaller skiff that we could paddle. If we were lucky enough to make it to the Mississippi, someone would surely see us and attempt a water rescue. The Mississippi River current could be treacherous, but no more so than a cult.

We hurried along the verge beside the bayou toward the gardens where Christa and Britta were being held. Thank goodness Cece had some knowledge of the grounds.

The fragrant smell of a flower slowed my steps. "This is the same as the scent from the Third Street property."

"It's sweet, isn't it?" She tapped her watch. "Our time

is running out to get them and get away. No time to stop and smell the roses."

"Right." We ran as fast as we could over ground we didn't know and couldn't see clearly. The moon, which had risen above the trees, helped a lot, but there were patches of shadowy ground where a hole or vine could be treacherous. I couldn't shake the sense that someone watched us. Someone who meant us harm.

When I heard the tinkling of water, I knew we were close. We were right on top of another fountain, which was centered in a beam of moonlight.

Cece stopped abruptly and I ran into her back, smacking my nose on her shoulder blade. "That's incredible," she said.

I peeked around her. The fountain was enormous and the artwork exquisite. The goddess Hebe poured water into the goblets of the other Olympian gods, renewing their immortality with her gift. I knew instantly this was the garden that Britta was supposed to paint for that commission. Yes, all of this was connected. But where the heck was Carlos?

"Let's move," Cece said.

"Britta was the original target. She was to be the blood sacrifice. Christa managed to find this place or at least find out things about Rhianna that Rhianna viewed as dangerous to her cult. So they took Christa, too." I relayed what Renaldo had told me about the blackmail, how Rhianna forced her followers to participate in murder and then used that to financially bleed them over the years.

"So that's the story Christa found. She's going to be one helluva journalist," Cece said. "She's got grit."

"And a death wish," I said.

Cece only scoffed at me. "The same might be said for you," she pointed out. "You came out here with only me to help you. I wouldn't exactly call that a desire for self-preservation."

That was enough plumbing the depths of my psyche. "Let's find the girls and vamoose."

The gardens were extensive and something of a maze, but we found a building tucked behind a curtain of vines. The structure was made from rocks and cement. It was stout, and airtight with high, barred windows near the roofline. The door was padlocked, which was a setback since we didn't have any tools. It would be a huge waste of time if it turned out to be merely a gardening shed.

I knocked gently on the door. "Christa. Are you in there?"

Silence.

I knocked again, louder. "Britta! Christa! Are you in there?"

"Yes!" The answer was clear. "Yes. We can't get out. I think Rhianna is going to kill us. Hurry!"

"Hang on. We'll get the door open." Easier said than done, but Cece was already on the job. She'd located a garden shed that actually held tools and she returned with a shovel, a sledgehammer, and a pickax, which was perfect to pry the lock hinge off the door. The old wood was tough, but Cece used the sledgehammer to hit the pickax while I held it in place. The door popped open.

I hesitated at the doorway. The interior was inky, and while I knew the women were in there, I didn't know who else might be waiting for me to plunge inside.

"Christa?"

"I'm here. So is Britta." Christa sounded breathless.

There was the sound of scuffling and someone cried out briefly.

"What's going on?" Cece demanded. "Who's in there with you?"

"Don't come in! It's a trap." Christa's warning was followed by more scuffling and the sound of someone crashing into something.

"Stop!" This cry came from someone with the hint of an accent. Britta, I assumed.

Cece motioned that she was going in, but on her hands and knees. I was to keep them talking. "Who's with you, Christa? Is it Rhianna? One of her guards?"

"Come in and find out." The voice was female. Young, also.

The skin on my arms erupted in goose bumps. I knew that voice. I couldn't place it, but I knew it. And I had a sudden thought. I caught Cece by her pants leg. "Give me your phone."

She didn't hesitate. She handed it over with her password. In a moment I had it set. "Go," I whispered.

Cece launched herself like a rocket straight into the heart of the darkness. I followed and hit the camera button on the phone. The flash illuminated the small room in rapid succession, one photo after another. As I'd intended the flash blinded everyone in the room but me and Cece because we weren't facing it, and I got a clear look at what I would have to deal with. Frozen in the blast of the flash was the person I now knew was responsible for the troubles that had befallen Christa and Britta. It didn't surprise me. It was almost as if I'd known, but just refused to acknowledge it. The missing computers, the stories suddenly found and then brought to us, the hints that Carlos was behind this. I just couldn't believe that a scholarship competition could turn into a plot for murder. But it had.

"Give it up, Addie," I said.

"Oh, you wish." I didn't have to see her to know she had a gun. I threw myself to the left and rolled on the cement floor while Cece rammed into her. The gun went off and someone screamed. Had Christa or Britta been hit? Cece?

Two bodies, thrashing together, fell on top of me. I added to the melee by trying to push them off. They had me pinned to the floor and my tailbone was screaming. I bucked like a rodeo bronc.

"The police are coming!" Britta called out. "I hear the sirens. They're coming to save us."

I felt fingers digging into my face and I swung blindly, as hard as I could. My fist connected with a face and I felt something warm and sticky gush over my hand.

There was more tussling until Cece said, "I've got her. Is there a light in this place?"

"We don't have time for a light," I reminded her. "We have to get out of here."

"We can't leave her. She'll get away. Or hurt someone else."

"Knock her out cold." I got to my feet and used the light from the cell phone to scan the room. Addie was on the floor in front of me, bleeding profusely. She glared at me but made no effort to stand up. Cece towered over her, and Christa and Britta inched closer. Britta drew back a leg and kicked Addie hard, in the ribs. The air went out of her in a whuff.

"Hey," Christa said, grabbing Britta's shoulders. "Stop."

"Bullshit. She lured me into being kidnapped. She was selling me for a human sacrifice." Britta drew back to kick again, but Cece stopped her.

"Not now. Maybe on the way to the road she can trip and fall a few times. Right now, we have to take quick action. If the cops are coming, Rhianna is going to do everything she can do to save herself. We have to stop her. Do we have anything to tie Addie up with?"

Christa shrugged out of her cotton overshirt that covered a dark, long-sleeved thermal. "We do now." She tore the sleeves from the cotton shirt and made strips. "We can use this."

"You'd better not leave me here," Addie said. "Rhianna is going to be pissed."

"Yeah, that sounds like a personal problem," I said. "Be sure and gag her, too."

"With great pleasure," Britta said. Christa and Britta went to work, none too gently. I couldn't say I blamed them.

I looked out the door and saw the flashing blue lights through the trees. The vehicle headlights highlighted the beautiful house and the mass of people milling about outside, reminding me of a television zombie show. The Jefferson Parish Sheriff's Office was going to have their hands full with this group.

"I guess Renaldo actually got help," Cece said. "I almost don't believe it. It's humbling that we suspected him and never realized Addie was part of the problem."

"There was always something about her . . . I just couldn't put my finger on it."

"She was willing to let me die so she could take my scholarship project and win." Christa was spitting mad.

"They were going to pay me fifty thousand dollars for each of you," Addie said right before Britta jammed the gag in her mouth and tightened it behind her head. Her muffled complaints were music to my ears.

When Addie was securely tied up, the four of us started across the lawn. We had to untie the boats and set them out in the current so Rhianna had no resources to escape. Coleman and the law officers were managing the big house and the cult, so it was up to us to cut off this possible exit.

"Addie watched us and eavesdropped on you and Frankie. She must have known every step we were taking," Cece said as we rushed across the lawn, the delicious smell of the coneflowers heavy in the night.

"She's a snake," Christa said. "She told Rhianna all about Britta, how she was alone here, how she was wanted for blackmail, how her parents didn't care about her."

"It was all a lie I made up so I could be bait," Britta said. "I came to New Orleans to find my friend who disappeared last year. Gerri. Rhianna and her cult were in Dresden three years ago and an Australian girl who was backpacking across Europe disappeared. Same MO. I knew if I could get inside, I could take them down. Christa and I were working together."

"And you almost got yourselves killed." I sounded just like Frankie and my mama. "You're telling me that Christa knew you were going to be kidnapped?"

"Not exactly," Christa said. "I knew about Gerri and how she'd disappeared. I suspected what Britta was doing. But when she disappeared a few days ago, I really freaked out. I hadn't found the location of this place and I didn't know where POE held their rituals. I was very worried."

"And then you managed to get yourself taken," I said. "You've about worried your mama into an early grave. Was it Renaldo who snatched you up?"

"No. Renaldo actually has tried to help me. He told me he was used by Rhianna. She sent him to bribe Britta with the offer of a commission. He figured it wasn't completely legitimate, but he had no idea Rhianna planned to kill Britta as a sacrifice to some goddess."

That sounded very convenient for Renaldo, but the truth was he'd brought the cops. Assigning blame was worry for tomorrow, though. Escaping was what mattered now. I didn't have a clear view of the house and what was going on, but I could hear shouting and a commotion up at the big house. I could only hope Rhianna and whoever was helping her were in custody. If the law officers didn't find Addie, we'd have to tell them where she was. After a while. A good long while of her lying on the cement floor bound and gagged.

We made it to the dock and halted. Something near the bonfire caught my eye, a flash of white in the moonlight. It was someone in a white dress, and she beckoned me toward her.

"Who is that?" I asked Christa.

"Who? I don't see anyone."

The woman in white stepped back into shadow and disappeared. I smiled at the thought of Marie Laveau. She was the queen here and she hadn't taken kindly to Rhianna coming along to corrupt her kingdom.

"What is it, Sarah Booth?" Cece asked.

"I thought I saw someone over by the bonfire."

Cece studied the area. "I'm going to check it out."

"Not by yourself!"

Christa put a hand on my shoulder. "Go with Ms. Falcon. Britta and I can keep the dock covered. If we can release the boats, we will."

I handed her the gun we'd taken from Addie. "Shoot first. Ask questions later."

"Oh, I promise," Christa said. "We'll be right here when you or the law officers come."

I hated to leave them but I couldn't let Cece head into possible danger alone. "We'll be back in ten minutes," I said. "Just keep your heads down and I'm serious, shoot anyone who tries to bother you."

I legged it after Cece, who was already jogging toward the dais that appeared empty to me. "What did you see?" I asked Cece. She'd obviously seen more than I had.

"Someone in a white dress. I think it's Rhianna, trying to escape."

"Are you sure you saw someone?"

"Absolutely. And so did you. Don't bother denying it."

I wasn't about to tell her that I thought I saw a voodoo queen long buried in St. Louis Cemetery No. 1. "Then let's check it out and get back to the young women. I'm hoping the law officers will head down this way quickly. I'd say we should go up to the house, but I don't want to run into any POE stragglers looking for revenge against us."

"There she is!" Cece pointed to the cleansing hut. She was right. A shadowy figure in a white dress was barely visible. Was she a spirit or a living person? We'd soon find out.

# 40

Cece took off at a run. She'd been itching to have it out with Rhianna, and she was taking the action to her. But neither Cece nor I was armed. And it was highly probable that Rhianna was. I wanted to yell out to her to be careful, but that would destroy the element of surprise, which was the only thing we had going for us.

I took off in hot pursuit, stopping only long enough to grab the tub of fireworks. Roman candles, Vesuvius fountains, spinners, bottle rockets—the gamut guaranteed for at least one practitioner to end up in an emergency room with an eye or hand injury. But if Rhianna was armed, I wasn't going in empty-handed. If I hurried, I could get there right after Cece.

Carrying the plastic tub was awkward, but I pushed

myself. The figure in white near the cleansing hut detached itself from the shadows, and Rhianna stepped out into the moonlight. It wasn't Marie, but the POE cult leader.

She pointed a gun right at Cece.

I didn't have time to think, but I called upon Marie Laveau for protection. "No!" I hurled myself forward, but not fast enough. A shot rang in the clear night and Cece went down. She hit the grass and didn't move. "Cece!" She didn't respond.

Before I could get to my friend, Rhianna came toward me. Her eyes seemed to glow with hatred in the night.

"You've ruined everything," she said. "You're going to pay for that. I'm going to snap your neck like a twig."

I'd left the gun I'd picked up in the shed with Christa but no way was I going to run off and leave Cece. My friend needed medical attention.

"The cops are here. You can't escape."

"I have nothing to lose by finishing you off. Why couldn't you just mind your own business?"

"Christa Moore is my business."

She advanced. "Those young women are a dime a dozen. No one cares what happens to them."

"Oh, you're very wrong about that."

I still clutched the box of fireworks to my chest, but there was nothing in there that would counteract a bullet.

When she was ten feet from me, she lifted her arm and I saw she clutched my pistol. I was about to be shot with my own weapon. Damn.

"I thought you were going to snap my neck." I couldn't think of anything else to say.

She leveled the gun and I wanted to close my eyes, but I didn't. I threw myself to the left, knowing it was futile, but as I was hurtling toward the grass, I saw Cece. She had a huge rock in her hand and she tossed it with deadly accuracy at Rhianna's back. The rock hit hard and Rhianna fired wild. I grabbed the cigarette lighter from my pocket and jammed it into the box of fireworks. A fuse caught and I pushed the plastic container into Rhianna's chest. She instinctively grabbed it just as the first Roman candle went off.

The explosion, trapped in the plastic tub, was a hot mess that lit everything else in the container. Rhianna ultimately held a bomb.

She threw the box down, but a Vesuvius fountain ignited and hot bolts of pink, blue, and green shot into the folds of her dress. Before I could get to my feet, she was on fire.

Cece came from behind and tackled her, and I helped roll her in the grass and dirt until we smothered the flames. She didn't look too badly hurt, just some burns on her legs.

"You caught her," Coleman said as he came up. "That was a helluva show, Sarah Booth."

"Cece's been shot," was my answer.

Coleman spoke into a radio on his shoulder. "Send the paramedics over here. One gunshot and one burn."

My knees felt a little wobbly, so I just sat on the ground where Cece had also plopped down. "You okay?" I asked.

"Not really."

Coleman brought a high-beam flashlight over to check Cece out, and I saw the blood seeping through her jacket at her waist.

"Let me take a look," he said. But before he could remove her jacket, the paramedics were there with a stretcher. They loaded Cece onto it—and the fact that she didn't try to fight them had me worried. Her jacket was soaked with blood.

The two paramedics worked over her for a few minutes before they loaded her into the ambulance.

"How is she?" I asked.

"Looks like the bullet grazed her. She should be fine. We'll clean the wound and bandage it and she'll be free to go." The paramedics were all about action, not talk.

Coleman put his arm around me. "They'll get her to the hospital to have it checked out. By the time we finish here, we can pick her up."

And with that I sat back on the ground, crying out when my tailbone hit the grass.

"What's wrong?" Coleman asked, kneeling beside me.

"Long story." I was so relieved Cece was okay that I wanted to weep, but now wasn't the time. "Christa and Britta are at the end of the dock, waiting for the cavalry. Where's Frankie?" I wanted to ask if there was any news of Carlos, but no one had even told Christa he was missing. I decided to keep silent, for a time at least.

"My daughter is on the dock?" Frankie stepped out from behind Coleman. "Thank you, Sarah Booth. Thank you so much." She had a big flashlight and she took off in the direction I pointed, but Christa and Britta had already come to see what had caused the fireworks explosion. I was able to watch Christa run into her mother's arms.

Coleman watched the scene, too, before he offered a hand to pull me to my feet. "You did it, Sarah Booth. You brought her daughter home safely."

"Me, you, Cece, Tinkie, and half the New Orleans police and Jefferson Parish Sheriff's Office. By the way, Addie Graham is tied up on the floor of a building in the middle of the gardens. That way." I pointed. "Make her tell us what happened to Carlos," I whispered to him.

Coleman called over some law officers and sent them to collect the prisoner while I told Coleman the role Addie had played in the abduction of both women. "She would have allowed Rhianna to kill Christa and Britta." I still found it a little hard to believe. I'd worked cases with some strange motives, but they normally boiled down to money, sex, or revenge. I suppose Addie's motive—a journalism scholarship that could lead to a high-level career—could be counted in the money department. And then there was the payment of fifty thousand each for human sacrifices. But how did one even attempt to justify the death of two "friends" for that?

I had a sudden thought and grabbed Coleman's hand. "Come with me."

I half dragged Coleman toward the gardens and then to the building where four law officers were bringing Addie out in handcuffs. I stopped right in front of her. "Did you have anything to do with the other German student's disappearance? Gerri."

Her slow smile was not the answer I wanted to see. "Why?" I demanded. "What had she ever done to you?"

"Nothing. It was strictly about money. Rhianna wasn't really established here yet. She didn't know anything. She spoke to Father Joseph about her desire to include younger people in her spiritual quest."

"Father Joseph?" I didn't believe a priest would dabble in this kind of thing.

Addie laughed. "He believed Rhianna was a good Catholic merely leading a spiritual quest with more of an emphasis on nature than the church building. I made it a point to meet her when she had a small temple in the

French Quarter. She was just connecting the dots among the New Orleans wealthy. She was particularly looking for beautiful, fresh young women, so I offered to introduce her to some. She picked Gerri because of her beauty." She shrugged. "For a world traveler, Gerri was really sweet and naïve. She didn't have a clue. She believed the whole thing about the painting commission, just like Britta did. They were so arrogant about their looks, their artistic talent, both of them."

She was mad with jealousy of everyone she met. She'd helped kill Gerri and had planned to do the same with Britta and Christa because she thought they had more than she did. More beauty. More creativity. More talent. More of everything. Only Addie had more of several things too—jealousy, cruelty, immorality. She had heaping servings of those.

What she needed was a punch in the snout, but I knew Coleman would be blamed for my bad behavior so I restrained myself. Christa and Britta were safe. Rhianna had been apprehended. It would take some time to sort through all of the craziness. I was ready to ride back to New Orleans in the car with Addie and force her to tell me what she'd done to Carlos. But I didn't have to. Coleman stepped in.

"You're in big trouble, Addie. I won't lie. But you can help yourself if you tell me where Carlos is."

She sneered at him. "I don't know."

"You do." I grabbed her shirt in my fist. "And you're going to tell."

"I'll speak up for you if you tell us," Coleman said. "That's the best offer you're ever going to get."

"Carlos?" Christa said. "Has something happened to him?"

"He's in the slave pens on the property. When he started getting in the way, I had to remove him. I had set it up so perfectly for him to be blamed for everything." She smirked at Christa, as if she would have the last word. "No need to rush to find him, he's probably dead by now."

"If you've hurt him . . ." Christa smiled. "You wouldn't. You've had a crush on him since I started seeing him. You thought you'd blame him, then fix it where he wasn't charged. You thought he'd be grateful and care about you. You are such a sicko."

I had nothing to add to that. I checked my watch. It was 11:30. We just had time to get back to New Orleans to see Tinkie and Maylin and celebrate the arrival of Samhain. I didn't have a costume and I didn't care. I was ready to hug a barstool with my butt and raise a glass with Coleman and my besties.

# 41

New Orleans was a madhouse of tourists, costumes, laughter, and mini-parades through the French Quarter as midnight arrived. Maylin snoozed in her carrier, oblivious to all the noise, and I found I couldn't take my eyes off her or her mom. Tinkie was positively gorgeous, in the full bloom of new motherhood. Cece was busy texting Millie back in Zinnia to get the whole story of Rhianna and the cult of youth in the Sunday newspaper. It was a tight deadline but Cece had reminded me to use her phone to photograph the arrest of Rhianna and her perp walk to the patrol car. And I got some great shots of the POE facilities. Cece had turned it all in as soon as we had a cell signal on the ride back to town.

Coleman had sent a police cruiser to the apartment

complex and they'd found Carlos, fit to be tied but not hurt. Addie had drugged him, trashed his place and Christa's computers, and left him in the slave pens. She'd also left him food and water, which made me think Christa's assumptions were correct. Addie had wanted Carlos for herself.

Cece gave me a thumbs-up as she hung up the phone. "It's all set to be printed. Millie is sick she wasn't here."

"Someone has to write the column and feed the town," Coleman said. He looked like ten years had dropped off him.

Christa and Carlos strolled up and joined us, doing their best to be cool. But Christa's emotional wall crumbled and she burst into tears and hugged her mother close. "Thank you for looking for me."

Coleman gave them a minute before he turned to Christa. "I'm sorry about Britta's friend who was killed last year. And Addie." He shook his head. "I'll never understand her desperate need to take everything you had. Even your life."

"She's messed up," Christa said.

"It's clear now that Addie was trying to set Carlos up as the person who abducted you and Britta. She planted your earring in his car and took your computers to his place and destroyed them. It was a masterful plan that almost worked."

Christa blinked back tears. "I haven't processed all that's happened. It's going to take some time."

"You busted a criminal ring, Christa. You and Britta." Coleman patted her shoulder.

"No one else will ever be hurt by these dangerous people," Britta said. She, too, fought back emotion. "I can't believe my parents brought counterfeit money to pay for my ransom. They're the most law-abiding people in the world."

"They were desperate," Coleman said. He'd convinced the NOPD not to charge them because of the extenuating circumstances. He gave Britta a wink. "And they got the idea from you, after all. When you went around telling everyone you were blackmailing rich men. You young people are world-class criminals." Coleman teased her to make her smile. "Getting your computer friend to create those fake arrests—your folks felt the horses were out of the barn on legal conduct."

"Of course they will blame me." Britta rolled her eyes.

Coleman held up his Jack and water. "To criminal masterminds. I seem to be sitting at a table full of them."

Britta beamed as if she'd won an award. "And I found out what happened to Gerri. I couldn't stop it, but the police collected her bones and once the DNA match is completed, they will send them home. At least her family will have closure."

"Rhianna was going to burn them tonight, after she killed me and Britta." At last Christa was showing anger. "And I'm pretty sure she ordered that man who owned the property, Rebus Mitchem, to be killed. I heard them arguing when I was first abducted. She was going to keep me at his place in the French Quarter, but he refused. And he threatened to call the law on her activities."

Frankie grasped Christa's hand and squeezed it. "Your friends Burt and Leitha are going to be very glad to see you both. Apparently you're the cooks."

"Yes," Britta said. "Christa and I have complementary culinary skills. And Carlos, too. He brings a little special zing to his recipes."

The long arm of justice had finally plucked up Rhianna,

but I still had questions. "What would have happened among her followers when several people were murdered and no one looked any younger?" I asked.

Christa nodded, thinking through her answer. "Rhianna would say that the goddess was disappointed in the sacrifice, or that the bloom of youth would come with the next blue moon, or some such deadline. She intended to be long gone by then."

"But she would keep bleeding her followers even from a distance, because they were complicit in murder," Frankie said. "It's a brilliant scheme for an eternal fountain of money for her."

"It's a good thing we nabbed her when we did," Coleman said. "The Jefferson Parish Sheriff's Office and the NOPD found out she was planning on fleeing for South America tomorrow."

"What will happen to all of her followers?" I asked. I was thinking of Pouty.

"Depends on how deep they're into this. Some have followed her for a long time. They're in it all the way. Some actually thought she was one day going to perform the miracle of eternal youth for them. They knew what was going on and wanted youth so desperately they were willing to keep killing. The newer members, they didn't have a clue what she was actually going to do. All of the talk of blood sacrifice, Pouty said they figured it was a chicken or something. Not that that's okay." Coleman, like me, didn't believe in harming animals for sport or religion.

"Will they be charged with anything?" Cece asked. She was, after all, writing another story for the newspaper. Pouty's arrest would be big news in Zinnia, and the appeal of a blood sacrifice and youth cult would be international. Cece's and Millie's sense of what the public wanted was keen and accurate. Everyone had made out okay in this episode except Tinkie, who'd missed Maylin's first Halloween in Zinnia. The baby was cute as could be in her little bug outfit. Even sleeping she totally captivated my attention.

"Room for three more?"

We looked up to find Oscar, our dear friend Harold Erkwell, and Deputy DeWayne Dattilo standing at our table, the last of whom was wearing the most ridiculous bumblebee outfit.

"Oscar!" Tinkie was on her feet, rushing into her husband's arms. "I'm so glad you're here." She turned to Harold and DeWayne and gave each one a hug in turn. "All of you. I can't believe you drove down here on Halloween."

"What's buzzing in Sunflower County?" Coleman asked DeWayne.

"Wouldn't have missed wearing this costume for the world," DeWayne said, totally ignoring his boss. "And what fun would it be if you didn't see me?" He bent over the baby. "I see our favorite bug is out for the night, though."

"I have photos of her. Now let's get more with everyone!"

Cece and I both took pictures. It was a happy celebration of Halloween. When I glanced at Frankie and saw the glint of tears in her eyes, I made a solemn vow. "I promise you that Addie will pay." I would make sure, and Coleman would help me.

"The NOPD is working on her confession right now," Coleman said. "I'm sure she'll admit to all of it. She might get some leniency in sentencing if she owns her crimes. Otherwise she'll never step outside of prison."

"I hope she never does," Christa said.

"I second that." Britta sighed. "I feel stupid. I do. I came to New Orleans to search for the people who kidnapped my friend Gerri. I knew they were dangerous. I knew they were ruthless. I thought I'd set the perfect trap. I even took shooting lessons so that I could take care of myself. I bought a gun."

"But you didn't have it with you when you were taken?" Coleman asked.

"No. I was working at my booth at Jackson Square, painting and planning on meeting Christa for lunch. Addie showed up an hour before lunchtime and asked me if I'd take some photos of her. Over on the levee. She said it was for her scholarship application and she wanted something that showed the flavor of New Orleans in the background. She said her focus was on some corruption at the docks, something about riverboat captains on the take, so the river in the background was important." Anger crackled in her eyes. "Of course it had to be at an isolated location. I should have seen this coming from a mile away."

"But you didn't," Christa said. "And neither did I." She leaned into her mother, and Frankie stroked her hair. "I trusted Addie."

"You can't go through life without trust," Frankie said with more wisdom than I could have mustered. Lack of trust kept us safe, but also only half living.

"I trusted Addie, too," Frankie said. "She seemed so genuinely concerned for both of you. And she'd pretend to come up with new information and rush over to tell me. I ate it with a damn spoon."

"I almost told Addie what I was really up to," Britta said with a wry grin. "I wonder what would have happened if she realized I was trying to set up Rhianna and her cult."

No one could answer that. Britta had played a wild hand of cards, and she'd almost died. I only had a few more questions. "So, Renaldo is in custody, too. What role did he play?"

"Renaldo was a patsy, as far as I can tell. He had no idea anyone was planning murders." Frankie signaled for another round of drinks.

Tinkie was being the perfect mom and had forgone alcohol for hot tea. I could only admire her fortitude and wonder if I could ever live up to her example of motherhood. I didn't know that I was willing to risk it and fail. I sure as heck wouldn't tell Jitty that, though.

"Why are you smiling?" Tinkie whispered in my ear. "You look like you know a secret."

"Oh, I know a lot of secrets."

"Spill it," Tinkie pressed.

"I'm in love with your daughter. I may have to steal her every now and again."

"Not until I watch you change a diaper."

Tinkie had me there. I cleaned out horse stalls and looked out after the dog and cat, but that was a far cry from the responsibility of caring for Maylin. I could certainly change a diaper, but she was so fragile, I was afraid I might hurt her in the process.

"When she's older and tougher, I want lots of time with her. And I'm going to teach her to cuss."

"Don't you dare!"

I had Tinkie now. Daddy's Girls did not curse or throw tantrums. They were the iron fist in the velvet glove. They got what they wanted by being smart. And by smiling. And by making men feel good about themselves. It wasn't exactly deceitful, it was what Tinkie called working with the elements she had.

"Yes, I think by first grade I'll have her dropping the F-bomb." I made my expression serious.

"You cannot cripple Maylin socially." Tinkie wasn't certain I meant to follow through, but she didn't want to risk it.

"Hey, I'm freeing her from the baggage of being a people pleaser."

Tinkie scoffed. "As if you ever knew what that meant."

Cece and Coleman snorted with laughter. "She got you there," he said.

"Sarah Booth, you've never set out to please people. Maybe on occasion a few special people"—Cece winked at Coleman—"but on the whole, I'd say you pretty much felt like people could take you or leave you as you are."

I couldn't argue that. "I just want Maylin to be tough. People don't pick on tough girls."

"That's true," Coleman said, pretending he was going to act like a referee. Ha! When it came down to it, he'd side with Tinkie every time where Maylin was involved. "But cursing girls are like a crowing hen." He fought the grin that threatened to spread. "I know your aunt Loulane told you this many times. 'A cussing girl and a crowing hen will never come to a good end.'"

I was up in arms. "You've bastardized her saying, Coleman. And you know it. It's whistling girl, not cussing girl."

Everyone laughed.

"I remember Loulane," Frankie said. "She sure loved your mama and you, Sarah Booth."

"Look!" Tinkie pointed down the street where a parade came toward us. It was led by La Catrina, the Lady of Bones in traditional celebrations of the Day of the Dead. The costumed young woman wore a black gown with glowing white bones to show the human skeleton. Her face was painted to look like a skull, and she wore an elaborate black hat with black plumes. She danced from one side of the street to the other, twirling a parasol decorated with what looked to be crow and peacock feathers, handing out bread she retrieved from a mule-drawn cart filled with marigolds. Behind her danced dozens of people in skeleton costumes or the bright, fanciful dresses La Catrina was famous for.

It was a colorful and delightful beginning to the celebration for the start of the two-day festivities for All Souls' Day. I'd forgotten that the calendar had flipped over to November 1. Halloween was over. The Day of the Dead was up to bat.

# 42

I wasn't really hungover when the sun came through the apartment window and forced me to accept that a new day was well underway. Coleman's side of the bed was empty, but he'd left a note.

"Gone to the PD. The Wagners have been released, no charges. Giving counterfeit money to criminals isn't a crime. I'll call when I'm headed back."

The day was off to a terrific start. I could smell fresh coffee, and I stretched and jumped out of bed. I was ready to head back to Zinnia. DeWayne, Harold, and Oscar had left early in the morning so they could attend to their professional duties and DeWayne could feed the horses. I had the morning to explore New Orleans and there was one place I especially wanted to go.

But first, coffee!

My gaggle of girlfriends was out on the front porch enjoying the crisp morning and hashing out the details of the case.

I slipped into jeans and a jacket, poured a mug of coffee, and went outside to join my girlfriends. For a moment I leaned on the balustrade and took in the view of a peaceful Esplanade and the chatter of songbirds.

I loved the balcony, which put us close to the tree branches of the big oaks that made New Orleans so beautiful. It was like a treehouse my dad had built for me as a kid in the small grove of oak trees beyond our back pasture. I'd insisted that fairies lived there and my parents had encouraged my imagination, leaving little gifts from the fairies in the treehouse.

"Remember the treehouse James Franklin built for you?" Frankie had slipped up beside me.

"You must be psychic. I was just thinking of that." I had a question for her. "Rhianna knew about Mama's Bedazzling phase. For just a moment, I almost believed she had powers."

"I'd mentioned that to Christa only last week. She could have mentioned it to Addie, who probably told Rhianna. Let me ask Christa."

That made a lot more sense than Rhianna communicating with my mother. "Thanks, but don't." I realized I wanted to believe my mother had been fighting to save me. I didn't get how Bedazzling would fit into it, but my mama was never easy to figure out.

Frankie's arm went around my shoulder. "Thank you for saving my daughter."

"We had some good luck." I wasn't exactly sure how everything had fallen into place, but the only important thing was that Christa and Britta were alive and safe and Rhianna and Addie were in jail.

"Good luck and good detecting work. And some help from that handsome sheriff you brought along." Christa and Britta came to the rail, too.

"It would have been a different outcome if Coleman hadn't arrived with the officers when he did. And you should know that Renaldo sent them. He was instrumental in Christa's and Britta's abduction, but I honestly don't think he knew what Rhianna intended. Coleman and the officers will sort it all out."

"It was Addie who lured me out to the levee where some of Rhianna's thugs snatched me," Britta said. "Renaldo left the photograph and mentioned the big commission, but he wasn't involved in snatching me. That was all Addie. That little—"

"Bitch," Christa said. "She told me she'd seen you at the French market, back where the service trucks were. She said you were injured. I rushed with her and the next thing I knew I'd been chloroformed and pushed into the back of a truck."

"Christa was getting too close to finding out the truth," Frankie said.

"She set Carlos up and she would have left him for dead in those pens. I'll never forgive her for that," Christa added.

"But why?"

"Carlos suspected Addie was not who she pretended to be. The last conversation I had with him, before I was kidnapped, he told me to watch out for her. She was always asking about my story, about the scholarship," Christa said. "Besides, he was one more thing I had that she didn't."

"I'm sorry, Christa. I know this has been horrible for you." So much had happened so quickly.

"I haven't really had time to process it," Christa admitted. "I was just so happy to see Mom. To get away from that place before . . ." Her voice broke and I realized she had a lot of experiences and emotions that she'd have to struggle with for months, maybe years.

"And that man who owned the properties. Rebus Mitchem? Who killed him?" Frankie asked. "Was it really Addie?"

"I'll find out." I dialed Coleman's cell phone. If he was busy, he'd let it go to voicemail, but he picked up.

"I know you're ready to go home, but it's going to be several more hours," he said.

"No worries. There's something I want to do anyway."

"That's rather enigmatic." He did love to tease me.

"I want to visit St. Louis Cemetery No. 1. It's All Saints' Day."

"Know someone buried there?" he asked.

My gal posse was watching me, and I only said, "I do. Someone I need to say thank you to. I'll tell you all about it when you're done. But I'm calling to find out who killed Rebus Mitchem. It's one detail we don't know. Oh, and was Pouty arrested?"

"Pouty wasn't arrested and she's returned home to try to work things out with the doctor. And Rebus was killed by Rhianna's security team. I found out a few more details. It seems he became a loose end with the property once you found the Third Street location. He was pushing Rhianna to build a permanent worship center on the Third Street property. He held a few rituals there to stir up the neighbors and get talk started once she refused. Obviously, you don't go against Rhianna's commands."

"What about Renaldo?"

"He's been cooperating with the police. He swears he didn't know about the plans for a blood ritual. He thought it was all talk that Rhianna used to control her followers. Once he realized she was going to kill Britta and Christa, he did what he could to help them escape."

I wasn't certain I believed that entirely, but he had sent help, as he'd promised. And he could have just kept driving my mama's car into the sunset. Christa tugged on my arm and pointed at Britta. "Are they going to deport her?"

I asked Coleman, who only laughed. "No. She isn't really a blackmailer. She's just a con artist." He laughed. "There are no charges. She's free to continue painting in Jackson Square."

"So we really can go home?" I was more than ready.

"Couple of hours and I'll be done. If you're packed, we'll throw the suitcases in the trunk and hit the road. We could be home before dark."

"Sounds like the perfect plan. And thanks for saving my life."

"You had it covered, Sarah Booth, but you're welcome. Now I have to finish up."

We hung up and I looked at my friends.

"Cece and I have to head back to Zinnia," Tinkie said. Maylin slept soundly in the papoose sling she wore. That baby looked like a little pink angel in her faux-fur-lined hoodie and her little pink fuzzy boots. "Ed called this morning and said if she wasn't back by lunch he was going to give her office to Toby Keene, that suck-up, and put Cece on the desk writing obits."

Ed was very tolerant of Cece's antics, but when the threats started, it was best not to beard the lion in his den, as Aunt Loulane would say. That newspaper was Ed's territory and the man could roar when he wanted to.

"Coleman and I will follow when he's done. Frankie, what about you?"

"Christa and I are going to Ocean Springs for some time together."

"And my parents are coming over." Britta stood up. "In fact, I think that's them pulling into the parking lot. Once the coroner runs the DNA on the bones Sarah Booth discovered, I'm sure they'll find they belong to Gerri. My parents and I will go back to Germany to tell her parents. In person."

The heartache they would suffer was palpable to all of us, all mothers or daughters, all bonded in ways that were strong, tenacious, and delicate. "Don't tell them about the blood ritual," I said. "There's no need."

"I agree," Frankie said. "I have my daughter, alive and sound, thanks to some very good friends. But I think the fewer details you share, the better for them to heal. Let them remember her as the bright, happy young woman she was."

"I should go pack," I said, standing up. "Coleman will be ready to hit the road the minute he finishes, and I'm eager to get home myself."

"Me, too," Tinkie said. "In fact, Maylin, Cece, and I are packed and ready to go. As we noted earlier, Ed Oakes is not to be thwarted."

Tinkie turned to Frankie and gave her a big hug, careful not to crush Maylin. "Thank goodness this turned out okay. A daughter . . ." Her voice broke and she didn't finish, but we all knew what she wanted to say. Motherhood had opened portals of feeling in Tinkie that nothing else had ever touched.

"See you in Zinnia," Cece said, helping Tinkie down the steps.

I watched them get into Tinkie's Cadillac in the parking lot. A moment later, they were zooming down Esplanade toward I-10 East.

"Thank you," Frankie said. She'd come to stand beside me at the balcony railing. "Thank you."

"I'm so glad it worked out. I'm sorry for Gerri's family."

"I know how lucky I am," Frankie said. "And how lucky you are, too, Sarah Booth. Libby loved you more than life itself. When you start out with that abundance, you can never be without riches."

She was right about that. "I have something I need to do. I'll be back in an hour or so. Will you be here?"

"Christa and I are ready to go home for a few days to recover. You and I will talk later, though."

"Indeed we will."

I stopped by the apartment and packed all of my things and Coleman's things and had them ready at the door. Then I took an Uber to St. Louis Cemetery No. 1. I had an obligation to fulfill. In my time of greatest need, I'd followed Tammy's advice and called upon Marie Laveau to help me. And she had. I'd seen her in the fringe of lush growth around the cult compound. Now I meant to pay my debt.

# 43

I joined a tour of St. Louis Cemetery No. 1, trailing along at the back of the pack, taking in the celebrations of All Souls' Day with families visiting the graves of their loved ones. Although this was technically *el Día de los Inocentes,* the Day of the Children, it was clear some were also celebrating *el Día de los Muertos,* the Day of the Dead. During these two days the gates of heaven were presumably opened and the dead—first the children on November 1 and then the adults on November 2—could join with their families for joyful reunions and sharing of memories.

Bright flowers, marigolds and mums, were everywhere, and many people had brought homemade altars where they burned candles and placed food and drink.

Though the festivities honored death, it was very much a celebration of life, too, and of the undying connection between those who remained earthbound with those who had transitioned to a spirit state.

The guide talked about the history of the cemetery and the famous people buried on this sacred ground. Fascinating information, but I was there for another purpose. Out of the corner of my eye, I caught a beautiful woman dressed in white moving among the mausoleums and tombs.

The cemetery was called the city of the dead, an accurate description. Each tomb was unique, a reflection of family, time, place, and social standing. I'd expected the visit to be a little creepy, but other than the white-clad woman drifting behind monuments, always just out of clear sight, the cemetery was sunny and filled with those honoring their loved ones. Not scary at all.

When at last we came to Marie Laveau's tomb, I edged forward, noting the altar someone had made for her that contained bottles of wine, bread, and coins left by those who paid tribute or had been granted a favor and had paid their debt. The gifts would soon be collected by the cemetery maintenance people, but Marie would know.

While the tour group moved on, I remained behind a sepulcher. When they were gone, I went to Marie's tomb. I felt a strange affinity with this woman who had lived so many years before me. Some believed her to be a sorceress, a voodoo practitioner who could hex or curse a person. Others revered her as a healer, a protector.

Out of the corner of my eye I saw the white-clad woman approach me. I focused on my business, before the tour guide became aware that I had slipped away from the group and came back to find me.

The area around Marie's grave was quiet, and I knelt in front of the tomb. Someone had left a dozen fresh roses, and I placed a gold chain that Aunt Loulane had given me for high school graduation on the fragrant flowers beside an assortment of Mardi Gras beads. The necklace was one of my most prized possessions, because it marked the end of so many things in my life, but also new beginnings. Aunt Loulane had loved me dearly, and she'd given up her own life to come and make one for me. The chain had been an acknowledgment that I'd left childhood behind and would soon leave for college.

"You pay your debt." The woman in the white dress stood just behind me. I looked over my shoulder. She was very beautiful.

"I do."

"Your connection with the dead is very strong, Sarah Booth."

I wasn't even surprised that she knew my name. I'd called upon her in my hour of need and she'd answered. "Thank you."

"Leave here now. Go home. Love your man and honor your friends."

That was easy enough to do. "I will."

"Remember, Sarah Booth, that you are protected. You have many who watch over you."

Jitty had told me that numerous times, but it was good to hear it from someone else. I slowly got to my feet. It was time to leave the cemetery and New Orleans. I had horses to ride at Dahlia House, cases to explore, animals to take care of. My place wasn't in a cemetery, not yet anyway.

"Life is passion, Sarah Booth. Give yourself to passion and live."

When I turned to answer her, there was no one there. Another group of tourists was coming down the path. It really was time to leave.

As I started back to the main gate, I saw a slender woman in a brightly colored dress walking parallel to me. When we met up at the entrance, I realized it was Jitty. "You've already given me your Marie Laveau impersonation."

"What are you whangin' on about?" she asked.

"You're pretty slick, Jitty. Showing up at the cult house, and then again back at the tomb. Nice one, making me think I had some supernatural help."

Jitty's smile was filled with delight. "I wasn't there, Sarah Booth. I've had things to do in the Great Beyond. Your mama was about to have a fit, you runnin' around in the swamp and fighting with cult leaders."

"Right, Jitty. Right. You were just over at Marie's tomb. I'm not hallucinating."

"I didn't say you were." She sighed and looked out over the cemetery. "Death is never what people think it's going to be."

This was the closest she'd ever come to sharing anything real about the Great Beyond with me. "What's it like? The Great Beyond. Are my parents dancing and enjoying themselves?"

"No need to ever worry about Libby and James Franklin, Sarah Booth."

That didn't answer my question. "If I could only know what they do, how they spend their time. That they have each other to love the way they did here."

"They have each other, and you. And that's all you need to know."

Down the street, another parade approached the cemetery. Dozens of La Catrinas danced and frolicked as they came toward us. The music was lively and fun. They would take their celebration into the city of the dead.

I looked at Jitty, who slowly shook her head. At the sound of rattling bones and the mariachi music from the parade, she swirled until her skirt was a blur of different colors, and then she was gone.

When I got back to the apartment, everyone had left. I made some coffee, washed out the pot, and took a cup to the balcony so I could watch for Coleman. I'd just finished my beverage when he pulled into the lot. He got out of the car and blew me a kiss. "Oh, Juliet, come down and we'll take the chariot to our love nest."

"Not exactly Shakespeare," I called down to him.

"How about I'm eager to get home. I still have the rest of this day off, and I have some things on my mind that we need to take care of."

I liked the sound of that. "Bags are at the front door. I'll lock up as I come down. I'm ready for whatever you're planning." And I was. Marie was right. Embrace the passion. It was one of the few untainted joys of life. I'd learned that from my parents.

# Acknowledgments

As always, enormous thanks go to the hardworking team at St. Martin's Press and my agent, Marian Young. Thank you all! Good editors, agents, and artists are hard to come by and I have been so very lucky.

Many readers tell me that Sarah Booth and the Zinnia gang are like family to them, and I truly feel the same. This fictional world has been a wonderful place for me to "hide out" during the hard times of a pandemic and a lot of personal loss. Thank you to all the readers who care about my characters, and the booksellers who recommend the books.

Special thanks to my niece, Jennifer Haines Williamson, who kept me on the straight and narrow with plot holes, dangling threads, and my usual writing calamities. It's always an adventure with each new book.